The Unexpected Adventures of Clive

By

Anthony Merton

Published by Constanzia Books, March 2017

www.constanziabooks.com

Chapter 1

Clive Evans was washing his hands in the cubicle, when the plane suddenly, and very dramatically, bounced in the air, sending him upwards, so that his head banged hard on the ceiling and then down again, leaving him crumpled on the floor. Then the plane's engines began to make an awful sound that suggested that their demise was very imminent, as indeed it was because they cut out altogether a few seconds later. After the initial feeling of panic had subsided, just a touch, Clive was struck by the thought that if he was going to die, he didn't want it to be in a toilet but when he tried to unlock the door he found that nothing he could do would shift it. He also realised that there was no point in shouting for assistance because such cries would never be heard above the terrible screaming that was coming from the cabin. So, as the plane hurtled earthwards, Clive reluctantly sat down on the seat and assumed the brace position. They say that your whole life can pass before you in such situations but the only thing that Clive thought about was for how long Mrs Elphick, his elderly neighbour, would remember to feed his cat.

It must have been Clive's presence in the toilet that saved him, for when the plane eventually hit the water, and the rest of it disintegrated and sank, the cubicle and its contents were ejected upwards and then splashed down relatively softly a few seconds later. While the initial impact had rendered Clive dazed, he was otherwise unharmed, except for a few cuts and bruises, and when he regained his senses his first impulse was

3

to question why he was having a cold bath, when he usually had hot showers. By the time reality dawned, the cubicle was already half full of water and filling up quickly, not that this was terribly obvious because the light had cut out. Groping for the door handle, Clive found it just as the water level reached his neck. By some stroke of luck the impact of the crash must have released the lock, and so, moments before the cubicle sank into the oblivion below, Clive was able to push the door open and emerge into the daylight and the broad expanse of the ocean.

Clive trod water and looked all around him; nothing. Within a little while however, the sea began to make rather disgusting belching noises as air bubbles from the sunken aircraft reached the surface. Pretty soon objects began to appear as well, including inflated life jackets, one of which Clive grabbed and struggled into, with much difficulty, since these things are designed to be put on before they are activated. The largest object amongst this growing mass of flotsam was a sizeable piece of fuselage and Clive swam to it in the expectation that he could clamber on and use it as a raft. This wasn't easy as the curve of the object, and its slipperiness in the water, meant that he kept falling off. Finally, just as he was almost on board, it rolled over. As it did so Clive desperately tried to find something to cling on to and grabbed at what looked like a metal rod. This came away in his hand, just as the slab of wreckage sank back down into the abyss.

Clive trod water. It took a few minutes for the magnitude of his predicament to hit him; he was the lone survivor of an air crash, there was no land in sight, and no ships, or any other sign of human life either. The daylight was beginning to fade. The water was cold.

'Let's face it, Clive,' he thought to himself, 'you're a dead duck.'

Clive continued to tread water. He still had the rod in his hand. It was about a metre in length. He wondered if he should drop it but then he thought about sharks and decided he might just be able to deter them by prodding. Clive looked at the detritus all around and realised that most of it was lifejackets. Then he had an idea. He could use the straps on the jackets to tie them together to make a raft. Clive wasn't sure if it was a good idea but it was the only thing he could think of and it had to be worth a go; he probably wouldn't last the night in the cold water. So Clive wedged the rod inside the belt round his waist and set to work. It wasn't easy, it took time, but eventually, just as the daylight was almost gone, he had a bundle of floating lifejackets that was large enough to support his weight. Once on top he took off his shoes and tied them onto his makeshift raft. Then he fell asleep.

Clive spent the next two days at sea. Time passed slowly; there was nothing to do. Once he saw an aircraft but it didn't see him. During the third day Clive saw a fin in the water, circling his raft. Then he saw the shark that it belonged to. The shark swam up to his raft and bit one of the lifejackets. The air hissed out of it. The shark swam away a little, then turned round, swam back and bit another one. It struck Clive that this was a particularly intelligent shark to have worked out how to wreck the raft, and eat him for lunch, with a minimum of effort. Clive remembered the rod after the shark had bitten four life jackets.

5

'I'm not giving in without a fight,' he thought, as he prodded the shark's snout when it homed in on a fifth.

The shark flinched, turned and swam away. It never came back. Clive was quite surprised.

'Thank God for the rod,' he thought, and then smiled because it rhymed.

During the fourth night, while Clive was asleep, the raft, with a slight bump, washed up on a beach. Clive didn't notice and slept on until morning. It was a nice surprise when he woke up. He couldn't have lasted much longer on the ocean.

Clive looked around. There wasn't much to see. It was misty so everything looked grey. He could just about make out a line of trees beyond the beach. Clive wondered if it was an island and whether there were people and if there would be anything to eat. He also wondered if there were any wild animals, just before he saw the lion. Actually it was a lioness. She was watching him. Clive jumped in fright, or surprise, or both when he saw her. The lion noticed and roared in response. That frightened Clive even more.

'It's just not fair,' thought Clive, 'how unlucky can one person get?'

He wondered if he would be dead before the lion started to eat him. He didn't like the idea of watching himself being eaten. The lioness stood up.

'That's it. I'm for it,' thought Clive.

The only possible escape was back to the sea. Maybe she couldn't swim and, after all, cats don't like water. Then Clive noticed that the tide had gone out.

'Oh bugger it,' thought Clive. 'I really am for it.'

The lioness began to move towards Clive, slowly at first, then breaking into a trot, while continuing to roar savagely. Clive grabbed the rod, there was nothing else. He held it firmly with both hands and pointed it at the onrushing lion. She stopped still in her tracks, ceased roaring and lay down. Clive and the lion surveyed each other; neither seemed to know what to do next. Clive didn't dare lower the rod and, pretty soon, his arms began to ache.

'This is stupid,' thought Clive, 'the lion is bound to win in the end. She's in better condition than me. I was already half-dead to start with.'

Clive lowered his arms. The lioness didn't flinch. It occurred to Clive that maybe she had had lunch already. Maybe she wouldn't eat him then and there, just kill him and save him for later. The only possibility was the ocean. The lioness might have other ideas but he'd have to try anyway, there was nothing else for it. After all, where there was one lion there were bound to be more, and the others might not be so amenable. Clive pondered his predicament. He'd have to take the raft with him. There was no point in getting into the water without it. He wouldn't last five minutes. It was worth a go.

Slowly, cautiously, Clive edged backwards off the raft until his knees were on the sand. Then he continued to edge backwards, pulling the raft and pointing the rod. It was rather disappointing that the lioness came too, still crouching down but shuffling forward on the sand.

'Damn it,' thought Clive.

Still, she wasn't charging or growling, just shuffling. Clive pointed the rod more purposefully at the lioness. Perhaps that would make her stop. It didn't; she was shuffling forward

7

faster than he was edging away and getting nearer. Finally, she was so near that she was almost touching the raft and the rod. Clive stopped, and so did the lioness. Then it occurred to Clive that she might be more interested in the rod than in him; her eyes were fixed on it. Perhaps if he threw the rod as far away as possible she would go after it and he could make his getaway. But then what would he do about sharks, and what if she didn't?

Clive started to edge backwards again. The lioness started to shuffle. Finally Clive reached the sea. He wasn't looking down, but he could tell because his feet and knees were getting wet. The lioness was still shuffling and staring at the rod. Then she did something that Clive hadn't anticipated. She leaned forward, sniffed the end of the rod, rubbed her face against it and licked it. Then she started to purr and rolled over onto her back.

'I think she wants me to tickle her tummy,' thought Clive.

Just then all hell broke loose. The lioness jumped up, growling angrily, and rushed into the sea. There was some violent thrashing about. Finally, after a few seconds, Clive saw a large fin heading out to sea.

'Goodness,' he thought, 'I've just been saved by a lion.'

The lioness came out of the water and nuzzled up to Clive, purring even more loudly. Clive patted her side. It seemed the least he could do by way of a thank you.

Clive stood up and looked around. It was still misty and grey, positively uninviting in fact but there must be fresh water somewhere and maybe something to eat. Going back on the raft would be positively suicidal, especially considering that there were now several fins gliding about in the water. Clive patted the lioness. She continued to purr.

'Perhaps it won't eat me after all,' thought Clive.

Clive pulled the raft back up the beach and beyond the waterline, just in case. The lioness followed and watched while Clive retrieved his shoes. Then she walked on towards the trees. When she reached them she turned round to look at Clive and waited. Clive wasn't quite sure what to do. Maybe she wanted him to follow or maybe she was saying goodbye. The lioness walked back to Clive and pushed him towards the trees. She wanted him to follow.

The lioness led Clive into the trees. Inside it was even more misty and grey. There was no proper path and Clive found it quite hard going. He was beginning to feel lightheaded, dizzy even. After all, he hadn't had anything to eat for days. Clive felt himself swoon and fell to the ground. The lioness came up and licked his face. Her tongue was rough. It brought him round. Clive forced himself up and the lioness walked on, more slowly this time and turning frequently as if to check he was okay. At length they came to a stream and the lioness began to drink. So did Clive. Water had never tasted so good. While Clive was drinking, the lioness walked away. When Clive looked up, she wasn't there anymore.

'Just as I was beginning to feel comfortable with her,' thought Clive. 'What on earth do I do now?' He needn't have worried. A minute or so later she reappeared, opened her mouth, and dropped an apple.

'She's feeding me now,' thought Clive. 'This is some lion. I shall call her Elsa. She was a nice lion too.'

Clive was careful to wash the apple, not knowing what else might have been in Elsa's mouth. Then he ate it, all of it, even the core and stalk. He ate it so quickly he didn't even properly taste it.

'I wonder where she got that from,' thought Clive. 'One apple isn't really enough when you've been starving for days. Perhaps she'll lead me to the tree.'

She didn't. As soon as Clive had finished the apple the lioness started off again, turning after a few seconds to make sure that he was following. Presently they came to a large clearing in the forest. At the far end the land rose up into a hill, into which was cut a series of steps. They wound their way up the hillside until they disappeared into the murk above. Clive looked at them for several seconds before it dawned on him that a staircase meant people. That was the only explanation. Staircases didn't make themselves and the lioness certainly couldn't have done it. The lioness walked over to the staircase and lay down beside it. Then she started to purr again. If she was happy, Clive was positively ecstatic.

"So this is where you've been leading me," he cried out loud, while hugging the lioness. "You're the best lion I've ever met."

Clive knew that this was a stupid thing to say, given his lack of acquaintances in the big cat world and that she couldn't understand him anyway, but it aptly conveyed his feelings at that moment.

"Come on then, Elsa, up we go. I wonder what we'll find."

Clive positively bounded up the first few steps and then looked back. The lion hadn't budged.

"It's only a few steps. You can manage."

The lioness looked up, and roared in a gentle kind of way. Then she stood up and walked away into the gloom. Clive never saw her again, at least not like that.

Chapter 2.

Clive had been climbing for what seemed like ages when he suddenly emerged out of the grey gloom and into bright sunlight. Ahead of him he could see that the steps ended in what looked like the entrance to a cave. Clive stood still and considered the situation. Perhaps it was a trap. Given his run of bad luck, he wouldn't be surprised if it was. Maybe, for example, it was the lion's den and she had effectively delivered her family its next meal. Clive dismissed the idea; she had been a nice lion. Clive continued to ponder and then he noticed a brown shape just within the entrance of the cave. Clive's immediate reaction was to thin that far from being the lion's den, the cave was, in fact, a bear's lair. At this point the brown thing stood up, revealing itself to be a person. It spotted Clive and beckoned him forward. Clive obeyed, relieved.

As Clive got nearer he could tell that the person was a man because it had a beard and moustache. He was wearing a long brown cloak or tunic that stretched almost to the ground. Clive thought he might be a monk or a hermit. Clive held out his hand in greeting.

"Hello, I'm so pleased to meet you. Are you a monk?" he asked.

"No," came the reply.

"A hermit?"

"I am the Keeper of the Door."

"It's an open cave. There isn't a door to keep."

"Do you always argue when you first meet people? Besides there is, inside. My name is Ggydren. Come in and sit down. You look done in. We'll bother about the formalities later, I expect you'd like something to eat and drink."

Clive was wondering why there was a door inside and not outside and what formalities there might be but he refrained from asking, having already seemingly got off on the wrong foot by arguing. Anyway, the appeal of food was overwhelming.

"Yes please,' he said, 'that would be great. I haven't had anything to eat or drink for days, well except for an apple and some water. Right now I could eat a horse. Of course, I don't mean I want a horse, I don't eat horses. Well, not knowingly, I mean, do you remember the lasagne scandal?"

Clive realised he was babbling nonsense, just before he fainted.

When he came round a few minutes later he found himself on a bed inside the cave. His rod was beside him. Being on a bed in a cave confused him as he usually woke up on a bed in his bedroom but after a few seconds he remembered where he was. Clive sat up and looked around. It wasn't bad, for a cave that is. It was quite a big space and there was a table and chairs and a nice comfy sofa. The walls had been whitewashed and the floor was quite flat. There was a fireplace, with a fire and a pot of something hanging over it. Right at the back of the cave there was a door. It was a big, antique looking, wooden door, with lots of iron work and an ornate key hole, from which protruded the end of a big key.

13

There was also a letter box which somehow, looked out of place.

Clive tried to get up and fainted again. When he awoke Ggydren was standing beside him holding a bowl of steaming broth.

"I think you'd better get this down you."

Clive sat up and took the bowl. His initial thought was that soup wouldn't have been his first choice after having been starved for ages but it was really very tasty and quite thick.

"No horse in there," said Ggydren.

Clive thought it was a strange thing to say. The soup refreshed him enormously. He looked around again and asked if there was anywhere he could have a wash or a bath.

"I'm caked in salt,' he explained, then thought that this might need a bit of explanation, and added that he had been marooned on a raft on the ocean for days.

Ggydren nodded and pointed to an alcove Clive hadn't noticed before.

"There isn't a bath but there's a basin over there and plenty of water. You'll find a change of clothing as well. It wouldn't do to be seen in the outlandish garb you have on now. Where on earth did you get it?"

"It's not outlandish where I come from. Everybody dresses like it; well, the men anyway."

"I hope the women have more sense."

The alcove was near the door.

"Is that the door that you're keeping?' asked Clive.

"You don't seem to be taking this very seriously,' replied Ggydren, 'I'm not keeping it, I am the Keeper. It's a very responsible job. I was lucky to get it, given the state of the economy. Regular pay and a pension, all meals provided."

"What's on the other side?" asked Clive.

"I'm not allowed to tell you, until we've been through the formalities and established your credentials; management rules. I think they think it adds to the suspense. You do ask a lot of questions. Could knock you up a sandwich while you're washing, if you're still peckish?"

"Sounds good," said Clive, being more famished than peckish, despite the broth, and already beginning to salivate.

The alcove affording some privacy, Clive decided to undress for his wash. Then he decided to go the whole hog and attempt a shower. This was possible because the water seemed to be flowing continuously from an opening in the cave wall down into the basin. The overflow then dropped to the floor where it drained away though another hole. Clive crouched down and moved under the overflow. The coldness of the water made him gasp but he persevered and got used to it. He even made himself more comfortable by changing to a sitting position with the water cascading down onto his head. After a few minutes Clive leant forward out of the water to find Ggydren standing a few feet away, staring at him.

"I'm beginning to think that you are rather strange," he said. "Anyway, I've brought you a towel. Choose whichever garment you want. There is no charge."

Clive dried himself off, feeling rather foolish for having been discovered in such a ridiculous position, but relieved to feel fresh and clean. The choice of garments was rather limited; long grey robes or brown ones. He chose the brown. There

15

were no underpants and no socks, so rather reluctantly, given their condition, he put his own back on again. There were, however, some stylish leather boots which fitted perfectly and would have looked rather dashing, if only they weren't covered up by the drab robe. As Clive dressed he considered his predicament. The steps had ended in the cave and the hillside above had looked too steep to climb. Apart from going down again, his only option seemed to be the door, wherever that led. Clive presumed it must be to some sort of tunnel, which hopefully emerged on the other side of the hill and where perhaps he might find people and civilisation. Strange though to have a door blocking it off. Maybe there was something within that Ggydren preferred to keep out, and what was it with Ggydren anyway?

Ggydren had prepared a cheese and cucumber sandwich. Clive bolted it down and asked for more. After the third Ggydren said that it was time to get on with the formalities and fetched a quill, some ink and a scroll from a sideboard.

"Name and address?"

"Clive Evans, 35 Hillside Crescent, Ealing."

"Ealing? Where's that?"

"London."

"London? Never heard of it."

"But you must have. Everyone's heard of London."

"Not me."

"London, you know, London England."

"England? Never heard of that either."

"You can't be serious. Everyone's heard of England and besides, you're speaking English."

"Look here, I'm speaking Aughphalian and so are you. Are you deliberately trying to be difficult?"

Clive was beginning to get exasperated. There couldn't be more than a handful of people on the whole planet who hadn't heard of London and England. He tried to explain.

"No, look, I'm sorry, I'm not trying to be difficult, I promise. You see where I came from everyone knows about London and England; we used to rule most of the world, after all. Maybe it would help if you told me where we are; I mean where this cave is, and where you come from because I really have no idea where I am. I was in a plane that crashed and everyone else was killed and I made a raft out of life jackets and was adrift on the ocean for days before I arrived here and, right now, I'm just completely bewildered."

"A plane? What's that?"

"A plane? An aeroplane! You know, they've got wings and fly in the sky and the one I was in crashed."

"You were inside a type of bird or dragon?"

"What? Of course not,"

Clive realised he was shouting.

"Well, what else has wings and flies and anyway, how could you have been inside one? Please try to calm down. Are you feeling alright? Maybe the hunger's made you delirious. Perhaps you'd better lie down again."

Clive took a deep breath and considered the situation. He knew that he wasn't delirious so perhaps it was Ggydren, perhaps Ggydren was just plain bonkers.

"Do you live alone? Is there anyone else I could talk to? Maybe that would be easier."

"No and no. I live with my wife but she's not here at the moment. She's down below. You must have met her earlier."

"No I didn't. The only thing I met down there was a lion."

"That's her."

"What?"

"That's her, the wife."

"What? Your wife is a lion?"

"Only some of the time."

Having had his suspicions about Ggydren's sanity confirmed, Clive decided he had better play along.

"Sorry, silly of me not to realise. What's her name?"

"The wife? Elendril."

"And some of the time she's a lion?"

"That's right, shape-shifter. She chooses whatever form she thinks is right for the job.   We're a team you see. She does the initial vetting and I make the final arrangements."

"Vetting? Arrangements? Could you explain in a bit more detail?"

"Well, basically her job is to keep the riff raff away. She checks them out and sees them off if they're unsuitable. We get quite a few idiots and time wasters. You wouldn't believe it. Last month this whole boat load turned up. All sorts of weirdo's, even some of those pointy ears. The leader was this old bloke dressed all in white, with a silly pointed hat and a long beard. Said they'd come a long way and had every right to be here, given he had a staff. Well, she just grabbed the staff, broke it in two and sent them off again."

"His name wasn't Gandalf, was it?"

"Does ring a bell. Know him?"

"Not exactly."

Clive tried very hard to keep calm. He didn't want to upset Ggydren because it occurred to him that Ggydren might be dangerous as well as mad, as mad people can sometimes be. Clearly Ggydren must be mad because the alternative to madness seemed to Clive that he'd been washed up in the fourth book of The Lord of the Rings.

"I presume that Elendril must have led you to the steps?" enquired Ggydren.

"Yes, and she saved me from a shark and she gave me an apple. I thought she was going to eat me at first."

"Was there anything that changed her mind, do you think?"

"Well, she seemed fascinated by the rod. Yes, that one on the bed. After she licked it, she turned over and started purring. Then she saved me from the shark and led me here."

"Would you mind if I had a closer look at it. I think it might bear closer examination. There is just a possibility..."

"Not at all, help yourself."

Ggydren looked at the rod for some seconds, stroking his chin as if deep in thought. Then he picked it up and turned it round and round in his hand and upside down for at least a minute until he had inspected every inch of it.

"Where did you get this?"

"It was on a part of the plane. I grabbed it and it came away in my hand."

"The plane? Oh yes, the thing that flies that isn't a bird or a dragon. What was it doing there?"

"Doing there?"

"Yes, why was it there? Do you always get them on these plane things, as you call them?"

19

"Well really, I have no idea. The plane crashed and broke up and part of it came to the surface and this was on it. I presume all planes must have them. I don't know; you don't normally see that bit of the plane when you're just a passenger."

"Have you tried heating it up?"

Clive was feeling exasperated again. Of all the places he could have washed up, this was not the one he would have chosen.

"No, and why would I do that? In fact, how could I do that? I've been adrift on the ocean. There was nothing to heat it up with. It never crossed my mind. Look, is there some point in all this? I'm sure you mean well but I just want to go home."

"Would you mind if I tried?"

"Heating it up?"

"Yes, in the fire."

"Oh, I suppose not. Go on then. It's made of metal, so it can't do any harm. What do you want to heat it up for anyway?"

"Oh, just to see."

Clive sighed. Ggydren approached the fire with the rod, then he pushed one end into the flames. He waited at least a minute before retrieving it. Then he took it over to the bowl in the niche and plunged the hot end into the water. There was a loud hissing noise and a burst of steam. Then Ggydren carefully examined every inch of it again. There was quite a lot of tutting.

"No, nothing at all," he muttered, a disappointed look on his face, "that's a shame. It's just a rod, like you said. Elendril must've made a mistake, that's all. Oh well, never mind. We'd better get on with the formalities instead. You'll be wanting to make a start."

Ggydren sat down at the table again and took up his quill. Clive sat down as well and leaned forward in anticipation.

"Was it the standard or the five star experience, and have you got the receipt?"

At this point Clive lost it, completely. He stood up, leant over, bent down and clutched at Ggydren's robe, where the lapels should have been, and pulled him up towards him.

"Now listen here. I've been in a plane crash, adrift at sea for days without food or water, attacked by a shark, scared half to death by a lion. I've had enough. Enough, do you hear? There is a limit to what I can take and you have just overstepped it. All this stuff and nonsense, shape-shifters, speaking Augwhatsit and all that. I want some plain answers, and I want them now. Do you understand? I want them now."

Clive, feeling somewhat better for his uncharacteristic outburst, released Ggydren from his grip. Ggydren sat down. Clive remained standing.

"It's Aughphalian actually. That's what we speak here in Aughphalia. I don't know what's come over you. I'm only doing my job. Violence isn't allowed. I could report you. Am I to take it you don't have a receipt? No-one goes in without proof of purchase, and what is it you don't understand anyway?"

Clive was calmer. The urge to throttle Ggydren had passed.

"Everything," he answered, "I don't understand any of this. You've never heard of England, yet you're speaking English to me, and I've never heard of Aughphalia and I'm speaking Aughphalian to you. It's as if we're from different worlds, yet

21

we're not. What is this place? Please try to explain it as simply as possible, like you would to a child or maybe someone from a different planet. That way there's just a chance I might begin to understand."

Ggydren explained. Calmly, and at some length, he explained as best and as simply as he could. At the end Clive was still completely mystified.

"So, let me see if I've got this right. In here it's Aughphalia and on the other side of the door, through the tunnel, it's Morgrnvia. And if you have a standard ticket you can go and spend the day in Morgrnvia, and with a five star ticket you can spend a few nights as well and come back later. That's right so far, is it?"

Ggydren nodded.

"And even a standard ticket costs an arm and a leg but people think it's worth it because Aughphalia is so boring that people would do anything to get away, even just for the day. But you're not allowed to tell me anything about Morgrnvia until we've been through the formalities but I can't go through the formalities because I haven't got a ticket, but anyway, it must be better in there than it is here because people will do anything just to go for the day?"

Ggydren kept nodding.

"And you are the doorman, sorry the Keeper of the Door, who checks people's tickets or receipts and lets them out and back in."

"Yes, sir."

"And your wife can change herself into a lion and back again, and there are real dragons."

"Exactly."

"That doesn't sound boring to me. In fact, it's very unusual where I come from, on Earth."

"You told me you came from London."

"Never mind about that, the thing is that even if I had a receipt, which I don't, I could only go in there for a few days at best and after that I'd be back here and have to go down into the gloom again?"

Ggydren resorted to nodding.

"So really, I'm just wasting my time here. I might as well just walk back down again."

Ggydren didn't nod or say anything. Neither said anything for at least a few seconds. Then Clive had a thought.

"Where do they go, when they've gone down again?"

"Home, I suppose."

Clive was beginning to get excited. Obviously there was more to 'down there' than just a beach and some trees.

"And where might that be and how do they get there?"

"Could be anywhere in Aughphalia. Mostly they come and go on horseback but a few of them walk or arrive by sea. Usually they're so bored after a few weeks back home they start saving up to come again."

"Where do they leave the horses while they're up here?"

"At the stables at the inn. They get a night in the inn on arrival and another on departure all included in the ticket price."

Clive would have found it hard to describe his actual feelings at that point, containing as they did several degrees of wild elation and just as many of extreme anger.

"You mean that there is an inn down there, with people and horses and beds and food and drink, and you didn't tell me?"

23

"You're shouting again. I didn't tell you because you never asked me, and besides, I assumed you knew. Everyone else does. It's famous, the Last Friendly Inn at the Edge of Aughphalia. People dream of it."

Just then both of them were startled by the rod. It had fallen, with a loud clang, from its upright position by the fireplace where Ggydren had placed it. As it lay there it started to twitch. They both watched intently. It started slowly, just a few twitches to begin but then the movements became stronger and more regular. First it got longer, then it became thicker and one end started to curl round. Then it started to glow until it became red hot. Then it cooled down again.

"Good heavens, this is absolutely incredible," said Clive, startled, "it's turned into a walking stick! How did it do that?"

"Stick my foot!" exclaimed Ggydren "That's no walking stick, it's a staff and no ordinary, two a penny staff, mark my word. I was right all along and so was Elendril. That, if I am not mistaken, is one of the four Staffs of Power. It must have been a delayed reaction. Maybe I didn't leave it in the fire long enough to happen immediately. You realise what this means, don't you?"

"I have absolutely no idea," replied Clive, totally amazed by what he had just observed. "I've never seen anything like it before. This is turning out to be the weirdest day in my whole life. I doubt if I'll understand but, go on then, explain it to me."

"Well, actually, now I think of it, I'm not too sure either. The four Staffs of Power were made ages ago. There's one in the main town but it hasn't been used for yonks and the other three disappeared generations past. I didn't know they could change themselves like that but I'm sure it must be one of them. It's about the right length, a bit too big for an ordinary man. My word, I'm more than a little bit flustered. Just let me think for a bit."

Clive looked at the staff. It was long enough to be a bishop's staff. Its trunk was twisted and there seemed to be symbols or designs anyway etched into it. One in particular, an Ж shape, stood out, near the handle that was not just curved but wound round three times and ended in the head of a serpent with its tongue protruding. Clive carefully picked it up and held it. Though the rod had been made of metal, the staff was brownish in colour and looked more like polished wood. It was surprisingly light for something so long. As he touched its end on the stone floor of the cave little sparks flew up. He did it again, more sparks. Then he banged it down quite hard. There was a loud explosion and a flash of light that shot up, hit the roof of the cave, bounced off it and rebounded several times off the walls and floor, until it shot out of the entrance and into the sky. Clive dropped the staff in surprise and wonder. It clanged on the floor and started to glow. Then it began to twitch and move again, getting shorter and thinner until, once more, it was just a plain metal rod. Clive and Ggydren stared at it.

"Why did you do that?" demanded Ggydren, "I told you I needed time to think."

"Well, I wasn't to know, was I? We could try heating it up again to see if it changes back."

"No, just leave it be. Don't touch it. I'm going to consult the manual. I seem to remember there's something about it in there."

Ggydren went over to a bookshelf and took out a thin volume entitled 'Aughphalia: Alphabetical Guide to All You Need to Know.' He leafed through until he came to the S pages.

"Here it is, 'Staffs of Power. Staffs of Power, handle with care, can cause fatalities. Best left alone.' Well, fat lot of good that was. Everyone knows Staffs of Power can kill. What did you say happened when Elendril saw it?"

"She was roaring and charging at me. I thought I was going to die, get eaten alive. There was nothing else, no weapon to use, the rod was all I had, so I held it up and pointed it at her and she stopped dead in her tracks. And when she'd smelt it, and touched and licked it, she rolled over and started to purr. I thought she wanted me to tickle her tummy. "

"So, even when it's a rod, it's still got the same power as a Staff of Power. It's just taken another form, a bit like the wife."

"And, now I think about it, it worked on the shark too. Not the one on the beach. Earlier, while I was at sea, there was this shark that was gradually biting its way through the raft to get at me and when I prodded it with the rod, it just swam away. I thought it was just the prodding but maybe, maybe it sensed the Staff."

"Probably; it's all beginning to make more sense now. I thought you were a bit of a nutter with all that talk of England and planes but there must be something about you to have a Staff of Power and the thing is the rules of this place say that

26

anyone who turns up with a Staff, not any old staff mind you, but anyone with a Staff of Power, gets to go into Morgrnvia for as long as they like and never come back at all if they want and while they're in there they gets to go on a quest. They can even put in a request for which sort of quest to go on. You lucky thing, I'd give anything to go on a quest."

Clive's reaction was not what Ggydren anticipated.

"Oh God, not a quest. Please God, let it not be a quest. After that stuff about Gandalf and the elves I knew there was going to be a quest, and there'll probably be a company and lots of fighting and magic and dark lords and I'm beginning to think I've gone mad and that none of this exists or it's just a dream or even a nightmare. I refuse to go on a quest. I absolutely refuse, hear. The only thing I want to do is to go home as soon as possible and feed the cat."

"Begging your pardon, Mr Clive, but I've already told you, there's no England to go home to round here, not even far away from here. There's only Aughphalia and a few other places and the sea. There's nowhere else."

"But there must be. You've just not discovered it yet, like America before Columbus. I got here by sea, so England must be somewhere across the ocean and England, well Britain is an island, so it all fits. You've just not discovered us yet, and we've not discovered you, even though we speak the same language, that's all. I'll just go back down, find the inn, get a proper boat and sail off until I find England. I don't want anything to do with quests and Staffs of Power."

"I'm sorry but you're wrong. You're barking up the wrong tree. Most of here is sea, hundreds and hundreds of miles of it, and in all the sea there's hardly any bits of land and only a few of them have people. Aughphalia is one and another is where the man with the pointy hat and the beard is from. There's one or two other bits of land but none of them have any places called London or things that people could fly up in the sky in. Apart from that there's nowhere else, just sea. Of course, we've looked to see if we could find other places with people; there's been a lot of voyages but none of them ever found anywhere else. Some of them even sailed all the way round and the only people they bumped into was on the other side of Aughphalia. There was even one person that sailed all the way round and missed us altogether and had to sail all the way round again, but he never found any more places either, with or without people. I tell you, there's just a few places and none of them is called London, or England or wherever else you mentioned. I don't see as you can ever go home. I don't really understand how you got here but you certainly can't go back again."

Clive's spirits sank until he was almost in a slough of despondency. It couldn't be true. He had to get home. Suddenly he jumped up.

"Poppycock, utter poppycock, complete and utter twaddle! Got you! I don't know what your game is but you've just tripped yourself up. Of course there's somewhere else, there's Morgrnvia! What have you got to say about that, ha? Explain that!"

"But that's the point. Morgrnvia isn't really here either. It's difficult to explain but if you climb to the top of this hill and look over, it's Aughphalia you see on the other side, the inn and the stables and the harbour but when you go through the hill, through the tunnel, it's not like that at all. You come out

28

at an altogether different place that's called Morgrnvia, and Morgrnvia is much bigger than Aughphalia, hundreds, maybe thousands of miles bigger. And another thing, the tunnel is shorter than it should be to reach the other side of the hill. It's like Morgrnvia is between the end of the tunnel and the bit of Aughphalia that's on the other side of the hill, but that's just plain impossible. No one can understand it. It's like there's a space for Morgrnvia inside the hill but Morgrnvia is too big for the space but even so, it's there. I know it sounds like nonsense but there you are. It's very difficult to explain."

Clive thought about it. Dr Who came to mind.

"You mean it's like a tardis, bigger on the inside than the outside."

"Never heard of no tardis but yes, that's exactly it, bigger on the inside that out. You know all about it then? Is that what it's called, a tardis? Got these tardises where you come from, in England?"

"No, it's just make-believe, a TV programme."

"TV?"

"Sorry, I was forgetting. As you were saying, it does seem very difficult to explain, but what I think you're getting at is that the door, or the tunnel, is a portal into another dimension. No, sorry, forget I said that. It's just silly anyway. Go on please, you were speaking."

"Well, the only way in, as far as we know, is through the door. It's not that long since it was first discovered, maybe twenty years or so. The person who found it was gone nearly two weeks and when he eventually came back he was half mad and ranting on about evil and monsters and magic and demons and stuff like that. Well, the authorities decided to send in an expedition to see if it was true or whether he really was mad. They was gone about ten days before they said they'd had enough and got back here as quick as could be. Apparently it was fair enough to begin with. There was a town with lots of things going on but after a while they came to this forest and inside it they came across all manner of weird and frightening things, some of them completely out of this world. Well, they didn't hang about and got back here just as soon as they could. After that some people wanted to block up the entrance with bricks and boulders but some of the Councillors thought it might be a good way to make some money by allowing people to go in but only for long enough so they wouldn't have time to get as far as the scary bits. It killed two birds with one stone really because it was just at that time that people were really starting to moan about how boring Aughphalia was and there was even talk of rebellion. They realised they could calm the situation down by offering people a really interesting experience once in a while, which, hopefully, would stop them moaning the rest of the time. So, instead of bricking it up, they put in a good strong door, set up a commercial venture and hired me in as Keeper. It's been a roaring success, sometimes the queue is half was down the hill."

"But there's no one else here."

"Because it's Wednesday. It's closed Wednesdays, my day off; everyone's entitled to a day off. By rights I could have turned you away. Look here, as far as I can see, you can either go into Morgrnvia now and go on a quest or you can go down the hill, find the inn and then settle down somewhere in Aughphalia. Even then you'll probably want to visit Morgrnvia sometime or other, just to relieve the boredom, so you might as well go in now. I'll tell you what, why not just think it over for an hour or two? Take your time to make a decision. I'll get us a nice drink and maybe rustle up something to eat. What do you say?"

"Yes. Perhaps that would be for the best. I do need time to think and I could murder a nice cup of tea."

"Tea, never heard of it. I was thinking of beer. Cask conditioned mind you, none of your gassy rubbish. One of the perks of the job. Fancy a pint?"

Two pints later, when Clive was feeling distinctly better, Ggydren had an idea.

"Listen Mr Clive, if you can't get back to England from here, maybe you can from inside Morgrnvia. I'd say that was the only possibility. Why don't you put in a request to go on a quest to go home?"

"Do you think it could work?"

"Well it must be worth a try. I can't see any other way you can get back. Shall I write it out? It has to be put down in writing and submitted properly."

"Submitted?"

"Posted, in the letter box, in the door."

Clive nodded. He was beyond caring.

"There," said Ggydren, a few minutes later and holding up a scroll of parchment for Clive to see,   'Mr Clive Evans of 35 Hillside Crescent, Ealing, London, England, being in possession of one of the four Staffs of Power and of sound mind and body, requests permission to go on a quest to go home and feed the cat. Signed Ggydren, Keeper of the Door.' There, that

31

should do it. All we have to do now is post it and wait. Are you sure you don't eat horse?"

"Positive, why do you ask?"

"I make a mean horse burger."

"I could give it a try."

Two more pints and a horse burger later, Clive asked Ggydren if there was any more he could tell him about the Staffs of Power, and if he could explain what was so boring about Aughphalia.

"Sit back and make yourself comfortable," replied Ggydren.

Chapter 3.

Ggydren lent back on the sofa, took a sip of beer and paused, as if collecting his thoughts. Then he took another sip and then he started to speak.

"If you really want to understand, Mr Clive, we have to go way back to the start of things, right to the beginning when there was just Aughphalia and the Sea. For a long time that was all there was but then things started growing, like grass and trees and beetles and ants and cows and fish and people, and plenty of other things besides. And these things didn't just keep growing till they were the size things are now, they kept on growing till they got really big, enormous in fact. The greatest of all these growing things was a huge oak tree that was taller and wider and heavier than anything else and this made some people think it was special, and that they ought to worship and adore it, and even hang things in its branches, and give it presents to please it. Most people were quite happy with this, except Eric who said that it was plain silly to worship a tree and, anyway, he was the biggest man, and men can do more things than trees, so people should worship and adore him instead. To prove his point, he chopped down the mighty oak tree with his axe and cut up the trunk for furniture and the branches for logs for his fire.

Not everyone was happy with this and a few of them managed to rescue a branch when Eric wasn't looking. They took it to the best carpenter for miles around and asked him to make something with it, so that people would always remember the mighty oak and hate Eric. The carpenter thought about it but said that the best he could come up with would be walking sticks because the branch was short and quite thin, even for an enormous oak. He made four of them and showed them to the people and the people grumbled because they were just plain walking sticks and couldn't he do better? So the carpenter took them away again, soaked them in water and heated them in fire and did lots of other things besides, until they became bendy and he was able to make twists in them and a big curly bit at the end and when, he was finished, he lined them up and showed them to the people and everyone was really impressed and said that they weren't simple walking sticks any more but magnificent staffs instead. Just then a big fiery thing fell out of the sky and landed on the staffs. All the people in the vicinity, including the carpenter, were instantly killed but the staffs just glowed red, twitched around a bit and cooled down later, and didn't seem to be hurt at all, and people think that was when the staffs got their special powers and became the Staffs of Power because they got some of the stuff that was inside the fiery thing, that came from up there, that we don't get down here.

The big people that weren't around when the fiery thing came down, were all relieved that they weren't there at the time, but they weren't so lucky because a few weeks later a really enormous fiery thing fell out of the sky and made a huge hole in the ground and everyone for miles around was instantly killed. The people who were near enough to see what had happened but not so near that they got killed, thought they were lucky but they weren't really because the fires started by the fiery thing spread all over Aughphalia, and all the big things were burned alive or choked to death. That was the end of the First Age of Aughphalia.

For the first few years after the Great Calamity, as it was known, Aughphalia was a pretty horrible place. Everything was black and sooty and there was nothing moving about. But not everything died in the Calamity. Lots of types of big things did die out completely but there had always been lots of little things anyway, that big things hadn't paid much attention to because they were small, and some of these little things managed to hold on in the sea that hadn't boiled away, and in holes and caves on the land. These little things were the forefathers or even the forefathers of the forefathers of the things around today, even people and horses. And other things, such as grass and trees, things that had roots underground that didn't get burnt in the fires, managed to survive even though their top bits got burnt up. So basically, we still have a lot of the things that were here before the Great Calamity, only most of them are much smaller.

Time passed by. People completely forgot about the First Age of Aughphalia and the Great Calamity. Most people even forgot about the four great Staffs of Power. Most, that is, but not all. Some people preserved the memory of the Staffs by writing odes and composing songs about them and they would recite and sing these on dark winter evenings, when everyone was huddled around the fire, especially after they'd had a few beers and were a bit merry. Children would listen with wonder at these tales and, in turn, would pass them on to their children, and so the legend of the Staffs lived on, even though nobody knew where they were, or even if they had ever really existed.

For generations after the Great Calamity most people were peaceful, except for the odd scrap over something and nothing. But then some people began to question how things started. They said that the sacred words, 'In the Beginning was Aughphalia and the Sea', couldn't be true because things couldn't just happen out of nothingness, so someone or something must have made Aughphalia and the Sea, and he, she or it or whatever, must have been pretty special to have done it and ought to be worshipped and adored. Then, some of these people started claiming that he, she or it had spoken to them personally and that made them special as well, while other people disputed this and said that whoever or whatever, weren't like that at all. Well, these two or three or four lots of people who claimed they knew all about it, started arguing with each other and it even came to blows at times, with more than a few people getting killed. It got even worse when some people started asking who had made he, she or it because things couldn't happen out of nothingness, and that if you followed it back logically, you'd just go on and on and never get to the beginning, and perhaps there wasn't even anyone special who'd started it all. Well, that really set the cat among the pigeons, with everyone arguing and fighting and killing one another. Eventually some people said you could never get to the bottom of it anyway, so you might as well just leave it at that, stop the arguing and killing,, and think about other things instead. A few sensible people agreed with this but there were plenty more stupid people, so the arguing and killing went on.

After a while even some of the stupid people were getting tired of all the killing, and hoping they wouldn't be next. Some of them were wishing for someone to come and put a stop to it all. There was even a meeting in the main square of the main town of Aughphalia, demanding peace and reconciliation. The meeting turned violent when people started to argue about which side should give in first because they were wrong anyway, or whether they should all give in together, when there was an almighty flash of lightning that made everyone jump, only it wasn't lightning, it was William. William had a staff in his hand which seemed a bit too big for him but, even so, when he thumped it on the ground it let off a loud bang and a streak of light that shot up into the sky. William told them that he was completely fed up with the whole ruddy lot of them and, if they didn't shut up and listen, he would burn them to cinders. A couple of people were annoyed at the interruption and said it was William who should shut up and stop getting above himself, and lots of other people muttered in agreement but absolutely everybody stopped muttering, when he said, 'So be it,' and burnt the two of them to cinders, on the spot, with his staff.

When people realised that William had a Staff of Power and that all the old stories were true, they were really impressed and a lot of them started to worship and adore him. Pretty soon they had made William king but he didn't let it go to his head and most people generally agreed that he did very well, especially considering he was only a blacksmith before, and a pretty rubbish one at that. He made people cut out the arguing and killing over how things started and threatened to use his Staff on anyone who didn't comply. He did have to use the Staff on a few of them but people said they had it coming anyway, as they'd always been troublemakers. So, by the time William died, Aughphalia was peaceful again and quite prosperous.

Having made William king, the people were lumbered with his son when he died. That's one of the problems of having kings. His son was William too, only he was called William the Bastard, and not because his mum and dad weren't properly married either. William the Bastard said that people not only had to worship and adore him but they also had to give him presents too. People moaned that these presents weren't really presents but were actually taxes, but William said no, they were just presents, only compulsory ones. These presents were usually in the form of money but sometimes people had to give William their tools or their land or both, or even their wives and daughters but that was usually just for the evening. People didn't like this but William had inherited the Staff so there was nothing much they could do about it. William became very rich, while everyone else got much poorer. He said this was only right, as he was king and they weren't. He even said that he, she or it had actually chosen him specially to be king, so people had better do what he told them. A few brave people had the nerve to say they weren't going to give him any more presents because it just wasn't fair but he used his Staff on them, or had his henchmen catch them and string them up on the gallows as a punishment and a warning to others. Pretty soon everyone hated William. Even his friends hated him after he began worrying that they might be plotting behind his back. Some of them were put on trial and executed for high treason. In the end William died all of a sudden. The official story was that he fell off a ladder and broke his neck but lots of people guessed he didn't fall off but was pushed or maybe there wasn't even a ladder, just someone slit his throat.

William's son was called Ian and he became known as Ian the Interferer. It might not be as catchy a title as William the Bastard but it does give you a good idea of what he was like. He started off by saying that his dad had done a lot of bad things and he was going to put them right again, so that people would worship and adore him out of respect, not because they had to. Then he started issuing decrees saying things like, shopkeepers had to stop cheating their customers and people shouldn't have their heads cut off unless they done something really bad. People liked this but he didn't stop there. He started making all sorts of new rules and regulations about this, that and everything, till it seemed there was at least one new decree every day. Then, after a few years, he said that being in charge was too much for one person, even for a king with a Staff, and he was setting up a council to give him a hand. The people he put on the Council each had his or her own special area to do things in, like crops or roads or houses, and pretty soon they were all issuing decrees as well, with each Councillor trying to out-decree the next one. The people on the Council appointed more people, very often their own relations, to make sure that ordinary people did what the decrees told them to do and eventually there were more people checking up, than there was actually doing things. That was when things started to get really boring. There wasn't any more killing or fighting, which was good, but there wasn't much fun either. For instance, one of the decrees said that there was too much beer drinking, especially at weekends, so inns had to shut from Thursday till Monday and close by half past seven the rest of the time, with home brewing forbidden. Another decree said that it wasn't fair that some people had bigger plots to grow vegetables on than others, so in future everyone would have to share each other's land and, to make it fairer still, they were only allowed to grow what things the Councillor decided, and he also decided when they were allowed to plant them, when to do the tending and weeding and when to harvest them, and even how much they got for them, so even growing things got boring because all the decisions were made for you, instead of you doing the deciding. Then the Councillor in charge of Wellbeing said that steak and mince was bad for you, so beef was banned, and the Councillor in charge of Dairy Products said that cows were a wasteful way to make milk and it would be much better to cut out the cows and just add this and that to grass mowing, and drink that instead. So now we don't have cattle anymore and even the countryside's boring, with so much grass and no cows. Next up, some Councillor or other, decided that people were getting too finicky about their appearance and issued a new decree saying that everyone had to wear these horrible gowns, the only choice being grey or brown. Of course, this didn't apply to Councillors or their cronies who are allowed to dress as fancy as they like and they do. And so it goes on. Nowadays you're only allowed to get married when you're at least twenty eight, have no more than 1.4 children, tell me how that's possible, drive your cart on the road every other day, and not at all at weekends, go to more than one party a year and even then jelly's not allowed. You're only allowed five days holiday a year, plus weekends but now they only start after work on Saturday and you're not even allowed to go away on holiday because it messes up the schedules and your lawn gets longer than allowed and looks untidy. What's more, you have to spend three days every week doing community work, like clipping hedges and road cleaning and repairing the Council offices and marching in line and doing press-ups and preparing for what to do if another fiery thing falls out of the sky. I tell you, the list of things you can't do and have to do is endless. That's how it became so boring and why it still is. Nobody's allowed to think for themselves. Basically there are rules and more rules and rules about rules, and you need a permit for anything and everything, even a haircut. By the way, we still have kings but mostly people don't pay them much attention and they're not really worshipped and adored, as we still have the Council too and that's what really gives the orders. The present king does a lot of hand waving and going to see things or meet people that everyone knows he's not the least bit interested in, so I suppose that even he's bored a lot of the time. Officially he's still the Holder of the Staff of Power but he's not allowed to use it and it sits on a special stand in the main Council Office, where only the cleaner is allowed to touch it. No one knows where the first William got his Staff from as he never would say, which makes people think there was something dodgy about it and nobody has ever seen any of the other three, so it was a bit of a surprise, well a jolly big one really, when you turned up with one today."

41

Chapter 4.

"Are you listening, Mr Clive? You look a bit sleepy to me."

Clive stirred.

"Eh, of course, sorry, really interesting," answered Clive, a few seconds before nodding off completely, this being mainly due to the effects of the beer.

When he woke up, a couple of hours later, the daylight was fading and Ggydren was lighting candles.

"Any reply yet?"

"Nothing, I expect they're deliberating."

"Who are they?"

"People on the other side. Don't really know actually. Authorities, I suppose. Probably won't be long. I should imagine they'll be keen to see the Staff."

"How do they know about the Staff?"

"Well obviously somebody must have told them," answered Ggydren. "It weren't me," he added, rather defensively, then remembered he'd written it in the letter. "Well, it was me but only for you, in the submission."

"Have you been there, to the other side? Are they just like us, the people there?"

"A few times, yes, but only a little way, not as far as anywhere, well, anywhere dangerous. Most of the people I came across are almost just like us, except some of them, well all of them in fact, have horns."

"Horns?" enquired Clive.

"Only little ones. You wouldn't even know it when they're wearing hats."

Clive wondered what other strange things there might be.

"You mentioned dragons."

"Did I?"

"Yes, you thought the plane I was in might have been a dragon."

"Oh yes."

"Where I come from, London, England, that is, dragons are only thought of as mythical creatures."

"Mythical?"

"Mythical, yes, things that only exist in our imagination, make believe. Do you really have dragons here?"

"Of course."

"Are they around now? I wouldn't mind seeing one."

"Not much to see really, they're only small; the biggest is no bigger than a robin. They can hardly raise a spark let alone breathe fire. We used to have big ones that came here in the summer when it got too hot for them further north."

"Why would the heat bother a creature that breathes fire?"

"But that's exactly it. If you're already hot enough to breathe fire, then summer temperatures can be a real killer."

"So dragons are migratory?"

"I don't know about that but the big ones only used to come here in summer."

"Why don't they come any more?"

"The Council ordered them out. Too many complaints of houses and crops getting burnt up, so they were exiled down south."

"And the dragons just agreed and left? Doesn't sound like dragons to me."

"They're quite cowardly actually, sneaky and cowardly. The Council threatened them with the Staff and the dragons shifted out as quick as could be. See, even dragons is afraid of Staffs of Power."

Just then a scroll popped through the letter box.

"They've said yes," said Ggydren, "only there's a proviso. Before you go on a quest to find your way home, you have to rescue a princess from somewhere called Besanto Castle, before a baron who's kidnapped her, has his wicked way with her. Seems fair enough."

"Princess, Besanto, baron?"

"No point asking me. Never heard of any of them. Still, it adds to the excitement, doesn't it? What do you say? Are you still game?"

Clive did not reply. He was mulling it over. He'd started out by categorically refusing to go on a quest, then he had been persuaded to apply for one and now he'd got two. Things were getting out of hand but then, what was the alternative? Mrs Elphick had only agreed to feed the cat for up to two weeks, if she remembered because 'my memory isn't what it was', and after that she was going to stay with her sister in Rotherham. It was no good. If the only way back was through the door and into another dimension where he had to complete two quests, then it had to be. Two other thoughts struck Clive. Firstly that a secret camera was probably filming all this for the type of TV show where they set you up to do ridiculous things, without you realising, and then have a good laugh about it afterwards at your expense, which actually wouldn't be as bad as having to go on two quests and the second was why, if he was so concerned about the bloody cat, had he never taken the trouble to give it a name?

"I'll do it."

"Good on you. Good on you."

"Do I start right away?"

"Well, not much point now it's dark. First thing in the morning will be fine. Have good night's sleep first. Actually, I've been thinking, I've always wanted to go on a quest..."

Clive guessed what was coming.

'Oh God, now there's going to be a company too, next it will be dwarves and elves,' he thought to himself.

"But what about Elendril? Wouldn't she be upset if you left?"

"Well, it wouldn't be forever and I could leave her a note to explain. Actually, she'd be quite useful to have along too, knowing the layout of the place more than me."

"How's that?"

"Well obviously she comes from there. We don't have shape-shifters here. I thought you would have realised."

"Does she have...?"

"Only titchy ones. Is that settled then? I'll make a few preparations and then we'd better turn in early. Big day in front of us tomorrow. You can have the bed, I'll make do."

A little later, Clive stood at the entrance to the cave looking up at the moon and lost in thought. It had been a strange day, a strange few days in fact. Normally he spent his days in the office, preparing invoices and sending them by email. It wasn't demanding work, it wasn't even interesting most of the time but it paid quite well and the hours were good. He didn't usually like adventures, more of a home bird really. This trip had been the first time he'd been on a plane in over four years and that had only been for a five day walking holiday on Madeira, well away from the tourist hot spots, nothing too adventurous. Yet, when Clive thought about it, he had to admit it had been quite exciting to survive a plane crash and fend off a shark, and to nearly get eaten by a lion, and everything else that had followed. So maybe a quest or two might not be so bad after all. And the idea of rescuing a princess, well that was something really quite exciting. She might even be sufficiently impressed with his gallantry to fall in love with him, something no one had done before. And Ggydren seemed a decent enough sort too, and it would really be quite interesting to meet Elendril and see her horns and maybe even watch her change shape, and who knows what might happen along the way or how long it would take, and whether he'd succeed and get back in time to feed the cat. Best just to try and approach things with an open mind. It was probably all a dream anyway. Just then Ggydren called out about something, stirring Clive from his reverie. It was only then that he noticed the other moons.

Chapter 5.

The bed was comfortable; Clive slept like a log. He woke to the sound of Ggydren telling him he'd better wake up as they hadn't got all day. Ggydren, it transpired, had been busy for a good few hours, preparing for the journey. There were two knapsacks on the table, each containing a packed lunch and a change of clothing.

"And while you were sleeping I've been down to the inn and arranged for a stand-in keeper. Had to have a good excuse so I told them my brother is laid up, ha ha, and I have to look after him. Well, a little fib once in a while can't do too much harm and I could hardly tell them I was going off on a quest, now could I? I've also had a word with Elendril and asked her if she wanted to come along but she decided it was better to stay behind in case any more weirdo's, like the bloke with the pointy hat, turned up. Would you mind shutting your eyes for a moment or two? I've got to do something private. I'll let you know when you can look."

Clive wondered what on earth Ggydren needed to do in private. When he was told, a few seconds later, that it was alright to look, there was quite a large leather pouch in front of him on the table.

"We'll be needing some money, I expect, and I don't suppose you've got anything that's legal tender here or in Morgrnvia."

He emptied a pile of golden coins on the table.

"Groats; quarters, halves and ones. Worth a pretty penny, this lot. I've been putting a few away each week ever since I got the job, saving up, just in case. I reckon a quest is a good enough excuse to spend a few."

Ggydren counted out twenty groats in various denominations and put the rest back. Clive had to close his eyes again. He remembered they'd had groats in England in earlier times and wondered if this might be significant or just coincidence.

"It's not that I don't trust you, just that a hidey hole wouldn't be a hidey hole if people knew about it. You'd think that someone could come up with a better place for people to keep their savings."

"Like in a bank."

Ggydren look at Clive with a slightly bewildered expression.

"Well no, actually I was thinking more of a big strong building, with guards and heavy metal doors and locks. Besides, what would happen when the river flooded?"

Clive decided not to take it any further.

"Time for breakfast," said Ggydren, "I'm out of cornflakes but there's eggs and bacon in the larder. No black pudding I'm afraid."

"Bacon and eggs sounds delicious. I'll have a quick wash, if that's okay. I don't suppose you've got a spare toothbrush?"

Half an hour or so later they were almost ready to go. Ggydren handed Clive a cloak of the same material and colour as the gown he was wearing.

"Regulations, you see. Cloaks and gowns must be matching,"

Ggydren also insisted that Clive keep the rod well hidden and handed him a belt so that he could hold it in place.

"We don't need to go advertising the fact that you've got a Staff of Power, even if it doesn't look like one. Besides it would look a bit strange to be seen wandering about holding a metal rod. People might start wondering what it was for, and why you're so attached to it. Now where is that Ggydon?"

Just then a young man came rushing up the last few steps and into the cave.

"Hello uncle," gasped Ggydon, "I'm not late am I? You must be Clive. Very pleased to meet you. I wish I was coming too, it's so boring here. Don't worry uncle, I'll look after everything."

"And mind you do. Make sure everyone has a ticket and write down all the details properly.   You know where everything is, and don't try looking for any hidey holes, there aren't any. Make sure you lock up after us until the first customer arrives and not a word to anyone about the quest. If anyone asks, I'm visiting your other uncle who's broke his leg. And make sure you keep everything tidy or Elendril will have your guts for garters when she gets back. And no parties. Got it?"

Ggydon nodded.

"Well, we'll be off then. You're a good lad Ggydon," said Ggydren, in a more kindly voice, "I know I can count on you."

Ggydon smiled and Ggydren and Clive gathered up their things in readiness for departure. Ggydren looked around as if to check that everything was in its place or maybe, as Clive wondered, as if he was saying goodbye. Finally, he approached the door.

"It's dark inside. Just try to keep right behind me."

With that he unlocked and opened the door. From the light of the cave Clive could see a narrow tunnel stretching ahead. When Ggydren shut the door behind them he could see nothing at all and was suddenly quite afraid.

"Just a few hundred yards like this. I didn't have time to light the lanterns this morning. I should warn you that there's a place in the middle where it gets a bit wobbly but just keep going."

Ggydren's voice sounded echoey and loud in the confines of the tunnel. The wobbly bit was very wobbly indeed. Clive felt unsteady, as if he was falling or about to fall, but he kept on creeping forward as Ggydren had told him and he was soon through it. A few minutes later Clive bumped into Ggydren who had stopped.

"Sorry," said Ggydren. "I should have said, we're here."

Clive heard the sound of another key turning and the creaking of another door opening. It took a few seconds for Clive's eyes to adjust to the bright sunlight. They seemed to be half way up a hill, with steps leading down. Countryside stretched out below.

'Another dimension my foot,' thought Clive, 'it's just the other side of the hill. What's he's playing at?'

"Morgrnvia," said Ggydren, "pretty isn't it? No gloom. Follow me."

Ggydren descended the steps rapidly. As they rounded a bend a small town came into view in the valley below.

"That's Buggiton, our first stop. I want to get a map."

Within half an hour they had reached the outskirts and Clive saw his first Morgrnvian.

'It's true', he thought, looking at the small, fawn coloured horns that protruded just above the Morgrnvian's ears. 'Maybe it is another dimension after all.'

Buggiton was picture postcard pretty, with cobbled, narrow streets and half-timbered buildings.

"It's a den of vice," warned Ggydren. "You can buy anything here, if you know what I mean. That's why people are so keen to come. No rules, no regulations."

Towards the centre Clive began to see why. Every other place seemed to be an inn and each inn seemed to have large gaudily painted signs saying things like, 'Gambling tables, Smoking permitted, Exotic dancers, Pretty women, Handsome men, Private rooms available, Discounts for parties, Aughphalians welcome'.

"I see what you mean," said Clive.

It seemed to be teeming with people, even at that hour. Ggydren explained that Buggiton was a magnet not just for Aughphalians but for Morgrnvians as well.

"They come from all over. It's famous. Mostly they get drunk and lose all their money gambling. A few arrive home with nasty diseases and not only the men. Some of them get so taken in with it all they just never leave. That's true of more than a few Aughphalians too."

Clive noticed more than a few establishments with signs advertising shape-shifters. Outside each were men who looked decidedly shifty, beckoning to the passers-by. One of them beckoned to Clive.

"Floor show inside, sir, all genuine shape-shifters, any shape, any pose, you do the choosing, only half a groat admission, unlimited time."

"Pay no attention," muttered Ggydren. "See what I mean, den of vice. Keep on your guard, lots of pickpockets."

Clive kept on his guard; there were more than a few shady characters about, even if the horns did lend them slightly comical appearance.

A few minutes further on Ggydren turned down a side street. Very soon they'd left the crowds behind. He stopped at the door of a shop selling antique books, maps and curios.

"Best let me do the talking," said Ggydren.

A bell rattled, rather than rang, as they entered. Inside each wall was lined with shelves and each shelf was stuffed with dusty books. Clive couldn't imagine there being many customers. Presently an old man emerged from a back room to stand before them at the counter. His face was wrinkled and what little hair he had was pure white.

"Good morning Sirs, are you looking for anything in particular?"

"It's a map we need," said Ggydren, "a map of Morgrnvia. We saw the sign on the door."

"Of course, of course, maps and maps, all kinds of maps. It's a pleasure to welcome you. I can't say I've ever had an Aughphalian customer before. Most Aughphalians come to Buggiton for its other delights. Would it be any particular kind of map you require?"

"Well, I'm hoping that you've got a map with England or London on."

"Sorry?"

"England or London. Have you got a map of Morgrnvia that shows where England or London is?"

"No."

"No, you don't have one in stock or no, there aren't any?"

"I've never heard of such places. Are you sure of the names?"

"Well, Besanto Castle then. That's the other place we have to go. Have you got a map that shows that?"

The shopkeeper looked surprised.

"Did you say Bes..."

Just then the bell rattled as the door opened for another customer. A Morgrnvian entered. The shopkeeper raised a finger in front of his mouth as a warning to keep quiet.

"Perhaps you'd like to come through to the office, good Sirs. Yes, I do have one or two fine specimens of books about Buggiton," he said, quite loudly and indicating with his eyes towards the back room door. "Really, no need to say anything, just in there, you'll find exactly what you need. Have a browse around. I'll be right in after I've dealt with this other customer."

Clive and Ggydren did as they were told.

"What was all that about?" asked Clive.

"Don't ask me. No idea. Did you see the way he reacted when I said Besanto? And I can't see any maps in here. What do you reckon; time for a hasty exit?"

"No," said Clive, rather decisively, "he was warning us to keep quiet and I think he got us in here for our own protection. I think we'd better wait and hear what he has to say."

When the shopkeeper entered he looked perturbed.

"By my horns, you two must be either stupid or just plain ignorant. Walking in here and announcing you have to go to Besanto. You're lucky that other fellow didn't hear or he'd have probably reported it and you'd be being carted off to prison by now. Don't you know about Besanto?"

"Well actually no." said Clive, taking the lead. "Perhaps you could explain it to us. This is our first holiday in Morgrnvia and we want to see more than Buggiton and its 'other delights,' as you put it. Is there a problem about going to Besanto? It was recommended to us."

"Must have been recommended by a practical joker then, Besanto is completely off limits. Don't you know there's a war on, for goodness sake? You'd better explain yourselves and make it convincing. All citizens of Morgrnvia are obliged to report spies, enemy agents and people acting suspiciously and saying you have to go to Besanto is certainly suspicious. Who are you? Who sent you?"

Clive and Ggydren just looked at each other. Neither really had a clue what to say or what to do next. Clive had a sinking feeling that whatever either of them said was only going to make matters worse. Just then he noticed the teapot, at least what looked like a teapot, sitting on the stove.

"That isn't a teapot, is it? I could murder a nice cup of tea."

"Of course it's a teapot and this isn't a café. I sell books, not hot drinks."

"I'm sorry," said Clive, genuinely disappointed, "I've had a difficult time the last few days. I shouldn't have asked. We'll get on our way."

"Not until you've explained yourselves. Oh, go on then, I was just brewing up anyway. One cup mind you. Milk and sugar?"

"Just milk for me. I don't think Ggydren's tried tea. They don't seem to have it in Aughphalia."

54

"You make it sound as though you don't come from there."

Clive thought about explaining then decided not to. It would only complicate the situation.

"Just a slip of the tongue. You said there's a war on. We didn't know. I don't know much at all about Morgrnvia or Besanto Castle. I don't even know where it is."

"You'd better sit down and I'll explain. Obviously neither of you has a clue."

The shopkeeper introduced himself as Reece, then poured tea into sturdy mugs and added milk. Clive took a tentative sip. Not exactly Twinings but definitely tea. He noticed that Ggydren pulled a face when he tasted it. How could anyone not like tea? He suggested sugar. Ggydren stirred in two teaspoons, tasted the tea again, then added a further two.

"I suppose you'd like a biscuit to go with it?" asked Reece, smiling. He fetched a wooden box and placed several biscuits on a plate.

"Oatmeal, go on, they're rather good. Let me see now......."

Reece told them all about it. Besanto wasn't just a castle, it was a province too. Far away on a high plateau, it was surrounded by mountains. As a remote province of Morgrnvia, it accepted the Morgrnvian king as overlord and paid annual tributes but the day to day government was controlled by the Baron of Besanto Castle, the highest ranking official. A year ago he had declared Besanto independent and stopped paying the tribute. A delegation sent to negotiate was turned away at the border but reported observing a small but steady stream or refugees fleeing the province. When questioned, they talked of the whole of Besanto being turned into an armed camp, with conscription for all males of fifteen to twenty five years of age and the forced requisition of crops and stores. On hearing the news, the King of Morgrnvia ordered an elite cavalry unit to enter Besanto, by force if necessary, to stop whatever was going on and to reimpose Morgrnvian rule. The unit was almost completely wiped out. The few survivors who managed to return home spoke not only of the quality of the troops set against them but also of a terrible new weapon, unknown and unseen, that killed from a distance using fire.

"Then, six months ago, the King's daughter, Princess Gretchen, was abducted by masked men, while on official business and smuggled off to Besanto. The King sent another unit to try to rescue her but they were almost wiped out too. Weeks later, a soldier who'd been captured in the attack arrived back with a message. The Princess was indeed held captive in Besanto Castle. Any further attack would result in her execution but only after...., well, I imagine you don't need me to explain any further. That's where we are now. The King is increasing the size of the army and has offered a large reward for the safe return of his daughter. People are afraid there's going to be all-out war. There, that's my side of story. Now it's time for yours."

Reece sat back and waited.

Once again Clive and Ggydren looked at each other. Ggydren spoke up.

"It's as we told you," said Ggydren, "we're on holiday with a mind to explore the country. We were told that Besanto Castle was interesting and wanted to find it but now we know better, we'll just give it a miss. Thank you for the tea but we'll best be on our way."

He started to rise but Clive interrupted.

"No, it's not entirely like that. You were right about me not coming from Aughphalia. I come from a city called London, in a country called England. No one here seems to have heard of it. I was shipwrecked and adrift for days before arriving in Aughphalia. I'd never heard of that either. I'm trying to find my way back home and Ggydren has kindly offered to help. For some reason we think that it may help if we can rescue the Princess first. I don't know why but maybe it has something to do with the reward. We need a map to show us the way. Will you help?"

Reece rubbed his chin, pondering.

"I'm not sure. It seems a very strange scheme to me. I don't quite know what to think. How do I know I can trust you? It could be you're working for the Baron."

"Please ask yourself," said Clive, "would an agent or spy from Besanto walk into your shop of all places and ask for a map of where he'd come from?"

Reece thought for a few seconds, then got up without speaking and went back through the door, into the shop. Ggydren and Clive sat in silence. Clive was more than slightly surprised at what he had said. It wasn't like him to speak out, to speak first, to contradict. He hoped he hadn't ruined everything. After a minute or so, Ggydren whispered.

"I thought we agreed to leave the talking to me. Do you think it was wise to tell him all that? I wonder what he's up to."

"I'm sorry. It just sort of came out. He must still be in there. I didn't hear the bell."

They waited for at least another minute before the door opened once more and Reece returned, clutching a scroll. He unwound it and placed it on the table.

"This is the most detailed map of Morgrnvia I possess. Here, have a look."

He pointed out Buggiton and then Besanto.

"What sort of scale is it? How far is Besanto?" asked Clive.

"I reckon, it's probably a good eighty miles as the crow flies but you wouldn't be able to go direct. All the roads and tracks avoid the Great Forest altogether and that probably adds another thirty. Then there are these afterwards," said Reece, pointing to some hills. "They look little enough here but some of the peaks are quite high. There are paths through but they're all rather windy and it's easy to get lost. There are brigands too, so they're dangerous. You can see how the main road goes around them but that would mean a long trek to the south-east and that route has its own dangers. If you do finally make it, you'll find that all the entrances into Besanto are heavily guarded and they're hardly going to let you just walk in, especially if you tell them you've come to rescue the Princess."

"Would there be lodgings along the way, places to find a bed and food to eat?' asked Ggydren.

"To begin with yes but after the forest the countryside gets wilder, with fewer villages and inns. You'd have to rough it for some of the time at least."

"And how much do inns cost, on average, for the night?"

"Maybe one or two groats per person, with the same again for dinner and breakfast."

Ggydren and Clive looked at each other again. Clive knew they were thinking the same thoughts; basically that what they intended was impossible. They had a packed lunch each, enough money for three of four nights' accommodation, almost nothing in the way of other possessions, and yet the long journey on foot that they faced would probably take several weeks, if not months, that is if they ever got there at all. Never mind the difficulties and dangers of rescuing a princess from the clutches of a megalomaniac. Impossible, simply impossible. It was all too ridiculous.

"You've gone quiet. Having second thoughts?" asked Reece.

"Well, we seem to be a little underprepared," said Clive. "Rather short on money and provisions and it seems a bit too far to walk. We might have to go with Plan B."

"Didn't know we had a plan B," said Ggydren.

"We haven't. Any ideas?"

"Search me, maybe something'll turn up along the way."

"You mean you're still willing to go?"

"Well, how else are you going to find your way back to your England? A quest's a quest, no one said it would be easy. Wouldn't be fun either, if it was too easy."

"Would it help if I made us another cup of tea?" asked Reece.

When they were finishing the second cup Reece had an idea.

"If you follow me upstairs, I have a few things that I think might come in useful."

He led them slowly up two flights of rickety stairs and into a dusty attic.

"I keep all my old junk up here and I don't suppose I'll make use of much of it again. Well past it, as you can see. I used to like hiking and camping out under the stars. There's a tent, a bit cramped for two but you could make do, and there's other stuff besides, cooking equipment and so on. Have a look. Help yourselves to anything. We'll say it's a loan but I wouldn't be bothered if it never came back."

Fifteen minutes later, Clive and Ggydren took their leave of Reece. Thanks to his generosity they had a tent, blankets, a flint for making fire, a frying pan and saucepan, sharp knives and forks and spoons, a leather water bottle, a fishing line and hooks, a map, not as detailed as the one Reece had shown them before but good enough, and several other things besides. Some of this was stuffed into a proper rucksack that Ggydren wore, while the rest went into the two knapsacks, together with the change of clothing and packed lunches, which Clive carried. Reece had also produced two woolly hats for them, obviously designed for people with horns.

"You'll probably look stupid in these but they may come in useful."

They left Reece, thanking him profusely for his generosity. Walking away, Clive was rather amazed to think that it had only been the previous day that he'd woken up on the beach in Aughphalia. Such a lot had happened since then and it still wasn't even lunchtime.

Chapter 6.

 Clive and Ggydren hurried out of Buggiton and into the countryside. The weather was bright and sunny, though not too hot for walking on that autumn day, with just a gentle breeze and no sign of rain. The map was easy to follow; there was only one road, though it was really no more than a track, deeply rutted by the carts that used it. They passed a few of those, laden with goods to sell in the town. The drivers smiled and nodded, friendly enough, though few words were exchanged. The countryside was dotted with farms and criss-crossed by hedges and dry stone walls. Some fields bore a golden hew, the stubble of harvested wheat and barley. In others, given over to pasture, sheep and cows grazed. Ggydren seemed particularly thrilled to see cows but then, of course, there were none in Aughphalia. There were only a few villages, most no more than a few houses and only one with an inn, although they resisted the temptation. After a couple of hours they stopped and rested, eating their sandwiches sat on the trunk of a fallen chestnut. Then they pressed on, although Clive found it increasingly hard going. He hadn't anticipated how much the days adrift on the ocean had taken out of him and they had to stop frequently for breaks. Eventually, well before the daylight began to fade they came across an isolated farmstead and knocked on the door to request permission to camp for the night. The farmer was generous and led them to a barn instead. He even fed them a decent stew with bread to soak up the gravy and fresh milk to drink and he gave them more bread and milk for breakfast.

During the second day Clive and Ggydren came across fewer farms and more open countryside. They bought lunch at a wayside inn and camped that night in a clearing beside a gently flowing stream. They'd kept back bread to use as bait if the opportunity for fishing arose and, taking it, they caught several plump trout. Clive proved adept at using the flint to make fire and Ggydren cleaned and cooked the fish. As they sat eating and talking under the open sky, the moons came out. Clive noticed that there were fewer of them than in Aughphalia but still more than he was used to.

So they continued onwards for several days, and all the while Clive's strength returning. As they walked, they talked. Ggydren found it hard to understand that there was something in England called electricity that made all sorts of things work, and other things with wheels that weren't carts and which could move you about from one town to another, many times faster than a horse could run, or that the things that weren't birds or dragons could transport hundreds of people, all at once and in the sky, many times faster than the things that weren't carts. From what Ggydren told Clive, on the other hand, it seemed that Aughphalia was hundreds of years behind home, certainly at a pre-industrial stage, although this didn't exactly tally with the artificial production of milk that Ggydren had mentioned earlier. And, from what Clive could tell, Morgrnvia was pretty much the same, though with the more traditional means of dairy production. In fact, Ggydren wasn't much use at all when it came to answering questions about Morgrnvia. It seems that Buggiton had been the furthest he'd ventured before. He did get more interesting though, when Clive asked him about shape-shifters and how he came to be married to one.

"Actually I call her the wife but we're not actually married. We can't have kiddies either, coming from different species. I don't mean that it isn't allowed, just that it can't be done. We don't have shape-shifters back home. They come from here; in fact I think they may only be from here. If you must know I used to go to the shifter shows quite a lot. Being the Keeper, I could always pop over on my day off without anyone knowing and I got in the habit of going. I know it's disgusting and I haven't done it for ages, since I met Elendril in fact."

Clive was rather intrigued to know more about the shows.

"You pay the admission, then you pay extra to get the shifter to do different things, like being a woman doing lewd things or becoming a monster with two heads or a thing with a long drinking spout coming out of its face and stuff like that. I was watching once when this new shifter came on and people threw down their money for her to do stuff and you could tell that she'd never done it before and was nervous and worried. The people in the audience started shouting and jeering and demanding their money back and then the manager came on and dragged her off and put on one of the regulars instead. I felt sorry for her and ashamed at myself for being there, so I got up and left. Outside I could hear crying from behind the building, and it was her. She had no money and nowhere to go and nobody to go to, so I told her not to worry and that she could come home with me. We've been together ever since."

"But where do they come from? I don't understand."

"It's not easy to say. She doesn't properly know herself, for sure. She told me all about it. How she grew up completely normal as a child with this family but when she got to the age of twelve or thirteen she started shifting shape. It wasn't on purpose, it just started naturally and to begin with she had no control over it, like when it happened or what she shifted into. She said the family were horrified and threw her out but not before they'd told her she wasn't their real daughter, had been bought in a baby auction and that they'd obviously been cheated. You can imagine how it all came as a terrible shock to her, being so young and not having had the slightest clue about it before. Well, she got by as best as she could, sleeping rough, stealing food, doing odd jobs for money and trying to hide the shape-shifting but she almost always got found out and had to move on again. People don't really like shape-shifters you see. Oh, they pays their money to get entertained or frightened half to death in the shows but they don't like the idea of them walking about, free like. Eventually Elendril ended up in Buggiton and was drawn into the shows. I think it was just that she wanted to be with her own kind, even in a place like that. And they trained her so that she could control the shifting and just do it, and come out of it, when she wanted or when they said. She was there some time before they said she was ready and, well, I've told you what happened when she first went on. The other shifters there all had basically the same story, growing up in normal families and then starting to change and finding out they'd been bought."

"That's horrible, the baby auction bit, I mean. Is it legal for babies to be bought and sold here?"

"Apparently yes. We don't have it in Aughphalia but they have it here. I think it's allowed when people already have too many kids, or can't afford to look after one, so it gets put in an auction, highest bidder getting the child. Only sometimes, not very often mind, the baby turns out to be a shifter."

"So it's natural then?"

"How do you mean?"

"Some ordinary babies here just develop into shape-shifters."

"No, I don't think so. You see it's only babies that were in auctions that turn out that way, like someone knew they had a shifter and wanted to get rid of it or maybe someone was deliberately planting them in amongst the ordinary babies for some devious purpose. It's another reason people don't trust shifters."

"And no one knows where they come from?"

"Elendril says that some people believe they come from the Great Forest because it's supposed to have weird things in it but then again people aren't allowed in the Great Forest, so they don't know for sure. Actually, the first people from Aughphalia who came exploring here and who returned terrified, said they'd got to a forest when weird and terrifying things happened. I suppose it could have been shape-shifters but then it might have been some sort of black magic or something else we don't rightly understand."

"How does she do it, change shape I mean, and how does she feel like when she's changed?"

"She just imagines what she wants to become and sort of wills it. That's what she says. While she is changed she still has regular thoughts but she can't do anything that the thing can't usually do. Like when she was the lion, she couldn't talk to you but was able to purr. She changes back again in the same way, by willing it."

'It's all very strange,' thought Clive. 'I'm not sure I believe a word of it but then again...'

The next day they passed through no villages at all and saw very few people. The countryside became less inviting, with fewer farms and fields until it was just uncultivated moorland. There was no inn in which to find lodgings or even a barn for shelter, so that night they camped out again, even though there was no stream and no food, and the air was decidedly chilly. Clive found it difficult to sleep. Having Ggydren pressed so close to him in the cramped tent and snoring didn't help. Neither did the hunger. Clive pondered on all that had happened and concluded that the only explanations were that he must have gone mad or be dreaming. In reality, he knew that there was only one moon, shape-shifters and Staffs of Power did not exist and nor did Aughphalia or Morgrnvia. Then another idea came to mind; that his earlier thoughts about the Lord of the Rings weren't so ridiculous after all. He hadn't really been serious when he'd mentioned Gandalf to Ggydren but the coincidences were becoming too numerous to be ignored. Gandalf had gone off to find the Grey Havens, and it had been really grey and gloomy in Aughphalia. In the book there were forests with elves and weird tree-like creatures called Ents, and here there was a Great Forest with weird and terrifying things. In the book, the evil Lord Sauron lived in a remote place called Mordor, that was surrounded and cut off by mountains, and this place had a bad baron who lived in a remote castle in a land called Besanto, that was similarly encircled. And although there didn't seem to be any powerful rings here, there were the Staffs of Power. Somehow, it was as if he had become a character in the pages of a book and yet that was just completely stupid. It was a conundrum to which he had no answers. All he could do was to press on with Ggydren in the hope that something might begin to make sense. The following day he remembered his thoughts about the Tolkien book and, once again, dismissed them. Even so, every once in a while he had a quick look behind to make sure that a wretched, slimy thing wasn't following.

Chapter 7.

The next day started even worse than the previous one had ended; it was raining. Not the hard driving rain that drenches in seconds but the fine drizzle that has the same effect in minutes. By the time they had packed up camp they were soaking. They trudged along for at least an hour before they came upon a house but hurried past when big dogs came running up to the fence to bark at them ferociously. A little further on they spied a farmhouse some way down a narrow lane and turned off the road. The lady who answered their knock and request to purchase food did not smile.

"Aughphalians? What are you doing so far from home? Food you want is it? Well, there's a loaf still left from yesterday, nothing else. One groat to you. Yes or no?"

It was an outrageous price for a loaf of bread but they had little choice; they hadn't eaten for nearly twenty four hours. The lady closed the door on them while she fetched the bread and opened it again only wide enough to take the money first, then hand the loaf over.

"And make sure you close the latch on the gate as you leave."

Under the shelter of a tree they divided the loaf into two, then wrapped one half for later and devoured the other between them. At least it was good wholesome bread and none the worse for being yesterday's bake.

They walked on, their spirits slightly raised by the food but soon dampened again by the persistent rain. Mostly they walked in silence, each wrapped in their own thoughts. Clive's were focussed for some time on the rod. He hadn't really considered it for days but then, as they walked along, he clutched it through the thickness of his robe and wondered about its powers. He'd seen the flash of light generated after it had changed into a staff and he'd banged its end on the cave floor, and he remembered the awe he felt when the light had flashed around the cave before shooting off into the sky. He also remembered Ggydren's account of how William had used a Staff of Power to silence the crowd and then to kill the dissenters and impose his authority on Aughphalia. How did he do it? Was it a flash of light that had burnt the two men to cinders, the same flash he'd seen in the cave? If the story was true, William must have learnt how to control the Staff and use its power. Was the light the extent of its power or could a Staff be used in other ways? And did the rod have the same powers as a Staff? It had worked on the shark, and the lion had been impressed with it, but could it really be used as a weapon to kill or did it need to be changed into a Staff to do that? Were they one and the same, only in different form, or was the rod an inferior version of the Staff. What had it been doing on the plane anyway? So many questions, but not a single answer. It struck Clive that he'd have to find out some for himself and that maybe the only way to do that was to experiment with the rod himself.

Clive's thoughts changed. It would soon be a week on the road. Thank goodness for Ggydren. It would have been far worse to have travelled alone but for how much longer would

Ggydren be content to continue? Ggydren had a job to return to. There was Elendril to consider. Would Ggydren suddenly announce that that was it and he was leaving? It was a horrible prospect. And what lay ahead anyway? Clive knew that they would soon be reaching the Great Forest. What then, what dangers lay within? Would they decide to face them or would they make the long detour around its borders, however long that might take? And how would they survive when their money ran out, as it must soon do? And how would they get into Besanto and rescue a princess without getting caught and killed, that is if they weren't killed before then or die of hunger first.

Clive was working himself up into a state and tried to pull himself together. Ggydren's voice took him by surprise but helped him to calm down.

"Begging you pardon, Mr Clive, but you remember when Reece told us about the goings on in Besanto?"

"Yes."

"And the Morgrnvian king sent out a unit to find out what was happening but most of them got wiped out?"

"Yes, I remember that too."

"The survivor that got back said that the ruler of Besanto had got hold of a brand new weapon that killed unseen from a distance, using fire?"

"Yes, I remember all that but what's your point?"

"Well, do you think it could be a Staff of Power?"

Clive took a few seconds to think. During the war the Americans had used flame throwers to root out and kill the Japanese in their foxholes and in England there were lots of things that could fit the bill, rocket propelled grenades, long range cannon, incendiary bombs, ballistic missiles. Only, he didn't suppose they had any of those in Morgrnvia. In the Middle Ages they'd used mangonels or was it trebuchets, to fire rocks and stuff at castles and sometimes the stuff had been set alight but that wasn't unseen or from any sort of distance.

"I haven't the faintest idea," said Clive, eventually.

Neither of them said anything more about it but both wondered what the implications might be, should it prove correct.

It drizzled for the rest of the morning. Eventually the sun started to peek through the clouds and the day brightened up a touch. Clive and Ggydren were still soaking though. They didn't bother to stop for lunch, there was nowhere dry to rest and, in any case, half a loaf of bread between them wasn't really worth stopping for. So they ate as they walked, munching as they went.

"I'm sorry about this," said Clive, a couple of hours or so after lunch.

It was drizzling again, he was fed up and bedraggled and somehow he felt responsible for the discomfort that Ggydren must also be feeling.

"It's not your fault. The weather's nobody's fault, it just happens. Rain or shine we just have to grin and bear it."

"I'm beginning to think it's hopeless," said Clive, "we're wet though, half-starved, in the middle of nowhere. Is there any point in going on?"

"More point going on than turning back. The last inn was yesterday. Besides I seem to remember the map shows a village a few miles before the forest. We must be quite near that now. Perhaps we'll find dry lodgings there. Here, I'll get the map out to check."

The map showed that Ggydren was correct, so they pressed on, walking quickly in the anticipation of some home comforts. After a while they found themselves climbing a low hill but as they neared the top two men suddenly jumped out from behind a tree and stood a few yards before them on the road, arms folded, muscles bulging and blocking the way. They were clad in leggings and short sleeved leather tunics. Most of the flesh that was visible was covered in tattoos.

'We're in trouble,' thought Clive, feeling an overwhelming sense of panic.

"Halt," ordered one of them. "Payment is due. The toll is two groats each."

"Toll for what?" demanded Ggydren.

"Road toll; pay up or turn back."

"Road toll my foot," said Ggydren. "This isn't a private road. We aren't going to pay and we're not turning back. Be off with you."

Clive was quite taken aback by Ggydren's bravery; the ruffians were much bigger than him and there were two of them. One of them stepped forward and punched him in the stomach. Ggydren fell to the floor, winded and groaning.

"It's three groats each now," said the other ruffian, looking at Clive and smiling.

Clive felt himself shaking. It was not the sort of situation he was used to.

"Look here"' he said, in a rather quivering voice, "we're almost out of money. We only have a couple of groats between us."

"Four groats each now. At this rate it will soon be ten. I'd pay up quick if I was you."

By this time Ggydren was staggering to his feet, only to be floored again by a second punch.

"Fancy some of the same?"

Clive was desperately searching for something to say or do when he suddenly remembered the rod and the effect it had had on the shark and the lion. He fumbled inside his robe and pulled it out. He banged it down hard on the ground. It let off a loud bang and a brilliant flash of light. Then Clive pointed it at his assailants.

"Fancy some of this?' he enquired.

The two ruffians looked in amazement at the rod, then at each other and then, without uttering a word, ran off as fast as they could.

'Thank God for the rod,' thought Clive, remembering it was the second time the phrase had come to mind.

By the time Clive had helped Ggydren to his feet and made sure that he was okay, he had just about finished shaking.

"I'm sorry," said Clive.

"Again?" asked Ggydren.

"The rod; I should have thought of it earlier, before they hit you. You were very brave."

"More stupid than brave. I should have thought of it too. We better get on before they decide to come back."

An hour later and they were at the edge of the village. A sign said it was called Mickelling. It was sizeable enough, with several side lanes leading off the main track and at least a few dozen houses. In the middle was a green, with a pond with ducks and other water fowl and to one side of that was an inn. It was a most welcome site.

"How much would it be for a room with two beds, dinner and breakfast and two or three pints of best beer?" asked Ggydren of the innkeeper.

The innkeeper looked up from the ledger in which he'd been writing.

"Aughphalian, eh," he said, noticing the absence of horns. "Can't say I've ever had an Aughphalian customer before. In fact the only Aughphalians I ever saw before were in Buggiton and that was a good few years' back. You're a long way from home. Is it business or pleasure you're on?"

Without waiting for them to answer he walked over to the till and started pressing keys.

"That would come to about nine groats, more or less, depending on how many courses and how many pints. Okay for you? Couldn't do it any cheaper. Payment in advance, I'm afraid. Not all customers recently have been exactly honest, not meaning any offence. I'll throw in the hot water for nothing. You both look like you could do with a bath, again no offence intended."

Ggydren counted out the money and the innkeeper led them to the top floor.

"Nice room this, always warm and quiet too. Bathroom's on the floor below. Food starts at seven of an evening until nine. I'll leave you to it then. You know where to find me if there's anything you need. If I'm not there, just ask for Bob."

It was a nice room but the bath was even more welcome, with hot water and carbolic soap to wash away the dirt and grime of several days, and a razor and comb provided to remove the stubble and untangle the tangles. Clive felt like a new man afterwards. When he returned to the room Ggydren was asleep. Clive considered leaving him be but thought better of it just in case it kept him awake later on; they both needed a good night's sleep. So Clive woke Ggydren and directed him to the bathroom. When Ggydren returned he looked very different but it was several seconds before Clive realised that his moustache and beard had gone.

"Been thinking about doing it for ages. Don't know when I'll get another chance. What do you think; takes years off me?"

Clive nodded in agreement, though he was actually thinking the reverse. With his whiskers it had been difficult to tell Ggydren's age but without them he looked at least fifty, maybe more.

A little later Clive and Ggydren made their way downstairs to the bar and found a table already laid and awaiting them.

"There's soup and main or main and pudding or all three if you want to pay a bit more. Soup is mushroom, pudding is jam roly-poly. The main is chicken á la something, only I'm not quite sure what the 'á la something' is, as the cook's gone all experimental on us but she's a good cook anyway so it's sure to be tasty. I'll fetch you each a pint of my best while you're deciding."

The deciding didn't take long. Two mains and two portions of jam roly-poly were soon on order.

The chicken was actually very tasty, served in a white sauce or gravy and with potatoes mashed and fried and two green vegetables besides. But if the chicken was tasty, then the pudding was divine, oozing hot strawberry jam and with lashings of custard. Ggydren seemed particularly impressed with the custard.

"Best I've ever had," he informed Clive. "I think milk must taste better when it comes out of a cow."

Later still and when they were, very contentedly, half way through their third pints of beer, the door opened and four men came in. Clive immediately recognised the two villains from earlier. They recognised him too and pointed him out to their friends. Clive motioned to Ggydren and after a hastily whispered discussion they finished their beers and retreated upstairs. Clive locked the door.

"What do we do now?" asked Ggydren, "I've half a mind to pack up and leave. Do you think they were deliberately looking for us?"

"Who can tell," answered Clive, "but if they were looking for us then I reckon we're better off here with the door locked, than out there in the dark and completely on our own. Maybe one of us should go down and explain to the innkeeper. He might be able to help."

"Yes, I suppose he might but then again maybe he might not want to get involved. They are in his inn after all and I don't suppose he wants to upset his regulars, even if they're hooligans; in fact, especially if they're hooligans."

They agreed to stay put. Clive took out the rod and held it firmly, knowing that two of the ruffians had already been frightened off by it but also wishing that he'd used the last few days to properly investigate its powers and understand its potential. They waited in silence, listening in trepidation for any sounds in the corridor outside.

"It just might be," said Clive in a low voice, after several minutes, "that they're just as frightened as us, worried that we might report them. Maybe they've already scarpered."

"Scarpered?" asked Ggydren.

"Run off,"' answered Clive, "maybe they aren't here anymore."

"They didn't run off when they saw us, just sat down and started drinking."

"Point taken," said Clive.

They waited in silence again.

"It's a real bugger," said Ggydren abruptly, several minutes later and much too loudly, considering the circumstances.

"Real bugger?" whispered Clive.

"Best evening I've had in ages. Nice warm inn, tasty food, good company and all ruined by those layabouts."

A few minutes later they did hear footsteps, followed by a gentle tap on the door. Clive and Ggydren looked at each other. Neither said a word. Clive felt himself starting to shake again. There was another tap, harder and louder.

"Who's there?" asked Ggydren.

"Bob, the landlord. Could we have a few words?"

Ggydren got up and went to the door. Then he looked towards Clive. Clive nodded, holding the rod firmly and pointing it forwards. Ggydren turned the key and opened the door, just a bit. He half expected the ruffians to burst in but it was Bob and by himself. Ggydren nodded him in and relocked the door. Clive put the rod down, so that Bob wouldn't see it.

"You'll forgive me and tell me to be gone if you think it's none of my business," said Bob earnestly and looking at Clive, "but I couldn't help seeing the look on your face when the

Hinckle boys walked in tonight or their expressions on seeing you and how you made a rather hasty exit soon after. The thing is that everyone knows the Hinckles are a bad lot, so I was concerned at what might be up and I made it my business to accidentally overhear their conversation. Well, they seem to think that you have something in your possession which is very unusual and probably worth an arm and a leg and I believe that they're intending to steal it off you. One of them came up to the bar and said he needed to talk to you and asked what room you were in. Well, I gave him the number of an empty room but I don't think it would take them very long to work out the correct one. I take it you've already come across the Hinckle boys?"

Clive explained what had happened on the road earlier, being careful not to mention the rod and rather exaggerating the part played by Ggydren to explain their escape.

"That was brave of you but there was only two of them then. You saw the four in tonight and there's another besides. I don't reckon you could do much against five. Do you mind if I ask what it might be that they're so keen to get their hands on and what your business here is?"

Clive took the lead again.

"I can't think what it is they want. We aren't rich and we don't have anything that's valuable or unusual. They must be mistaken. As for our business here, well we have none, just travellers passing through."

"If you'll pardon me saying, it's a might unusual to have Aughphalians here at all, let alone passing through and in the direction of the Great Forest. Do you have a destination in mind?"

Clive thought about and decided to be frank.

"I suppose you know that there is a reward for anyone who rescues a princess who is being held prisoner in a castle in Besanto. We thought we'd have a go."

Bob smiled.

"Well that's very laudable of you but don't you think you might be taking on a bit too much? Did you know that the King sent a squad of twenty men to rescue the princess and nearly all of them got massacred? Perhaps it might be better to turn round now. I don't see much chance of you getting past the Hinckle boys again unscathed, let alone taking on the Baron."

"We can't turn back and perhaps the Baron might be expecting another army but he's almost certainly not expecting two Aughphalians. Maybe we can sneak in unnoticed and rescue the princess that way."

"And what about the Hinckle boys?"

"Isn't there a policeman or a magistrate we could report them too? It can't be legal to hold up travellers and demand money."

"We've never had much use for magistrates and such like round here. Mostly we're an honest bunch. The Hinckles only moved in a few months ago. Came from somewhere up north. Always got plenty of money to spend, though nobody knows where it comes from."

"So we're not the first people to be held up by them?"

"You're the first I've heard of and I think we'd know if there were others besides. No, their money comes from somewhere else. I wouldn't be surprised if it had something to do with Besanto. There are rumours that the Baron's forces have invaded the lands to the north of the Great Forest. Maybe we'll be next on his list. Could be he's got intentions for the whole of Morgrnvia. Everybody is fearful that dark times are on their way. Maybe the Hinckle boys are working for the Baron, like agents or spies."

"Perhaps we ought to just pack up and leave now under cover of darkness."

"It's chucking it down out there and besides, if they want whatever it is so much, they're probably already watching the road. Mind you, I wouldn't be surprised if they decide to pay you a visit up here tonight. Why else would they have asked for your room number? Listen, I'd like to help; I've got no time for the Hinckles. Here's a suggestion; I've got a spare room in my part of the inn, the private bit. You could have that tonight and tomorrow morning you could get off early at first light. There's a path down the back garden that leads into the countryside. I'll draw you a map to show what directions to take so that you rejoin the road a few miles on. It should at least give you the chance to get past any trap the Hinckle boys might be preparing. What do you say?"

Clive and Ggydren nodded in agreement; neither wanted to spend the night waiting to be attacked. Quickly they packed up their belongings and followed Bob. He led them down by a different staircase, into his private apartment and into the spare room.

"Sorry, it's not as good as upstairs but you should be safe here. Try to make yourselves comfortable. I'd best get back to the bar. I'll get you up early. Try not to worry."

There was only one bed. Clive told Ggydren to take it and made do with an armchair. Neither of them even took off their boots, wanting to be ready to get out in a hurry if need be. They spoke only in whispers and spent a largely sleepless night. It seemed to Clive that he had hardly slept at all before the dawn chorus started and Bob knocked gently on the door.

"I've been up to the room; still locked and no sign of disturbance. They're probably waiting on the road. Best not to waste time over breakfast, I've packed you up some provisions for later. Oh, and I've got these for you."

Bob handed over two belted scabbards, each containing a short sword.

"I've had them hanging up in the bar for ages, only for show mind you, but you might as well make use of them. The blades are all rusty but a blade is a blade, after all, and the Hinckle boys might not feel so brave if they see that you've got weapons. I haven't had time to draw a map but, in any case, I thought I might come with you the first part of the way and then point you in the right direction. Three is better than two, as they say. What do you think? Rain's stopped, although I'm not sure that's to your advantage."

Clive thought that Ggydren looked quite fetching with a sword and hoped he did too.

A short while later Bob quietly opened the back door and listened. It was still too dark to see much but he glanced around anyway and then beckoned them out. He led them along a cinder path to a style at the bottom of the garden. They crossed over into the field beyond and, keeping close by the hedges, the better to avoid detection, followed Bob. He stayed with them for at least an hour, always avoiding open spaces where they might be spotted. While they walked the day dawned and the sun made an appearance through breaks in the cloud. Eventually they came out of the fields to a narrow lane. Bob explained that, after a mile or so, it joined the road they would have otherwise taken.

"I'll leave you here. There's no mistaking the way but make sure you turn left, not right when you reach the main road. I don't think the Hinckles will be a problem. If they've set a trap I should imagine we've bypassed it by coming across the fields. Hopefully they'll be waiting wherever they are for hours before they realise they've missed you. However, you should camp well away from the road tonight in case they're following. You'll soon be coming upon the Great Forest. I expect you've heard the stories about it. Whatever you do don't be tempted into going in, it's far too dangerous. Stick to the road that goes round it. It's a long way round but much safer. I wish you well in your quest and if you do rescue the princess, I hope the reward is a good one. You know where my inn is and if you ever make it there again, the first night will be as my guests."

Clive and Ggydren thanked Bob profusely and sincerely for everything he had done. With a final handshake he turned to make his way home. They watched him for at least a minute before he gave a final wave just before disappearing from view. There was a brief discussion about food but they thought it better to put more distance behind them than stop for breakfast, and so they set off once more, walking quickly, down the lane. After a quarter of an hour they came to the main road and glancing towards the right to make sure there was no one in sight, turned left onto it.

The Great Forest loomed before them after just a short while. The road appeared to be heading straight into it but veered to the left just before reaching it. Thereafter the edges of the Forest were never more than a few yards away. In those autumn days most of the trees had already lost their leaves, so that it had a dark and forbidding air about in. They could see inside just a few yards but never once, in all the rest of that morning, did they see a living thing, not even a bird.

Presently they decided to eat and looked for a place to stop. A small copse, off to their left, seemed suitable and they found a spot where they were invisible from the road. They had two packs of provisions and unwrapped the largest. Bob had been generous; it contained a large pork pie, slices of ham, a pot of chutney and several pickled onions. They ate until there was nothing left and then, feeling contented and sleepy in the gentle midday warmth, decided to rest up for half an hour or so before setting off again. With so little sleep the night before, both of them soon nodded off and it was nearly two hours later before they took to the road again.

Clive heard it first, a low rumbling. It occurred to him that it might be distant thunder, except that it was too steady. Then the constant hum of a busy motorway came to mind; impossible. He stopped and motioned to Ggydren. They listened as it gradually became louder. It was coming towards them from the direction in which they were headed. They needed to find cover and fast. Back, maybe three hundred yards back, was a thicket of gorse that stretched away from the road. It would have to do. They started to run towards it and had gone only a few yards when Ggydren stopped and called out.

"No, Mr Clive, look, ahead, in the distance, could be the Hinckle boys!"

There were several of them but too far away to tell how many for sure but they were coming towards them. Clive and Ggydren ducked low and turned towards the Forest to get out of sight. Then for a few seconds they waited. The rumble was even louder. Both groups were getting nearer. Two forces were converging on them and either or both could be malign. Clive knew that he and Ggydren needed to be hidden, if only for the time being. There was no alternative, no other choice. With a quick look around to make sure that Ggydren was following, he ran into the forest.

Chapter 8.

Clive and Ggydren ran a few yards into the forest and crouched down behind two trees. The rumble became louder and more distinct; it was the sound of marching feet. Presently they came into view, a column of soldiers, about thirty of them, all heavily armed with swords and some with crossbows slung over their soldiers. Each was helmeted and clad in chain mail that hung down to their knees, except the officer in charge who also wore a scarlet cloak and whose helmet sported a scarlet crest. Almost immediately after they had passed, the rumble ceased. Clive crawled forward to the edge of the trees to look. The column had stopped and the officer was talking with the men who had come from the opposite direction. Clive recognised them as the Hinckles. There was quite a lot of gesticulating backwards and forwards along the road and Clive guessed that they were telling the officer about him and Ggydren. After a few minutes the officer barked out orders and the squad resumed its march. His last words were quite audible.

"March in step lads, at journey's end is plunder for all and hostages for the Baron. Keep up, no slacking."

The Hinckles waited a few minutes, talking among themselves, before they too resumed their journey. Clive crawled back and quietly explained to Ggydren what he had seen.

"I expect the Hinckles told them about us. It was really stupid to have fallen asleep back there. We would be miles ahead of them if we hadn't. I don't feel that the road is safe for us now, with them so near. Maybe we should take to the forest. I know we've been warned against it but I don't see any alternative. What do you think?"

"Search me. I agree the road is dangerous but the forest is too. Remember what Bob said and even if we try to keep near the edge, who knows what nasty things it might have in store for us. Maybe we should just wait here for a few hours until the Hinckles and the soldiers are far away. It might be safe for us to take to the road then."

"Perhaps, but then again, perhaps not. Who knows what's best. Even if we do wait a few hours there could be more soldiers on the way and the Hinckles might just stop for a rest themselves half a mile down the road. I'm sorry Ggydren; it all seems to be getting a bit out of hand. It just felt as if it was a bit of an adventure at first, you getting your wish to go on a quest and me trying to find my way home but this is getting serious and dangerous too. I told you what the officer said. It might be that the plunder and hostages he was talking about are intended to come from Mickelling or Buggiton. It's a pretty bleak situation; it seems there's a war going on, the Hinckles are out to get us and I don't suppose it'll be long before the Baron will be after us too."

"Well, that's as maybe, Mr Clive but we're here now and even if there's danger ahead and danger behind, there's not a lot we can do about it. Look on the bright side, we've still got the rod and that's a pretty strong power to have on our side. Thinking about it, maybe your suggestion about the forest isn't so bad. The rod's worked so far, so maybe it will protect us against whatever there might be in here. Let's give it a go anyway. If we try to keep near to the road but hidden by the forest, we should be able to get away from danger wherever it comes from. Mind you, best to take out the rod, I think, and have it at hand, just in case."

"I agree," said Clive, reaching for it, "and you should unsheathe your sword too. The forest it is then. We'll use the cover of the trees and hope for the best."

Ggydren pulled his sword from its scabbard.

"Never used a sword before," he said.

Clive smiled.

"It might be better to keep that to yourself if we get attacked."

They set off, crawling at first, until they were well away from the road, and then on foot, trying to make as little sound as possible. The going was easy enough. The forest trees were close together, blocking out direct sunlight, so there was little undergrowth. After a while they moved to the very edge of the forest again and looked along the road in each direction but saw no sign of any people. Thereafter they stayed within a few yards of the edge of the forest, keeping the road in view as they walked. Within the forest nothing stirred, there was not even any birdsong. While they had been apprehensive at first, fearful of what the forest might hold, their fears soon began to abate. After half an hour or so they were sufficiently relaxed to start talking again, albeit quietly and Clive noticed that Ggydren had put away his sword.

The lull didn't last long; very soon they came upon the Hinckles again. They were between the road and the edge of the forest and it was only because Clive heard them talking that they didn't walk right into them. They seemed to have stopped for a rest. Very carefully, Clive and Ggydren backed away from the danger and moved deeper into the forest. This time the going quickly became more difficult. The ground fell away into a steep sided valley, with a little stream at the bottom. They followed it for some way as it meandered around and soon lost all sense of where they were in relation to the edge of the forest and the road. When they climbed up again and set off to their left, they walked for a good half hour and still there was no sign of the road. They could only continue. As the daylight began to fade, they knew they were completely lost.

Their intention, of course, although it was not discussed, had been to leave the forest before nightfall and find some spot where it would be safe to camp. That was no longer possible. They debated whether to put the tent up but Ggydren said he thought he would feel safer being able to see any horrible creature coming towards them, that is if you could see anything at all, once it got dark, than have it come upon them unseen in the tent, and Clive rather agreed. So, just before the light was gone completely, they found a broad tree, spread out the tent beside it to use as a groundsheet, and took out the second packet of food. It contained sausages, a good pound in weight, but uncooked. They debated the wisdom of a fire and agreed there was no wisdom in it at all. The smoke, not to mention the aroma of sausages, would alert anyone or anything else that might be around to their presence. So they packed away the sausages, wrapped themselves in their blankets and prepared for an uncomfortable and hungry night.

Much later, after Clive had drifted off to sleep, he was awakened by Ggydren shaking him.

"Wake up, Mr Clive, there's eyes, over there."

In front and quite high up, as if they were in the trees, Clive could see two green eyes blinking. Then another pair came into view and then another, until there were lots of them, all green, all eyes, blinking. Then there came a whispering, as though whatever the eyes belonged to were talking to each other. It became louder and, even though the words were indistinct, it seemed hostile and very threatening, as if evil things were deciding what to do with them. Ggydren drew his sword and Clive held the rod out firmly before him.

"Who's there?" he called out. "Show yourself, we mean no harm. Who are you?"

The whispering intensified and Clive raised the rod firmly towards it again. Then the whispers faded and the eyes went out, two by two. In a few seconds they were all gone.

"I was scared stiff, Mr Clive," said Ggydren, a little later. "I wonder what those things were, what they belonged to; I mean, if they were people or not. They seemed too high up. I think it worked again, Mr Clive, the rod I mean, the eyes went out when you held it forward. That's how it seemed to me."

"Maybe," answered Clive, "yes, maybe it was the rod but who can tell? The rod always seems to get me out of sticky situations. But it might not have been the rod at all. Maybe they were just insects or frogs or something like that, looking at us, not something horrible at all. I was scared too. We should take it in turns to watch from now. One should sleep while the other keeps watch, taking turns until morning. You sleep first. You must have been awake. You had to shake me out of my sleep."

"Alright, Mr Clive, I can't say I feel like sleeping after that though. No more than an hour, then get me up."

Clive sat, his back against the tree, looking out for more eyes and waiting for himself to stop shaking. He wished that he didn't shake with fear, or was it nervousness, in difficult circumstances, and he also wondered why Ggydren almost always called him Mr Clive.

'Actually,' thought Clive, 'I quite like it. It's sort of deferential, as if Ggydren sees me as being in charge, as if I'm the leader. I don't think I've ever been the leader of anything before. Maybe he thinks I've got a leader's personality or air about me. Or maybe not, maybe it's just that I've got the rod.'

Then he fell asleep and when he awoke it was morning and he guessed they had both slept through the night. Ggydren didn't let on that he'd woken much earlier, seen that Clive was asleep and left him be, keeping watch himself for hours and pretending to be asleep when Clive had finally opened his eyes.

Within a few minutes they set off again, although they had no idea whether they were heading in the direction of the road or away from it, or even going round and round in circles. They came to a stream but neither of them knew if it was the same one as the day before. The water seemed clean though and they stopped to drink and wash their faces and felt better for it. All through the morning they walked and saw no one and nothing, other than trees and bushes and the occasional creepy crawly. As they walked their hunger grew and their thoughts turned to sausages. Finally, around lunchtime, Ggydren stopped and sat down against a tree trunk.

"Look here, Mr Clive," he said wearily, "we've been walking for miles and as far as we know we've got nowhere. I mean we don't know if we're any nearer the road than when we started off. We could be in here for days. We might never get out. We could starve to death. Sooner or later those sausages are going to go off and I think we would be stupid to let that happen. I say we cook them now, here and now. I know it means a fire and a fire could attract unfriendly things, but frankly, Mr Clive, I don't care. I'm for the sausages and hang the consequences."

Clive could think of no good reason to disagree so they collected up dead branches and as much dry stuff as they could find and Ggydren made sparks with the flint and soon the dry stuff was smouldering and Clive gently blew it into flame. The sausages sizzled in the pan and soon the pan was empty and four sausages each had been greedily devoured.

"I could eat that again," said Ggydren, "at least twice over."

They waited, resting, until the fire had burned low and then kicked earth over to cover the embers and set off again.

A few minutes later they stopped abruptly. Something was out there. They could hear a faint rustling and sensed, rather than saw, movement. Something seemed to be darting between the trees, so quickly that by the time their eyes had focussed, it was no longer there. Then came a wail, not loud but piercing nevertheless, like the cry of a banshee or a terrified creature. They quaked in terror. It came again, then again, but always from a different direction. It seemed to be taunting them. They stood back to back, Clive with the rod, Ggydren with his sword. Momentarily Clive saw something dart between the trees. It seemed almost human in shape but it had no substance, as if it were just mist. It melted away even before he could raise the rod against it.

It lasted perhaps a few minutes and then all was still.

"What did you see?" asked Clive.

"I didn't really see anything, but that wailing, that was something evil, something dangerous. It seemed to be playing with us, like a cat plays with a mouse before killing it. I wish we'd never come into this dreadful place. The Hinckle boys are only human after all, whereas whatever's out there definitely isn't. We should have paid more heed to the warnings."

Clive tried to calm down. He was aware of the need for clear thinking. What he had heard, what he had briefly seen, reminded him of ghosts or of those wicked things that tempted travellers from the safe paths into mires and deadly pools, will o' the wisps, as he remembered from childhood stories. But whatever it was, whatever they were, had merely frightened and done no lasting harm. It was as if they were being warned out of the forest. That was all well and good but how to get out of the forest, that was the problem.

They walked on, sword and rod in hand and ever watchful, turning often to look behind, listening for any rustle, any sound. They came to an incline and climbed in anticipation that the peak would offer a view of the surroundings and show them the edge of the forest and the road but the peak was as wooded as everywhere else and no view was to be had. One of the trees had some low branches and Clive tried to climb it. He climbed as high as he was able, as high as he dared, but that was not high enough to see above the treetops. At the bottom again he rested briefly and then they made their descent to lower ground.

The rustle of leaves alerted them. Through the forest came a hooded shape wrapped in black rags and carrying a broom over its shoulder. Clive and Ggydren stopped still. The shape stopped and looked directly at them, revealing itself to be an old woman, hideous in appearance, with dark sunken eyes, a thin gaunt face and skin that seemed to have no colour at all. When she was no more than a few yards away, she stopped and smiled, the thin lips parting to reveal a mouth with no more than a few blackened teeth. She said nothing. After a few seconds she bent her head again and went on her way. It was only when she was well past and out of sight that either of them spoke.

"Well, she was mighty horrible. I'm glad to see the back of her. At least she was human, not like those other things before. Have you got any ideas? What about that broom? What would there be to sweep up in here?"

From back in his mind Clive was trying to remember boyhood tales. Suddenly it came to him, Pesta, the bringer of pestilence, the deliverer of plague.

"No, not human, Ggydren," he replied, "human in shape but supernatural or ghostly in nature. It was the broom that brought it to mind. Hundreds of years ago, where I come from, all over in fact, there was a terrible plague that caused millions of people to die horrible deaths. It was known as the Black Death. Nowadays we know what caused it but back in those days, people were ignorant and superstitious. In some places they thought that the disease was spread by an evil spirit called Pesta who took the form of a ghastly old woman. Sometimes she carried a broom and sometimes a rake. If it was a rake it meant that a few people would survive but if it was a broom then everyone would die."

"What does it mean? Do you think there is pestilence in here? Are we doomed? "

"I don't know Ggydren. The idea of Pesta is just a myth, an invention by people to explain something that was happening that they didn't understand, so I don't see how she could have been right here before us like that. Not unless she actually did exist and really did spread the plague but that's just too stupid for words. She's gone now anyway; let's get on. We need to find a way out of here before it gets dark. I don't want to spend another night in here. I'll think about it. Maybe I'm missing something, something that will make it make sense."

Clive thought. Since entering the forest there had been three incidents. In each of them something malicious seemed to be threatening them but they had been unharmed. In the first whatever it was had gone away when he had raised the rod against it. In the second and third the rod had been in his hand all the time anyway. Each of the incidents seemed related to human experience, to human fears; eyes in the dark, will o' the wisp, the Grim Reaper or Pesta, as in this case. It was as if long standing nightmares were being used against them. But that was also puzzling because these were nightmares from his own experience, from the Earth in fact, so how could whatever it was out there know about them, or were nightmares the same everywhere? Ggydren had told him that Elendril said that some people thought that shape-shifters came from the Great Forest. Maybe these shapes did not exist as such, but something was turning itself into them to frighten them away. If so, what was so special about this forest that the beings that lived in it wanted to keep everyone else out? Clive continued to ponder, and then he had an idea. On their own they couldn't find a way out. Maybe the beings in here could be called upon to show them the way. Maybe he could use the power of the rod to force that to happen. Clive made up his mind; he would do it. He would do it with whatever shape appeared next. He didn't know if it would work but he decided he must try, and he also decided that perhaps it was better not to tell Ggydren about it just yet.

Clive and Ggydren came to another stream, more of a trickle really, but it seemed clean enough, so they drank and felt refreshed. They followed its course for some time, hoping against hope that it might lead them somewhere. Eventually its meanderings became too tortuous and difficult to follow and they climbed away from its banks. As the afternoon wore on the gentle warmth of the autumn day gave way to a cold chill. Knowing that it would soon be dark they searched dejectedly for a place to spend another miserable night and came across a small patch where the trees were less dense. There they collected wood for a fire but could find nothing dry enough for kindling, until they spotted a silver birch and pulled off strips of its papery thin bark that, Ggydren assured Clive, would burn as easily as anything. They did and soon the fire was taking hold. It was then that they heard the unmistakeable howl of a wolf and from the sound of it, not very far away. Just as quickly as they could and leaving everything else on the ground, except their weapons and the rod, they scrambled up the nearest tree that had branches low enough to climb onto. Then they climbed as high as they could. The wolf was quickly upon them but looked like no wolf that Clive had seen before, for those he had seen on television or in the zoo had been no bigger than big dogs and were always thin and mangy looking, while the creature that snarled up at them from the ground below was huge in comparison and in magnificent condition. As it snarled, its lips curled revealing deadly fangs and Clive wondered if he hadn't been too hasty in deciding to put his theory to the test with the next thing that appeared. The previous ones had been frightening enough but this looked as if it could and would rip him to pieces, given half a chance.

Clive pointed the rod at the creature. The creature stopped snarling. Clive pointed it again and the creature started to slink away. Clive wasn't daring or brave by nature but he did something quite daring then.

"Halt," he shouted, "I haven't given you permission to leave. Come back here."

The creature turned and took a step towards the tree. Then it stopped.

"Come back here. That's an order."

The creature stood still, its eyes transfixed on Clive or perhaps on the rod.

"I said all the way," shouted Clive.

With that he banged the end of the rod as hard as possible onto the tree trunk. There was a loud bang and a flash of light that shot upwards, hit an adjacent tree and caused it to burst into flame.

Ggydren watched all this in astonished silence. The wolf responded by lying down and whimpering. Clive, also astonished and not a little impressed by what he'd done, decided to go the whole hog.

"Show us who you really are," he ordered the wolf. "Transform yourself right now and stand before us as your true self or I will start a fire that will burn down this whole forest, and you and all your kind with it."

Clive raised the rod once more and held it aloft, ready to strike it down against the tree again. As he waited the wolf seemed to melt away in front of his eyes until, in its place, stood a woman.

Chapter 9.

Clive and Ggydren climbed down from the tree and stood before the lady. She was fair skinned and clad in a gown of white that reached to her ankles. Two short horns protruded just above the dark hair that hung down to her shoulders. Her face was not exactly beautiful but certainly striking. She might have been in her twenties or thirties or forties; somehow she seemed ageless. It struck Clive how calm she was, given what had happened. After being so decisive and in the face of such serenity, Clive was rather struck for words. He tried to think of something appropriate to say, given the situation.

"Take me to your leader."

'I can't believe I just said that,' thought Clive.

"We have no leader. We are equal," she replied.

He hadn't expected that and was even more flummoxed.

"Who are you?" he asked.

"I am Angharind."

"Then take me to the others, Angharind."

He didn't know why he said that either. It just came out.

"Excuse me for butting in, Mr Clive," said Ggydren, "but shouldn't we be telling her to take us out of the forest?"

Clive suddenly felt pressured. He didn't want Ggydren or Angharind to think him indecisive and stupid.

"Maybe they can help us and, in any case, I'm rather intrigued to find out more. It's not every day that this sort of thing happens."

"It would be better for you to leave the forest." said Angharind. "Strangers are not allowed in here."

"Maybe not, but I've got the rod," said Clive, being assertive again. "Take us to the others."

Angharind pointed to the rod.

"I will obey, but that thing is powerful. Please put it hidden from view or things may go very badly."

Clive waited a few seconds, deliberating, and then pushed the rod into the belt inside his gown.

Angharind turned and started to walk. Ggydren and Clive followed.

"Do you think this is wise, Mr Clive? It could be a trap."

"I don't think so," said Clive. "I think the rod will keep us safe. It's worked on everything so far. It worked on her, when she was a wolf. Is Elendril like her? Do you think this is where Elendril comes from?"

"Well, they're both shape-shifters, that's for sure. Maybe Elendril does come from here. I'd like to know, one way or another. Perhaps it is a good idea to get this Anghar..., whatever her name is, to take us to the others. You were very firm and insistent back there, Mr Clive. I wasn't sure if you had it in you, to take on this quest when we started, but you seem to be, how can I put it, rising, yes, that's it, rising to the challenge."

Clive didn't say anything. He wasn't quite sure whether he just been paid a compliment or an insult.

Angharind led them on through the forest for over an hour. She followed no trail or path but seemed completely sure of the way. Eventually Clive spied something ahead of her, through the trees, something almost white, like a cloud.

Angharind walked straight up to it but did not stop or turn away. Instead she seemed to walk into it and disappear. Clive and Ggydren stopped and looked at each other. Cautiously they edged forward. Up close it seemed more translucent than white. It rose up from the ground, arching away from them, and, when Clive looked to either side, he could see that they curved away too. It appeared to be some sort of dome. Clive put out his hand to touch it but there was nothing to touch. Instead, his hand went straight into it and disappeared from sight, just as Angharind had done. Without waiting to consult Ggydren, stepped forward and went through.

On the other side, Angharind was waiting. She smiled as Clive appeared and lifted her arm as if to direct his eyes to all that was around her. And what was around her was a complete wonder to him, for where the forest outside had been dense and dark and bleak and cold, in there it was light and warm, and there was no forest, just a cultivated landscape, where everything was green and luscious. There were trees but they were in full leaf and many were ripe with fruits and nuts and there were many other things besides, flowers and bushes and vegetables, all growing in healthy abundance. The wall through which they had passed, curved over him towards a central point, high up in the distance and which was supported by a tall pillar, which seemed to be made of the same translucent stuff. Around its base were buildings, white walled and flat roofed, like some ancient Greek village.

Ggydren appeared. He was as equally amazed at the sight before him. Angharind waited a few seconds and then led them on again. In front of the houses people were gathering.

All of them women and all dressed in the same long white gowns, but they did not smile and they were not welcoming. Their faces displayed shock and unease, hostility even. Clive noticed that they also seemed ageless, like Angharind and he wondered where the men and children were.

Angharind stopped a few yards from the women and spoke in some language that was unknown to Clive. The others responded, sounding agitated. The conversation went on for some time. Eventually Angharind turned to Clive.

"I have explained why I brought you here. They are angry. Elisiu is forbidden to outsiders. There will be a meeting tonight to decide what we will do. You will be allowed to speak in your defence. In the meantime, I am held responsible for your actions. You must do what I say. My dwelling is near. Come with me; you will be safe there."

She led them through the houses until she reached her own. The door was not locked. It opened onto a room, white walled and sparsely furnished.

"Wait in here. I will prepare food. Do not go outside and whatever you do, do not use the staff."

They sat down at a table and looked at each other.

"I don't know about this"' whispered Ggydren, "I don't feel safe. What is this place? Who are they? I didn't ever hear of anywhere inside the forest other than the forest itself. I've half a mind we should make a run for it; I don't trust her or any of them, and what do you think she meant about speaking in our own defence? Are we to be put on trial?"

"Did you notice their faces?" asked Clive, also whispering. "They all looked the same; no, not the same in appearance

101

but all the same sort of age, not young but not old either and where are all the men and children?"

"Actually," replied Ggydren, "I never did hear of shape-shifters being anything but women. All the ones in Buggiton were women but their faces were different, more like normal. I wonder if they're all shape-shifters here."

"Is Elendril like them, I mean like Angharind? Do you think this is where she came from originally?"

"Yes and no; she is like them in some ways but she's more normal, like those in Buggiton. I suppose she and the rest of them could be from here but why, why would they turn up in baby auctions?"

"Maybe this place is a kind of nunnery."

"Nunnery?" asked Ggydren.

"Nunneries or convents; we have them where I come from, not many mind. Places that are only for women. They cut themselves off from ordinary life and they all dress the same, like here, only different."

"And they live in these dome things?"

"No, that's different. We have a few of them too but not for nuns. There's a place in Cornwall, that's part of England too, that has domes a bit like this one only much smaller. The glass walls make it warmer inside so they can grow tropical plants. I went once. You couldn't walk through the walls though, like we just did. I don't understand that."

Just then Angharind came back carrying a tray. There was bread, a pot of honey and a plate of nuts, berries and fruits.

"Eat"' said Angharind. "Will you drink water or juice?"

The food was good, even if the bread was rather chewy. Angharind explained it was made from ground up nuts; they grew all their own food but there was not enough space to grow wheat.

"Before the meeting"' said Angharind, after they had finished eating, "I need to know why you are here and why you did not try to escape from the forest when I sought to frighten you away."

Ggydren beckoned to Clive to answer.

"Neither of us had any idea that this place existed, that there was somewhere else inside the forest," Clive explained. "We only came into the forest because bad men and soldiers were threatening us outside it. We had no choice but to run into the trees to hide but once inside we got lost and couldn't find a way out. That is all. We had no other purpose, no ulterior motive. As for asking you to take us to the others, well I was angry that you were threatening us. I wanted to find out why. I had no idea it would lead us into here. How could I? We are just ordinary travellers, that's all."

Clive hoped he had said enough and not too much. He wasn't sure that talking about England or the plane crash or about the rod would help the situation. Ggydren came to the rescue by suddenly asking a question.

"Excuse me, but are you all shape-shifters here?"

Angharind glared at him.

"We do not use that term. We find it insulting. Yes, we can transmute but we only do it if it is absolutely necessary."

"But do you all come from here? I'm sorry if I shouldn't be asking but it's important to me. My....well someone I know is a ....transmuter, if you like, and there are a few of them too in Buggiton. Did they all come from here originally?"

Angharind looked vexed.

"It is not a question for me to answer."

"But they are looked down on, treated like dirt. Most of them end up in cheap, nasty shows doing this transmuting before men for money. And as far as I know, they all were sold in baby auctions. It's not right. Why can't you answer the question?"

"I told you, it is not my place to answer. The subject is closed. I have work to do before the meeting. Stay here. If you try to leave the building you will be killed. There are guards."

With that she left the room.

"Well, Mr Clive, it might not be her place to answer but she certainly knows what the answer is. There's something that's not right here. She's hiding something. This place gives me the creeps. All those women and all looking the same. "

"I expect we'll find out more later, at the meeting or trial or whatever it is. I'm worried now too Ggydren and sorry I made her bring us here. I should have followed your advice. Please forgive me."

"Well, you weren't to know, neither of us was, and at least we've still got the rod. She's obviously afraid of its power."

Clive didn't answer. He tried to think, tried to work out what to do. She had been very direct; they would be killed if they went outside. Maybe she was bluffing but then again. What would it be like at the meeting and what should they say? She said they would have the chance to speak. He had been truthful with Angharind but maybe he needed to say more. Did they know about Besanto and the princess? Would that help?

Angharind returned after an hour.

"They are ready for you now. You must leave your swords here. I will not ask you to leave that thing but keep it inside your gown. Let me advise you; when they question you, answer truthfully and without evasion. You are in violation of our most important rule simply by being here. You do not seem to me to be evil men or to have evil intentions, but you must convince them of your integrity if you are to avoid...well to avoid the consequences. I will say no more. Follow me."

Outside the street was deserted. Angharind led them to a building that was set apart from the others. Square in shape and with a small rounded dome on top, it was white, windowless and with a single wooden door. It reminded Clive of a temple.

"This is the Chamber," said Angharind, as they approached it. "In here the whole community assembles to make our decisions. Here they will judge you. I will not take my usual place but will remain at your side. They are to question me too, for bringing you here. I have not yet told them about your weapon. Keep it hidden until I say."

She pushed the door open to reveal an entrance hall that led to an enclosed staircase, from beyond which came the hum of conversation. The steps led up into the Chamber. Clive emerged onto what seemed to be the dock of a court, bounded on all sides by wooden railings. Above and completely encircling it was a balcony from which twenty three seated women looked down at him in silence, all conversation having ceased as soon as he and Ggydren appeared. There was one space and one empty chair, Angharind's. In front of each of the women was a flickering candle that created a shadow on the wall behind, so that the place had an eerie, even threatening air about it. Clive turned round to try to take it all in. Presently Angharind directed his eyes to one of the women. Behind and above her and hanging from the ceiling was a staff, of exactly the same size and shape as the one Clive's rod had changed into in Ggydren's cave.

"I am Bronghar. I have been appointed as spokeswoman to conduct these proceedings," she said. "We are gathered to consider the charge that you have entered Elisiu illegally. Since permission to enter is dependent on our prior and unanimous agreement, and since no such permission was sought, then your guilt is beyond doubt and our only purpose is to pronounce sentence. I should warn you that only in the most exceptional circumstances can the usual punishment be avoided. Firstly we will question Angharind, since she bears the responsibility for having brought you here. Afterwards you may speak in mitigation of your crime, if any such mitigation exists."

The lady focussed her attention on Angharind.

"You were supposed to frighten these two away from the forest but instead you led them here, in full knowledge of, and in violation of our laws. You have already told us that they commanded you and that you had no choice. Now you must explain how it was so."

"My ladies," answered Angharind, "the one called Clive has in his possession a thing which I believe to be a Staff of Power. He used it to order me to bring them here."

There was an audible gasp of astonishment from the other women. Then they started talking together in some foreign tongue Clive did not understand. Angharind silenced them by speaking again.

"This thing, he calls it a rod, does not look like one of the Staffs, so I did not recognise it at first, but when he commanded me, I felt a strong need to obey. This, as you know, is a sign of a Staff of Power, that the command of the Staff-holder is very powerful. And when I did briefly try to resist his command, he caused the thing to issue a bolt of light that shot through the air and set fire to one of the trees. This is another sign, that a Staff can be used as a unique and deadly weapon. So, although the thing did not and does not look like the Staff that hangs above us, I was convinced that it was indeed one and, when he ordered me to transmute into this form and to lead him here, I felt compelled to obey. Compelled, because of the power of the command, and because I feared for the consequences for us all, and for the forest, had I refused him and he had used the thing in anger."

Angharind paused and the others all began to speak at once. It went on for some time. Clive felt confused and frightened. His hand clutched at the rod inside his gown as if for protection. He looked at Ggydren and they exchanged weak smiles.

"My ladies," continued Angharind, "this is a situation that is new to us. The penalty for trespass here is death and we have had to deal with trespassers before but this is different. This person has a mighty power at his command. Let us hear him out. I do not believe that he has evil intentions. He has explained that he and his compatriot were pursued by enemies and had no choice but to flee into the forest to escape them. Once inside they became lost. He was angry

107

about the attempts we made to frighten him and wanted to know our reasons. Let him speak and then decide his fate."

She looked at Clive and waited. Clive, almost lost for words having just heard that they faced the prospect of execution, nervously repeated what he had already told Angharind and what she had just told the court.

"But what of the Staff that does not look like a Staff?" asked Bronghar. "Where is this thing, this rod? Let us see it."

Angharind whispered to Clive,

"Show them the rod but do not strike it on the floor under any circumstances. The power in it could destroy Elisiu and all of us along with it. I mean it; do not strike it on the floor."

Slowly Clive drew the rod out from his gown and held it before them. The women stared at it.

"This cannot be a Staff of Power"' snapped the leader. "It is a small thing, a puny thing. There is some mischief here. You have been deceived, Angharind, fooled by these men into bringing them here. You should bear the punishment too."

The others nodded in agreement and all at once they began to chant,

"The punishment is death, the punishment is death. Kill the prisoners, kill the prisoners."

They repeated it over and over. Ggydren looked terrified, Clive felt the same. Angharind was about to speak when Clive felt a sudden surge of rage and courage, or perhaps it was just blind panic, but anyway, a surge of something that overwhelmed him. He lifted the rod high and shook it hard. Then he screamed at them as loudly and as forcefully as he could.

"Silence, silence! Be quiet all of you. I order you to cease this awful racket."

Almost instantly the Chamber became quiet, although whether they obeyed out of surprise or because of the power of the rod, Clive wasn't sure. Still they were silent and this was his moment.

"How dare you threaten us, how dare you! This is a Staff of Power and you may not threaten me while it is in my hands. It has protected me in the past and it will protect me now. I will use it against you if I must. It is not for you to hold us to account. We should be your guests, not your prisoners. Now enough of this charade, I want the rest of you to leave right away but you," said Clive, pointing at the leader, "you will stay. I have questions and I want some answers. Everybody else out. Do it now, right away!"

Quietly, their eyes cast down as if they were afraid to look at him directly, the women shuffled out. Clive felt exhilarated and even though he knew that it was the power of the Staff that was forcing them to leave, he was surprised and thrilled at what he had just done. Soon only the leader and Angharind were left. Clive spoke again.

"What we need now is safe passage out of here and out of the forest. Angharind can show us the way and then she will be free to return here. I hope that is alright, Angharind," he said, turning towards her, "you at least, have shown us some consideration. I said that we had no evil intentions and I promise that we will not reveal the existence of this place to anyone and we will never return. But before we go I want some answers of my own. Why is Elisiu forbidden to strangers on pain of execution? What is so special about it? And you and all the others, why do you all look the same? Why don't

109

some of you look older or younger and where are all the men and children?"

"And why do shape-shifters turn up in baby auctions in Morgrnvia?" added Ggydren, who was also recovering his composure after what had just happened.

"Actually," said Clive, "I don't like it much in here with you glaring down at us from behind that candle. I suggest we go back to Angharind's. You can explain there."

"As you wish," said Angharind, "but I caution you again, be careful not to use the rod."

She turned and led them back down the stairs. They waited a few seconds for the leader to join them. Outside the other women were gathered. They moved aside to let Angharind and the others through. Clive could see the venom in their eyes but they said nothing and did nothing either.

"I said you were rising to it," said Ggydren quietly as they walked on, "I don't mind admitting I was worried sick back there. Who knows what might have happened if you hadn't taken control of the situation."

"It wasn't really me. It's the power of the rod. It didn't only silence them, it gave me strength too. Once we get out of here, we really must try to understand how to harness its power."

The four sat round the table in Angharind's dwelling, Ggydren with his sword in hand and Clive with the rod.

"So, we want some information," said Clive, "and I've got the rod so it seems that you must provide it. I want you to tell me about this place. You are the leader, you can explain."

"I am not the leader. We are a community of equals. I was merely selected to lead the trial but I will try to answer

110

anyway. Elisiu is a paradise. We are its handmaidens. We care for it and in return it provides for all our needs."

"But who made it, who created it and the dome, why were we able to simply walk through it without damaging it?"

"It is a living thing. We do not know how it came about or if any others exist."

Clive found it difficult to take in.

"What do you mean, 'it is a living thing'?"

"Simply that. It lives; it has lived for thousands of years and it will continue to do so as long as we care for it."

"Then where are the others, the old people who looked after it before you and the children who will care for it in the future?"

Bronghar paused, as if resisting the question. Clive raised the rod slightly to reinforce it.

"There are no others."

"Then you were sent here, like on a tour of duty or something like that?"

"No."

"You must explain this. It doesn't make sense."

"There are two dozen of us. It is a perfect number. Twenty four are needed to care for and maintain Elisiu, and twenty four is the number of people that it can sustain. Any more would be too many for Elisiu. It would be weakened and in the end Elisiu would wither and die and we with it. There can be no others, except...."

Bronghar paused again, as if she had given away too much already.

"Except what?' demanded Clive.

"It is not necessary for you to know. Some things are difficult to understand. Please do not make me say."

"You must tell me. I order it."

"Sometimes there are children."

She paused again. Clive and Ggydren waited. There had to be more. Eventually Clive tried to explain it.

"So sometimes you leave Elisiu and come back pregnant? Where are these children?"

"No, it is not like that. We are not like other women, not like women on the outside. We do not need men. Elisiu is perfect and we are perfect too. We do not need men to have babies."

"I caution you Bronghar,' said Angharind, interrupting, 'they are men, they do not need to know everything."

"Why should I care?" said Bronghar, clearly getting agitated. "They demand to know and I will tell them so that they will understand how weak and insignificant they are compared with us. You think we are just women," she said, turning to Clive again, "and that we are a little strange because we have learned to transmute into different shapes but that is only the beginning of it. We are the survivors. We survived the catastrophe that men brought upon this world with their aggression and war. You cannot begin to imagine how dreadful it was, when the vile weapons of man unleashed such death and destruction on the whole world. But we survived, we among so very few in all the world, we survived. And out of that chaos, Elisiu was born, and we found it and cherished it and it has cherished us for thousands of years. It is the perfect symbiosis. Now do you understand?"

"I don't think I understand a word of it," answered Clive.

"Me neither," added Ggydren. "We know about the Calamity when the thing fell out of the sky but that was in Aughphalia, not here. I never heard about any catastrophe or war when nothing survived except your ancestors."

"No, you stupid man," said Bronghar angrily, "not our ancestors. Us, us here; we survived. We have lived for thousands of years."

As she said it Clive understood why they all looked the same. They didn't age. Their faces were ageless.

"This is why outsiders are forbidden in Elisiu on pain of death," said Angharind. "Elisiu is unique, a paradise. Those inside it do not age. If those on the outside received such news it would mean the end of Elisiu. So many would come that we could not resist. We would be overwhelmed, Elisiu would wither and we would die with it."

"It all sounds like stuff and nonsense to me," said Ggydren, "but then nobody in Aughphalia can explain how Morgrnvia even exists, so who knows what could happen here. The thing is I still haven't had an answer to my question. How come shape-shifters, sorry, transmuters, turn up in baby auctions in Morgrnvia? You started to say that there are children sometimes."

"I don't think you need to know that," said Angharind.

"Answer him, it's important," instructed Clive.

"We told you, we can only be two dozen," said Bronghar. "If babies are born, they cannot remain."

"So you put them in baby auctions?" asked Ggydren.

"The girls, yes, after they have weaned."

"And the boys?" demanded Clive.

"Boys are smothered at birth," said Bronghar in a defiant tone. "Men brought us to this. They are, you are, a scourge."

There was silence. A minute or two earlier Clive had been fascinated by the idea that these women had lived for eons and could continue to as long as their dome persisted. It was pure Shangri-la but that their longevity was sustained by killing male babies and giving away the girls, well that seemed utterly repugnant.

"You kill or give away your own babies so you can go on living forever in this place, that's horrible, detestable. What sort of people are you?"

"What we do is necessary. In here things are perfect; out there is greed and suffering and hatred and disease and war and cold. We have evolved into higher beings. We are not restricted or governed by your foolish morals or ethics. We do what we must. This is becoming tiresome. You have the Staff so we cannot enforce the law, but you must leave now and we hold you to your promise. Tell no one about Elisiu or about us."

"I think she's right Mr Clive. It would be best to leave now. I don't want to stay here a moment longer than necessary."

"Maybe you're right; we should go while we can. Maybe Angharind could provide a few supplies to keep us going for a day or two. Would that be possible Angharind and how long will it take to get to the edge of the forest?"

Angharind did not answer. Instead she got up from the table and moved to the window. Then she smiled and beckoned Clive and Ggydren to join her.

"Behold, Elisiu at its most lovely."

Outside there had been a magical transformation. Where before the dome had been a translucent whitish colour, it was now glowing in soft pastel colours that seemed to emanate from millions of strands of shimmering lights that curved down from the apex. Not only that but the whole thing appeared to be pulsating, as if it was breathing. It was beautiful.

'It's like being inside a glowing, deep sea jellyfish,' thought Clive and the analogy was true enough for such creatures do generate their own light, as this thing did.

"To us this dome, as you put it, is the Cerridwine. Each evening, when the daylight fades, it reveals itself in all its glory. It bestows longevity and the power of transmutation and much more besides. See how precious it is."

"It's beautiful," said Ggydren, staring open mouthed.

"Yes," said Clive.

"I will give you food for a few days," said Angharind at last, "but you cannot leave now. Even I could not easily find my way through the forest at night and besides," at this she paused to look reprovingly at Bronghar, "at night you would be more easily assailed by malicious creatures. Tonight you may stay here. Tomorrow I will lead you to the forest's edge."

"You are too generous," said Bronghar, "much more generous than these trespassers deserve. The others will not be happy."

"I told you, they do not seem evil to me or to have evil intent. They have asked me to lead them and I will do my best. If the others disapprove then so be it; my conscience guides me."

"As you will," replied Bronghar. "Now, if we are finished here I wish to leave, or am I to be your prisoner, you who holds the Staff?"

Clive looked at Ggydren before replying.

"You may go but don't try any tricks. As you say, I am the Staff-holder and I am completely prepared to use it if needs be," he answered.

Bronghar got up and left without further word. Clive was glad to see her go. She had seemed cold and devoid of compassion. He wondered if that was just her nature or whether they were all like that. Perhaps that's what happened to people when they had been alive for who knows how long. But Angharind seemed different. She had given them some protection, spoken up for them, warned about leaving in darkness; perhaps Angharind different and could be trusted.

She said little else that evening, except to apologise that there was no spare room or even beds for them, just a few blankets to keep them warm and provide a little comfort. She showed them where they could wash, asked if they needed more to eat and drink and when they declined, took her leave of them. They talked for a bit, reflecting on all that had happened that day. Ggydren was particularly incensed by the treatment of babies and asked whether Clive thought it best for him to explain it all to Elendril or to keep quiet about it.

"She's bound to be mightily upset to think that her mother got rid of her, and maybe even killed her baby brothers, so that she could live on forever. I can't even begin to think of what kind of mother could do that. I wish them all to damnation. I've a good mind to use the Staff myself to destroy this place."

Clive understood his feelings but kept hold of the rod. A little later he got up to gaze out of the window. The lovely glow of the Cerridwine was fading. Soon Elisiu would be in darkness. He promised himself to keep awake this time. He certainly didn't trust the other women and he wasn't entirely convinced about Angharind. His eyes searched for any sign of people outside. He couldn't see anyone but that didn't mean they weren't there, in some form or other. They divided the night into four watches, Ggydren staying awake first, Clive next. Shortly into the final watch, while it was still dark outside, Angharind roused them.

"We should leave at first light. The others will still be asleep and it would be best to be away before they are up. I have packed provisions, enough for a few days. Ready yourselves quickly now; we must be off."

A few minutes later she opened the door for them, putting a raised finger in front of her mouth to warn them to be quiet. Clive and Ggydren both wondered if she was leading them away from danger or into a trap. Elisiu was still in darkness and they could see no one else about. Even so, they both walked with sword in hand, Clive with the rod as well. Within a few minutes they reached the Cerridwine and crossed through it into the forest. Inside it was still almost pitch black and Clive and Ggydren found it difficult to keep up with Angharind. At last the first rays of daylight eased their way through the trees and made the going faster. After another half hour without incident they began to feel more relaxed. Clive caught up with Angharind.

"Which way are we going? Our travels will take us to the north of the forest, so it would be better if you led us in that direction."

She replied quietly.

"It is better not to speak, that way we won't be overheard but I will answer. My sisters will not trouble you once you are out of the forest, so I am leading you by the quickest route. This will bring you out at the south-eastern corner. Not ideal for you perhaps, but even that will take until mid- afternoon. If I were to lead you to the north, it would be tomorrow before you left the forest and it is at night time that you would be at your most vulnerable. Trust me; I am trying to lead you to safety."

"I do trust you. I'm not sure you will be well received when you return but I am grateful for your help. May I ask one further question, please? I understand that in Elisiu you do not age but what about here in the forest? Are you starting to get older now?"

"The power of the Cerridwine persists a little way outside it. Here in the forest we may spend a day or so before its influence is gone, and that influence declines anyway the further away we are. I cannot be exact. We don't take chances but we must always be aware of who may be about in the forest, so that we can deter them, but we try to stay out of Elisiu for as short a time as we can. There will always be risks."

"Excuse me," said Ggydren, who had also caught up and been listening, "but how do you put the little girls into the baby auctions then? I've been puzzling about it half the night. You see yesterday the other lady, Bronghar, said you survived

118

the catastrophe, you lot and just a few others. Surely there couldn't have been baby auctions then, so what happened to the girls then, and how did they start getting put into auctions, when they take place so far away. It's important to me to know; the person... well, the person I live with is one of you. I rescued her from the shape-shifting shows."

Angharind stopped abruptly and looked at him.

"We know about the shows but we prefer not to talk about them. Maybe that is because of our shame. You seem a kindly man and if you have rescued one of us, then I am in your debt; she might even be my own daughter. We were many years, very many, before any children were born; the Cerridwine was still in its infancy when we found it. Later, when babies first happened they were all smothered; it was not only in our own self interest but it was also the will of the Cerridwine. Much later we captured a woman who had come into the forest to gather wood for fire. She lived in a shack just beyond the forest's edge. In pleading for her life she told us that women brought her children to put into baby auctions. One who was present was with child. You may think us cold but it was never easy, is never easy, to smother one's own child. This sister asked us why we should not give our children to this woman instead of smothering them. We deliberated long but eventually we agreed among ourselves and consulted the Cerridwine. Permission was granted but only for female children. So we made an agreement with the woman. In return for her life she would take the baby girls whenever they were old enough. The woman is long dead but we have maintained the contact with her family and her granddaughter continues to help us."

"You make it sound like the Cerridwine is a person," said Clive.

"There is a place in Elisiu, a sacred place, a grove where the Cerridwine communicates with us. No outsider has ever been there. It is also where the Cerridwine takes us at his pleasure to be the mother of his children. Now.... we have talked for too long and I have said too much. We must be on our way; the others will know by now that we have left."

She set off at pace and Clive and Ggydren followed, each wrapped in his own thoughts. Clive wondered yet again if he was in a dream and would wake up to find himself at home with the cat. It had already been too incredible to believe and now to think that these women were impregnated by something akin to a giant jellyfish. It was enough to get him certified or was it sectioned?

Making their way through the forest was slow going and tiring. With no paths to follow they had to pick their ways through the trees and never seemed to go further than a few steps in a straight line. After three or so hours of this, Ggydren and Clive were dog tired and when they came to a small clearing they flopped down and threw off their loads to rest. Angharind was not pleased.

"This is not good. If they come upon us here we will be open to their attack. Rest within the trees if you must."

The warning was too late. At that moment piercing cries came from all around and in a few moments hideous creatures began to emerge from the shadows. They took different forms but all of them were malicious and threatening. Some seemed like the gargoyles that look down from ancient churches, the demons that haunt nightmares;

some were wild animals, vicious, slavering, hyena like dogs or slithering, many headed snakes and other creatures besides. Clive and Ggydren stood up, back to back, weapons drawn and quaking in terror. Angharind stood a few yards aside, stony faced, silent. Then another figure emerged from the trees, a woman, Bronghar.

"Come to us, Angharind, you have done well to lead them here. We have come to deliver the punishment of the court. They cannot be allowed to leave the forest and here they must die."

All this was terrifying enough but what made it even worse the sense of betrayal, for Clive had come to trust, even to like Angharind, and now it seemed she had led them into a trap.

The feeling last only seconds for Angharind did not go to them. Instead she moved closer to Clive and Ggydren and spoke.

"I cannot allow it. These are not bad men; they intend no harm to Elisiu. I trust them. The one called Ggydren has befriended one of us, a daughter we discarded, and rescued her from ignominy. The other has the Staff. He could do untold damage to the forest were he to use it. Elisiu would lose its protection from the outside world."

"The law is the law, Angharind. You have always been soft. What happens to daughters when they leave us is not our concern. As for the Staff, well it is true that a little damage may be done at first but the Staff-holder cannot endure against so many. He will quickly fall and the Staff will be ours. Cease this idiocy, Angharind, you are one of us. Stand aside so the punishment may be done."

"I will not stand aside. I will fight with them. They have swords as well as the Staff. We do not age but we can be slain; some sisters are bound to perish. You say I am soft but you have always been hard. In our community of equals your voice has always been the most strident and the one to prevail. Now you are prepared to sacrifice any number of us so that your will can be enforced; well I say no. I will resist you. I challenge you. We should fight it out, you and I. One of us will live and one will die but the other sisters will live. If I die you may try to carry out the sentence on these men but if I live they will go free. Do you accept?"

Clive, still trying to control his fear, felt slightly ashamed that he had doubted Angharind. Without really meaning to he suddenly felt himself moving forward and speaking.

"You won't fight alone, Angharind. I will fight beside you. Let them see what the Staff can do."

"And I'll fight as well," said Ggydren. "My sword may be rusty but a rusty sword can still kill. I won't be taken without a fight."

"You are both brave, but no," said Angharind, "if we fight together, they will all join in. Some, a few maybe, or even many, will die, and you will too. That is what I am trying to avoid. They are my sisters. I will fight Bronghar for them."

While this has been happening the savage beasts all around had begun to transmute. Within a few more seconds they had all become women. Clive called to them.

"Will you allow this? Can't you stop it? Won't you help Angharind?"

They looked at each other. Then one of them stepped forward.

"This has been long in the coming. These two have never seen eye to eye and now it shall be resolved. Bronghar and Angharind shall fight alone. If Angharind prevails we will allow you to go. If Bronghar wins you must accept you fate and surrender to us."

"I accept the challenge," said Bronghar defiantly. "What form shall we take for the contest?"

"You may choose," answered Angharind.

"Then let us be bears. When bears fight it is until one is torn and bloodied or even unto death. I will tear you limb from limb. You will never return to Elisiu. Come, let us prepare."

Angharind and Bronghar began to change before their eyes, becoming twisted and contorted until the shapes of two enormous black bears emerged. They reared up on their hind legs, revealing curved, vicious claws and long pointed snouts, wide open, teeth bared, grunting, spewing spittle that fell to the ground. For some time they circled each other, each searching for the opportunity to attack, until suddenly, one sprang at the other and then they were locked together in frenzied action, with claws slashing and tearing into flesh and their teeth in each other's necks. They fell to the ground and rolled over and over in savage, brutal combat and very soon there was fur ripped off and blood and gore from open wounds. It was terrifying to behold, even to hear, for they grunted and roared with aggression and screamed in pain. Clive quickly lost his sense of which one was Angharind. All he could do was watch and hope. So it continued for many minutes. At times each bear seemed to be on the point of victory but somehow the other always came back until, at last, both fell to the ground, bleeding and exhausted. Then one, with a final, supreme effort, raised itself onto its back legs once more, until it towered over the other on the ground below it. From its mouth came a mighty roar, a roar of victory, of supremacy, and then its arm came down and with a swinging slash its claws tore into the other's throat, ripping through the fur and skin and deep into its flesh, until the blood spewed out. The stricken creature whimpered a few times and raised its head momentarily in one final gesture of defiance. Then its breathing laboured and it died.

The victorious bear dropped down onto all fours and turned to face Clive and Ggydren. Both were struck with a new terror that it was Bronghar who faced them. The bear roared again but weakly this time. Then it collapsed before them. One of the women walked forward, the one who had spoken before.

"Bronghar is dead. We will mourn her loss. Angharind has prevailed but at what cost we cannot tell. We honour the promise. You are free to leave. Go quickly before we change our minds. Go that way," she said pointing. "You will come to a stream. Follow its course; it leads out of the forest. A few hours, no longer. Go now, you two who have brought such tragedy onto us, go."

"But what of Angharind," asked Clive, "will she survive?"

"We cannot tell. We will take her back to Elisiu and care for her as best we can but who can say whether her injuries will prove fatal and she cannot transmute while she is so weak. Only time will tell, we cannot."

Clive bent down and, lost for words, gently stroked the stricken beast. After a few seconds he felt a tug on his shoulder.

"Come now, Mr Clive, let's do what the lady says. This is no place for the likes of us."

Ggydren pulled Clive up and then gathered their things. Without a word he started to walk in the direction the lady had indicated. Clive followed, almost instinctively. As they reached the end of the clearing he turned to look one final time. Then they were into the trees again.

Chapter 10.

Ggydren moved ahead at pace. Eventually they came to the stream that followed a meandering course. In places the banks were steep and in others the trees grew right up to the water's edge, so the going was slow. Even so, Ggydren walked as quickly as possible.

"Hang on Ggydren, I can hardly keep up," gasped Clive after a while and short of breath, "what's the rush?"

"I can sense them. They're following us, close behind. I don't trust any of them, not one little bit and this forest gives me the creeps. The sooner we're out the better."

"But they had us at their mercy back there. If they wanted to kill us, they would have done it then."

"Maybe, but I still don't like it in here. I'll only feel safe when we're out. Keep the rod in your hand."

So Ggydren cracked on, even wading through the stream at times, when the going along banks became too difficult. He kept glancing behind too, looking out for any creatures that might be around and continually muttering to himself. Clive had not seen him so agitated before. Eventually, after they had been trudging for at least two hours, the forest cover broke abruptly and before them lay the road and the open countryside beyond.

Both felt relieved to have come through the forest ordeal but, even so, they crouched low to check for danger along the road.

"Well, we've certainly come out further back from where we went in. This is where the road from Mickelling meets the forest and veers left. Look, over there, in the distance," whispered Ggydren.

Far away, where Ggydren had pointed, a pall of smoke hung in the air. Clive remembered the words of the officer from two days before.

"Remember what the soldier said. Do you think that could be the village burning?"

Even before Ggydren could answer, their attention was seized by movement along the road, coming from the direction of the smoke.

"I wonder what that is, could be soldiers again, if I'm not mistaken. I tell you what though, I'm not going back in the forest again come what may. What do you think?"

"Keep low and follow me," answered Clive. "I think they're too far away to spot us against the trees. We should be safer over there."

With that Clive, keeping low, moved along the verge between edge of the forest and the road, towards and past the turning to Mickelling. A couple of hundred yards further along he stopped at a place where the ground dipped away slightly and where they would be hidden from view from whoever was coming towards them. There they pulled off their packs and lay low to watch. Gradually a column of soldiers came into view and, in their midst, something more disturbing, men, women and children, all roped together and pulling a heavily laden cart. They looked a wretched lot, some with bandaged wounds but all downcast and forlorn and struggling to keep an even pace. The children, some little

127

more than toddlers but tied up all the same, looked particularly distressed. At least the innkeeper didn't seem to be among them but Clive realised that that didn't mean he was actually still alive. Finally, at the end of the line came the same officer he had seen and heard before, and next to him two of the Hinckle boys. They were talking, their words drowned out by the sound of the marching footsteps. Eventually they passed out of sight but the rumble of their boots continued for some time. When it had grown feint, Clive and Ggydren edged forward again. It was Ggydren who spoke first.

"It probably is Mickelling burning. The map doesn't show another village for miles around. I hope Bob is okay. I wonder why they've taken prisoners; bargaining pieces, hostages for ransom maybe or perhaps to be sold as slaves. I wish there was something we could do. Listen, Mr Clive, I have something to say. I've come to a decision. I know I was edgy back there in the forest but it's been doing my head in thinking about those horrible women and what they do with children. I've decided I need to get back to Elendril. I don't know what I'm going to say to her, whether I should tell her about it all, where she comes from and such like. In fact, I don't know how I feel about her after all this. It was difficult enough getting to terms with her shape-shifting but to find that her father isn't even a man, just some big blob thing that glows in the dark; well I don't know what to say. All I know is that I need to get back to her. I'm going back Mr Clive. I'm not going on. I'm sorry but I've made my decision. Will you come back with me? It's plainly far too dangerous to continue towards Besanto on this road. We could run into more soldiers any time and the Hinckle boys have probably got everyone hereabouts looking out for two Aughphalians and we must stand out a mile. I don't see how you can possibly succeed in this quest of yours and even if you did you'd still have to start looking for your London or wherever it is. What do you say? Will you come back with me? We could be a team, working at the cave, and you'd meet Elendril, as she really is I mean, not as a lion."

Clive thought about it. The road was certainly dangerous. If he was to go on, he would have to leave it and head across the open countryside and that would take much longer. And what would he live on and what would he do even if he did get to Besanto? Having to rescue a princess was bad enough but now there definitely was a war going on and a proper army to contend with as well. And if he did go on, it would be alone, without the company and comfort of Ggydren at his side. It was as plain as a pike staff that going on would be suicidal.

"I'm going on," said Clive, after a few seconds. "It's alright, don't feel guilty. It's been good to have you along this far and I completely understand your feelings. Of course, you must go back to Elendril but I need to get home too and Besanto seems my only hope. I have to carry on."

Actually it wasn't so much the need to go home or the desire to see the cat that decided Clive. Rather, it was the thought of going to live in a cave with Ggydren and a shape-shifter. Ggydren wasn't such a bad chap but having to live with him and also with someone who was sometimes a lioness as well as a lady, well, that was taking things a bit too far.

129

The next few minutes were a bit difficult. Ggydren tried to get Clive to change his mind but Clive rather got the impression that this was just a matter of courtesy. Then they argued about what belongings each should take. In the end it was agreed that Clive should take everything, except for a blanket and half the provisions Angharind had given them, as he might be travelling for months, while Ggydren would only be on the road a few days. This was all well and good but Clive struggled under the weight of the resultant load and feared he wouldn't get far at all. Finally it was time for goodbyes.

"Which way will you go? The road back might be just as dangerous as the way forward," said Clive.

"I'll try to find the route that Bob led us across the fields. That way I should come to the inn without being seen. Hopefully I'll find that Bob and his inn are both intact. Remember he promised us hospitality next time we are around, so I might be getting a soft bed and some good food. That is, if the soldiers haven't burnt the place down. Don't worry, I'll be careful. You keep a sharp lookout too. You never know, we may meet again. It's been quite a journey. I hate goodbyes, so I'll be off without further ado."

Ggydren held out his hand for Clive to shake but Clive thought that this would be too formal a way to part after all they had been through together, so he hugged him instead.

"Bloody hell," swore Ggydren, "I aint never been hugged by a man before. Must be a right strange place, your London, if that's how grown men behave," he said.

With that and with a quick look in each direction to check for soldiers, he set off.

Clive watched Ggydren walk away until he was just a speck in the distance and suddenly felt downcast. Ggydren had been a good companion and he realised he would be lonely without him. It was a big thing he was going to do, to set off alone in a strange land and walk into danger.

'Wish I'd never gone to sodding Madeira,' thought Clive, 'and I bet the cat isn't missing me at all.'

He looked at the map. In order to keep clear of the road he would have to set off in a diagonal direction away from it, in almost completely the opposite direction to the place he was trying to reach.

'Stupid,' he thought, 'but everything else that has happened so far has been stupid, so if that's what must be done then so be it.'

With that he packed up the map and set forth. He walked away from the road for about an hour and then turned northwards so that he was walking adjacent to it. There was no path or track to follow but it was open countryside, moorland with just the occasional bush or tree and easy enough going. At length the ground rose up in front of him. The hill seemed too wide to go round, so Clive trudged upwards, stopping often to catch his breath and ease his legs. Eventually he reached the summit and threw off his load to lay down to rest. From that height Clive could just see the road, thankfully empty and the forest beyond, although he could not make out any dome shape within it. Turning, there was no sign of habitation until his eyes reached the burning village that surely was Mickelling and he wondered if Ggydren was there yet and if he would find Bob alive. Eventually, after another bite to eat, he stood up and readied himself to move onwards. He looked all around to check for danger but from his location it was impossible for him to see the detachment of soldiers resting by the edge of the forest side or the two individuals who'd noticed him against the horizon and who were now moving towards him.

All through the rest of the day Clive struggled on, sometimes almost carefree, enjoying the solitude, the sheer physical effort of walking and the beauty of the open countryside but at others, deep in thought, focussed on the impossibility of his predicament and feeling downcast, even homesick. Eventually before the sun had set he came upon a stream with fishes swimming and decided to rest for the night. The clouds had gathered and he feared rain so he put up the tent, gathered wood for a fire and set about catching his supper. The fish seemed to take to Angharind's 'bread' and he soon had enough to eat. Gutting them in the water he found it only mildly chilly and decided to bathe. He stripped off his clothes and waded in, exhilarated. A few minutes later, just as he started to wade back to the bank, Clive glanced up to find two Hinckle boys looking down on him, self-satisfied grins on their faces. One of them had the rod in his hand. He banged it down hard on the ground. It let off a loud bang and a brilliant flash of light.

"Fancy some of this?"

Chapter 11

Ggydren soon found the lane that took him away from the road and any imminent danger and also recognised the place where he and Clive had joined it. He was full of apprehension, wondering what he would find at Mickelling, whether Bob would still be there and if any of the enemy remained. He didn't have to wait long to find out. At the end of Bob's garden a horrible sight confronted him; the inn was a smouldering ruin, almost nothing remaining. Ggydren clambered over the style, crouched down and edged forward until he had a good view of the village. One or two cottages remained relatively unscathed but most were burnt out shells. The few people he could see looked dazed, simply standing around and staring, as if bewildered at what had befallen them. At least there were no soldiers.

Ggydren kept still, contemplating whether to go back and take to the safety of the fields or to go forward and ask for information. He chose the latter, stood up and moved slowly ahead.

"Please, don't be alarmed," he called out, "I mean you no harm. I only want to know what happened to the landlord, to Bob. I was here just a few days ago and he helped me."

Most walked away, fearful of strangers after what had happened but one, an aged woman, turned to face him. She studied him for a few moments then called out to the others.

"It's alright, I recognise him. Aughphalian, he was in the inn the other night; him and another. The Hinckles were after them but Bob helped them to get away."

With that the others turned and walked quickly towards him, still wary but anxious for any information he might have. The old woman silenced them with a gesture of her finger, then spoke.

"Bob is dead. They made him serve them all the beer and food he had, then they strung him up on one of the beams and set fire to the place. By way of payment, they said."

Ggydren's heart sank at the news.

"Is there anything I can do, to help I mean?"

"To help? Nothing can help us now. The village is destroyed, half the folk taken off into captivity and my grandson among them. There's only a few old people and children left. One or two have already headed off to Trianja to seek the King's protection but I'm too old for that. I'd get away if I were you. People are bound to be suspicious of any strangers. There were two of you. What happened to the other? Did they get him too?"

"No, he's alright. We've just gone our separate ways. He's on a quest, an impossible one I'd say and I have to get home. The soldiers, did they all go back or did any of them carry on towards Buggiton? It would ease my way if I knew there were none of the enemy ahead."

"I can't say for sure but I would guess that they've all gone back to Besanto. There weren't many of them to begin with and what with all the loot they've stolen, and the captives too, they'll have their hands full."

"Besanto eh, I thought so. The Hinckles, are they from there too?"

"The Hinckle lot? No, I don't think so, the accent is wrong. I'm not sure where they're from. Most likely they're just working for the Baron, hired hands at his bidding. But the soldiers, yes they're Besantons. When I was working in the kitchen and forced to cook for them, I heard them bragging about how the Baron was going to conquer the whole of Morgrnvia. I have food if you need it; Buggiton is a long way off."

Ggydren was tempted, Angharind's stuff was not exactly delicious but he thought the better of it. The enemy had probably eaten or destroyed most of what food these people had.

"No, but thank you kindly, I reckon your need is greater than mine," he answered.

Then he felt uncomfortable, wondering how he should take his leave of them, as if to go was a form of desertion. She came to his rescue, telling him to be off and that once he had reached Buggiton, he should make sure that word was sent to the King of what had happened. He promised.

So Ggydren departed Mickelling, taking the road and keeping to it. He walked long that day, stopping seldom for rests and when at last night fell he wrapped his blanket around him and slept soundly under the cover of a tree. In the morning the blanket was wet with dew but he was dry and warm within it. The sun had not yet risen and the early morning air was still chilly when he set off. Once again he walked quickly, taking only a few breaks to rest and munch a handful of nuts. On that second day he met not a soul on the road, nor did he call at any of the few houses he passed. Further on there was the occasional cart and Ggydren wondered if he should warn the drivers of the fate of Mickelling but said nothing.

It had taken Clive and Ggydren almost a week to reach Mickelling from Buggiton but then they had been in no particular hurry and Clive had walked slowly, at least at first, after his ordeal at sea. But with Ggydren walking alone and at pace, he reached Buggiton quite early on the fourth day. His food had run out the previous afternoon and he was starving but he also remembered his promise to the old woman and, knowing no one else in the town, made his way back to the bookshop. Reece smiled to see him and closed the shop so they could talk without interruption. While Ggydren told his story, including much of what had happened in the forest and Elisiu, Reece prepared food, a simple meal of bread and cheese but very much appreciated. Reece offered tea to drink but Ggydren asked for milk instead and gulped down the glass in one.

"It really does taste better out of a cow. It doesn't come that way in Aughphalia. Will you be able to send word to the King?"

"I'll go to the Council as soon as you've left. They're sure to take it seriously; we could be next. The King will hear within two days I promise, not that he's renowned for acting decisively. Should I also send him word about that place, Elisiu wasn't it, in the Great Forest? Strangest thing I've ever heard of. Who would've guessed it? Under our noses, so to speak, all this time and nobody knew. They certainly did a good job of scaring people away. Should I send word to the King about

136

that as well? He would be sure to investigate, send a squad in. Maybe it would be best to keep it to ourselves. Who knows what sort of hornet's nest we might stir up if we start interfering there?"

"I agree," said Ggydren, "best to say nothing, for now at least. Someone I know from Buggiton is a shape-shifter and I'd like to get her ideas on it before anything is done. There's one thing I don't understand," he continued, "there are only twenty four women in Elisiu, well one less now, and none of them looked like they were expecting a baby. There can't be more than one or two babies born each year and half of them must be boys but there are half a dozen shape-shifting shows in Buggiton with several girls in each and I guess that all of them look about the same age as my friend or younger."

Reece smiled.

"Appearances can be deceptive when it comes to shape-shifters. Of course it's obvious that they can change into other things, animals and demons and so on but they can also change the way they look themselves. They might all look quite young but some of them are really getting on a bit. Eventually they get too old to continue and get thrown out but a few of us here have formed a society, well a conspiracy really because we have to keep it quiet, to help them out when that happens. It has to be in secret though because nobody round here trusts shape-shifters. As for there being a lot of them, well that's deceptive as well. You see the shape-shifting shows are all run by one business and the shape-shifters have to work in all of them. They do a shift in one and then have to pack up and go to another till they have gone round all of them. Some of the punters go from show to show thinking they're seeing new shifters each time but really it's just the same ones again and again."

Somehow Ggydren felt relieved. His question had been answered and he had found in Reece, a person who showed compassion to shape-shifters, just as he had done with Elendril.

"What happens to them, the ones you help out?"

"We take them in, usually as servants because that's easy to explain away. Nobody else knows that they're really shape-shifters. I have one myself. They seem to age very quickly, more quickly than we do. Usually they don't live for more than a few years."

"Couldn't you do something about it; get the shows closed down?"

"Money talks, my friend. They bring in lots of business. Besides, the shows also draw the shape-shifters. Some of them are utterly destitute when they arrive. At least it gives them a place where they can be together and where they are relatively safe, at least initially. It's a difficult dilemma, what to do for the best."

Ggydren left Reece, feeling he had found a kindred spirit and promising to return one day. As he walked past the shape-shifter shows he felt ashamed at his earlier weaknesses and hurried on. Outside the town, the hill leading to Aughphalia loomed and soon he was in the tunnel, in darkness again and approaching the door. It was shut and locked. Ggydren was puzzled. Maybe it was a Wednesday; he'd lost track of the days.

"Ggydon, are you there? It's Ggydren, let me in."

The person who unlocked and opened the door was not Ggydon. A tall, lean, mean looking fellow in official dress stood before him.

"Ah Ggydren, returned at last from your little holiday, have you? You are relieved of your duties and will be escorted to the Council offices to explain yourself. Next time you decide to go gallivanting please try to come up with a better excuse. Your brother, the one with the broken leg, must have made a miraculous recovery. Either that or his leg was never broken at all because he managed to trot up to the town hall to pay his garden water facility tax, just a few hours after we got your message."

Ggydren was dumfounded. He stood in silent shock for several seconds, and then he felt a wave of anger.

"You can't just sack me after all the years of hard service I've put in, living up here all alone half way up this mountain. It's not fair."

"We can and we have and the question of fairness does not arise. You broke the rules."

"But I had urgent business to attend to. I had to go."

"Urgent business, in Morgrnvia, I think not and besides, you should have followed the proper procedures if you wanted time off."

"Proper procedures! Proper procedures would have taken months, filling in forms, more forms, interviews, more forms. Proper procedures take an eternity in Aughphalia."

"Criticism of the system will not help your case. The Council's judgement will be much more severe if they learn that they are dealing with a dangerous extremist. We want no radicals in Aughphalia, and anyway, did I detect another lie? Have you really been living here alone?"

Ggydren's anger suddenly turned to fear.

"Elendril, my Elendril, what's happened to her?"

"Nothing's happened to her except that she's been returned to whence she came. Shown the door, so to speak. We want none of her filth here."

Ggydren was lost for words. His whole world seemed to be tumbling down around him. He had no idea of what to say or do.

"Guards," called the man.

A few seconds later two men in uniform entered the cave.

"Escort this wretch to the town hall. Make sure you get him there or your fate will be even worse than his."

They seized Ggydren by the arms and pulled him forward.
"My earnest wish is that they deal with you as severely as the law will allow. It's because of you I have to stay here in this stinking hole and perform your duties until a new Keeper is appointed and who knows how long that will take."

"Years probably," answered Ggydren, suddenly feeling a bit brighter, "especially if they follow proper procedures."

With that he was led away, down the hill and to the Last Friendly Inn at the Edge of Aughphalia where three horses had been requisitioned and were quickly made ready. At least the journey to the town hall would not be arduous. For some time they trotted along in silence. Ggydren's heart was full of sadness, not for the loss of his job and his home; he didn't give a toss about that, but for the loss of Elendril. All of his thoughts were about her and whether he would ever see her again. Where would she have gone? Maybe back to the shows but maybe not. In any case they would probably never give him permission to visit Morgrnvia again; she might be lost to him forever.

"You're a quiet one," said the guard on his left, in a not at all unfriendly voice.

"Oh, just thinking, you know. It's a lot to take in, getting the sack, becoming your prisoner," answered Ggydren, not wanting to talk about Elendril.

"I like that," said the guard on his right, "becoming your prisoner, makes us sound proper important, powerful even. Truth is we ain't never had a prisoner before. Most of the time we just has to stand still either side of the doors to the town hall. Must be the most boring job in the whole of Aughphalia, ain't it, Alf?"

"Bloody well is," answered Alf.

"What will happen to me?" asked Ggydren.

"Could be the chop," said the guard on his right.

"What, my head cut off?" asked Ggydren, feeling a sudden rush of panic.

"Or bollocks," said Alf. "In fact, most probably bollocks,"

"But all I did was take a few days off," said Ggydren.

"A few days too many," said the guard on his right. "He he, we're only kidding. Probably just a year or two in clink."

"Couldn't you just let me go?" asked Ggydren. "Pretend that I'd overpowered you or tricked you and escaped."

"Well," said Alf, "we could do that but then again we're rather fond of our own bollocks, so don't go getting any ideas now."

"Alright, I won't cause any problems," said Ggydren. "I don't rightly know what I'd do if I were to escape anyway. One question though."

"Yes?"

"What's a garden water facility?"

"Pond."

They delivered him to the town hall where he spent two hours filling in forms before his case could be heard. Then he spent three hours in a cell, while the officials who were to hear the case filled in their forms. Eventually someone came for him and took him to the Council chamber. The place was empty.

"There's no one here," said Ggydren.

"None of my business, I was told to take you to the chamber, that's all," said the attendant before leaving.

Ggydren sat down on one of the fancy chamber chairs and waited. Nobody came. While Ggydren waited he noticed the Staff resting on its special stand in the centre of the room. Underneath it a sign read 'Do not touch'. Ggydren picked up the Staff and examined it. It was exactly like the one Clive's rod had turned into in the cave. He gently tapped the end on the floor; little sparks flew up.

'It really is a Staff of Power,' thought Ggydren and almost immediately he smiled to think what he would like to do with it to the nasty tall man, who'd sacked him and banished Elendril. Then another more serious thought came to him, about what he could do to Elisiu with it.

Ggydren looked around for something to hide the Staff in. One of the wall hangings seemed the right size. Ggydren walked out of the chamber with the Staff, wrapped in the

142

cloth, under his arm. Outside the chamber various official looking people were milling about but nobody paid him any attention. He walked straight to the main door and opened it.

"Halt, who goes there?" said Alf, who had resumed his usual duties with the other guard whose name Ggydren did not know.

"Don't be silly. It's me, Ggydren. Case dismissed and I'm to be given my job back. You have to escort me back to the cave. Fetch the horses."

"Are you sure?" asked Alf.

"Course I'm sure. Do you think I'd be standing here otherwise?"

Alf and his fellow guard seemed very pleased that Ggydren had got off.

"That's one up for the common people," he said and when they got to the Last Friendly Inn at the Edge of Aughphalia he bought Ggydren a pint of best bitter to celebrate.

Actually it was several pints and all three of them were slightly 'merry' by the time they reached the cave. The tall, thin, mean looking man did not seem happy to see them.

"You were told to take him to the town hall. Explain yourselves."

"Alright now," said Alf, "don't be getting on your high horse. Case dismissed and he's got his job back."

"Are you sure?"

"Course I'm sure. Do you think we'd be standing here otherwise?"

"Most irregular. Didn't they give you any forms?"

"No."

"What's that?" said the tall man, looking at what Ggydren had under his arm.

"A wall hanging for the cave, to brighten it up a bit. Compensation for all the trouble I've had."

"It's rather stiff for a wall hanging."

"Yes, I noticed that too. Now, if you don't mind, I'd like my cave back and you better not have spoiled anything while I've been away. "

"Spoiled anything? What on earth is there in here to spoil? You're welcome to it."

With that, the tall, thin, mean looking man gathered up his things.

"I can't think what must have come over them. Cut and dry case. Guilty as charged. They've obviously gone soft," he muttered as he walked away.

"Bye," said Alf, "glad it turned out so well. Power to the people and all that."

The other guard, whose name Ggydren still did not know, just waved. Ggydren felt a bit guilty at what might be in store for them once they returned to the town hall but hoped that the more important, nasty, tall man would bear the brunt of the repercussions.

Chapter 12

Ggydren knew that they would be back once the deceit had been uncovered, so he moved quickly once they were out of sight. First he checked the hidey hole, found its contents intact and emptied them into a small sack. Then he packed up what food there was and a change of clothing. Next he looked around and gathered a few small, sentimental mementos, not knowing if he would ever return. With that he was off, through the door, locking it behind him and keeping the key, just in case, and then along the tunnel and out into Morgrnvia again. The light was already beginning to fade when he rounded the bend and saw Buggiton below. This time he did not head directly for the main street but skirted round it until he found a side road that took him into the town from the west. That way and with the gathering gloom he was able to approach the bookshop unseen. It was closed and Ggydren had to ring the bell several times until a flickering light was seen within and Reece opened the door.

"My word, Ggydren again, twice in one day, this is becoming a habit. You look dressed for a journey. What can I do for you?"

"I'm on the run. I've got to find Elendril. It's all gone haywire. I need some help..."

"Slow down my friend," interrupted Reece, "you're not making any sense. Come in and calm down."

Half an hour later, after Ggydren had been given two stiff drinks and had recounted the day's events, Reece went upstairs to prepare the spare room for the unexpected visitor.

"Of course not, I wouldn't hear of it. Keep your money, tonight you are my guest. Tomorrow we will search to see if Elendril is here in Buggiton. There is much to discuss. May I see the Staff?"

Ggydren unwrapped the Staff but felt a strange reluctance to hand it over.

"It's alright Ggydren; just tap it on the floor to show me the sparks."

Ggydren did as he was bid.

"So it really is a Staff of Power. They do exist after all. My word, this is a surprise and in my humble house too. And you say that your friend Clive has one as well. I don't suppose you know where the other two are, do you?"

Up to that point Ggydren had not mentioned the Staff in the chamber in Elisiu, nor his suspicions about the weapon in Besanto that could kill unseen and from a distance.

"Quite remarkable and very dangerous too if what you told me about the other ones. All four of the great Staffs of Power here in Morgrnvia at the same time. If I am not mistaken this could mean that we are on the verge of something momentous. Tell me, what do you know about the Staffs?"

"Well, I know that they seem to protect and can be used as a weapon and also that, how can I put it, oh yes, I remember what she said, 'the command of the Staff-holder is powerful'. But beyond that I don't really know anything, like how they can be controlled to use as a weapon. I don't know that."

146

"And what about their origins, how much do you know about that?"

"I know that they came from a great oak that Eric cut down. A branch was saved and made into staffs and then a great fiery thing came down from the sky and gave them its special powers. After that they were lost until William turned up with one of them and became king."

Reece smiled.

"It seems a rather simple tale, don't you think? Rather unlikely. I have something that will shed a little more light on it. Excuse me for a few moments."

A minute or so later Reece returned clutching a book. It was thick and heavy. He placed it gently on the table and blew away the dust on the cover.

"This, Ggydren, is my most treasured possession, the Book of Transition. It is the second volume of a set of three that charts the history of this world from earliest times until the start of the present Age. The originals were handwritten by scholars over a thousand years ago and have long since been lost to us but this is one of the copies made by apprentice scribes in order to learn their craft. It is almost as old as the originals and very valuable. I keep it hidden away and it is definitely not for sale."

He opened the book at the first page.

"This is the preface. It explains the main points of the first book. I think you'll find it interesting. Let me read."

Reece read aloud.

'The world is a sphere that floats in the ether between the Heavens and the Sea of Oblivion. The Heavens is the realm of the spirit world and is in a state of constant conflict between

the forces of good and evil. Everything in this world, be it mankind, animals, birds, trees, even the very earth and air, can be influenced by the spirit world. So good spirits may induce a welcome, gentle breeze to ease the heat of a summer's day, while evil spirits may send winter storms that wreak havoc and destruction. Although everything in this world is connected to the spirit world, mankind is unique in that only he may seek to communicate with that world to beseech the spirits to intercede on his behalf. At the time of death also, only man's life force can travel to become part of the spirit world, while all other things are lost forever in the Sea of Oblivion.

In the first great Age of the world, one man, whose name has never been revealed, learned how to free his vital life force from his physical body and travel to the spirit world and return from it. He was able to do this after purifying himself by induced vomiting and then by eating the ground up seeds of a certain plant, though the name of that plant remains a mystery. Within the spirit world he learned much that is outside the comprehension of other men and on his return to this world he had such powers that seemed incredible and magical to everyone else. Yet, each time, he also returned much wearied, for within the spirit world the forces of evil had sought to dominate him and it had taken all his strength to resist. At long last he returned a final time to warn of an impending doom, for the forces of darkness had achieved supremacy in the spirit world and mankind's future was in danger.'

"It does ramble on a bit here but basically it says that he was afraid that the evil spirits would try to act through him and using his special powers, to destroy the world and that he was too weak to stop them, so he endowed or transferred those powers to four artefacts and bade his disciples take them and hide them in faraway places at the ends of the world. Then he made a prophecy that although chaos was coming, one day far in the future, another man would find and gather the artefacts together and wield them against the forces of darkness and free the world. There, what do you think?"

"I've got no idea. What am I supposed to think? It all seems a bit gobbledygook to me."

"But the four artefacts, they could be the Staffs of Power."

"Well, who knows but all that other stuff, the spirit world, the Sea of Oblivion, forces of darkness, impending doom, it sounds like the person who wrote the book had a very vivid imagination. Surely, you can't believe that it's true. I know that everything's not perfect here and in Aughphalia but they're hardly in the grip of evil spirits."

"But terrible things did come about. This book goes on to tell how the whole world was engulfed in flames and how the smoke blotted out the sun for years and most things died. It was all eons ago but archaeologists have found evidence of it in their excavations of the ruins outside Trianja, a thick layer of soot that must have come from a great fire."

"We have something like that in our folk tales too, the big fiery thing that fell out of the sky and caused terrible fires. But it still doesn't make everything else true. It's all too far-fetched."

"Some of us do believe it. Not many, that's true, and we have to gather in secret; the authorities here don't like us, think of us as heretics who challenge the official view of

149

things and they don't like the idea of someone else who will come and have power over them. We have a special sign to reveal ourselves to each other. We carve it high up on the walls of our houses where most people wouldn't notice it. Here, I'll trust you, let me show you..."

Reece traced the outline of a shape on the table with his finger.

Ggydren recognised it at once. It was the same symbol that had been on Clive's rod in the cave, after it had changed into a Staff. He told Reece about it and they looked again at Ggydren's Staff. They couldn't see it at first at but after they had washed away years of engrained dirt, it emerged before them.

"What does it mean?" asked Ggydren.

"What does the symbol mean or what is its significance?" answered Reece.

"Both."

"Well, we don't know what the symbol means but we think it comes from an ancient language that was in use before our own. As for its significance, I'm still trying to work that one out. Our secret society is very ancient and it has always been our symbol. We have always believed the old stories, the ones in the book. Finding it on the Staff and you say it is on your friend's too, seems to confirm that our beliefs are correct. Tell me more about your friend, this Clive. Maybe he is the one to fulfil the prophesy. He said he was from a place called London that nobody in Aughphalia knows about. Is that so?"

"I think there's more to it than that. He said that in this place he comes from there is only one moon in the sky at night, so it must be another world, just like Aughphalia is another world from Morgrnvia. He explained he was in a thing he called a plane and it wasn't a bird or a dragon but it flew in the sky and something went wrong and it crashed into the sea. Everyone else was killed but he made a raft and survived. Part of the plane thing came away in his hand, a metal rod. It helped him fight off a shark. Elendril, that's my shape-shifter friend, realised it was a Staff of Power but in a different form. When we were in my cave we heated it up. Nothing happened at first but then, a bit later, it turned into the Staff and then it turned back again. But even in the form of a rod it still seems to have the power of a Staff. Certainly the ladies in Elisiu were afraid of it."

"You're right; it must be a different world if it has only one moon. It makes you wonder how many worlds there are and how easy it is to travel between them."

"I'm totally confused," said Ggydren, "nothing makes sense. It's not many years since we discovered the tunnel and found Morgrnvia, since contact was made that is, but this Staff has been in our Council chamber for much, much longer than that. The Staff that is hanging up in Elisiu either got put there in the last few years or there must have been comings and goings between our two worlds long before the tunnel was discovered. Probably between our three worlds when you think of Clive's staff."

"It does fit in with the prophesy though. Here, let me find the part."

151

Reece turned the pages of the book until he found the paragraph.

'One will come, not one of us, a Staff-holder who will gather the other Staffs about him and wield such power as will make the forces of darkness quake in his presence and he will smite them down and banish them from the world and there will be peace and prosperity everywhere.'

"See, your Clive is not 'one of us'. Maybe he is the Staff - holder."

"I'm not one of you either," said Ggydren, with a smile, "and I've got a Staff too."

"You say it lightly Ggydren but who knows. There is more though and it's not very encouraging."

'Not all those who possess a Staff are to be trusted. There is only one true Staff-bearer but there will be others, envoys of the dark spirits, who will come with malice and evil intent.'

"Blimey, well that can't be me"' said Ggydren. "I don't think I'm a representative of the dark spirits. I'm not the sort of person to hurt a fly."

"Enough of this talk," said Reece, "my mind is confused too. Let's leave it for now. Later on we might have some fresh ideas. I wasn't expecting company and I eat rather frugally myself and I don't have much food in, so I'll pop out to do a spot of shopping for dinner. It's late but something should still be open. Anything in particular you'd like?"

"Well," answered Ggydren, "I'm not a fussy eater so whatever will be fine but there is one thing...."

"Yes?" asked Reece.

"We aren't allowed beef in Aughphalia. It's been years since I've had a good steak. Here, let me pay."

A few hours later and relaxing after a satisfying meal of steak and mushrooms, washed down with golden ale, Reece asked Ggydren to tell him about Elisiu again. Ggydren related all that he had seen and all that had happened.

"She was very concerned that Clive shouldn't use the Staff in there. It made me wonder if the Staff could destroy the place and if that's true then I'd gladly go there right away to do it myself, now that I have Staff of my own, except of course, I've got to find Elendril before I do anything else. One thing I don't understand, I know I keep saying that I don't understand things, but anyway, the thing I can't get my mind round is why this Cerridwine thing should insist on having the boy babies killed or why it should want babies at all if it is only going to get rid of them. What do you think?"

"Maybe it has needs, lusts, if you like and babies are the result and there are lots of examples in nature where the father rejects its male offspring because there can be only one dominant male. You said, as well, that the place could only support twenty four people, so they would have to get rid of babies. It seems heartless but maybe it's necessary. Tell me again about the catastrophe she spoke of."

"She said it was brought about by people, actually by men. They unleashed vile weapons of war and that brought death and destruction on the whole world and only a few survived it, including them. That's when they found Elisiu. I think it must have come about because of the destruction and once they'd found it they cherished it."

"If only the third volume wasn't lost to us. We only have the second but there are stories about the third, rumours if you like, about a time when man learned to fly, we presumed like a bird but maybe in something like one of Clive's planes, and when men built cities that reached up into the sky and developed machines that could do his work for him. The stories also tell of a terrible war, when man used weapons of enormous power, so much so that a single one could completely destroy one of their cities and poison the air around. We've never been totally convinced about these stories because we don't have the book to back them up but maybe there is some truth in them after all. They certainly fit in with what she told you. I must say it gets even more interesting. My friends will be fascinated. Tell me, do you have any thoughts of what you'll do next, I mean if and when you find Elendril? You are a Staff-holder after all."

"Well, I told you I'd like to destroy Elisiu but perhaps that's only a whim and not serious. I can't say I've had time to give it any thought, given all that has happened today, and as for being a Staff-holder, well I've only had it a few hours."

Just then Ggydren heard a banging noise from above. He looked up, slightly startled.

"Matilda," said Reece, "I told you about her this morning. My servant, my own shape-shifter. Come with me."

Ggydren was excited, perhaps Matilda might know of Elendril's whereabouts. Reece led him to the very top floor and there, in a little attic bedroom, lay Matilda, a very aged, white haired lady.

Reece spoke quietly to her, introducing Ggydren but she made no visible reaction.

"I told you they age quickly once they get to a certain point," he whispered. "She's virtually bedridden now and in her dotage. I have to do everything for her, hardly my servant

154

at all, more the other way round. You'll excuse me now Ggydren but I have to attend to her personal needs. I'll see you in the morning. Sleep well and tomorrow we'll search out Elendril."

The following morning Ggydren slept in late, mainly due to the quantity of ale he had supped, not to mention the earlier stiff drinks. Downstairs there was no Reece, only a note that said 'Gone shopping again'. A little later Reece returned clutching a bag.

"You stand out a mile as an Aughphalian, dressed like that and with no horns to boot, so I've got you a few things to help you blend in more. Not new, I'm afraid but clean nevertheless."

He handed the bag to Ggydren and told him to try on the contents. When Ggydren returned downstairs he was dressed in a green shirt, brown fitted waistcoat and knee length brown breeches.

"I feel right peculiar, I can say. All we're allowed to wear in Aughphalia is the long gown. Do I look completely stupid?"

"Not at all, dear chap, quite fetching in fact."

"I'll still stand out a mile. No horns."

"I've thought about that too," said Reece with a smile. "Have you still got that woolly hat I gave you the first time you were here? The one with tufts to fit over horns. "

Ggydren rummaged around inside his sack and pulled out the hat. Reece lit a candle and tipped it so that the wax melted and dripped onto a plate. When he had enough he squeezed it into the horn shapes and placed them in the tufts.

"There, now you have become Morgrnvian."

Ggydren looked at himself in the mirror that Reece held out to him.

"Blimey," he exclaimed, "now I do look completely daft."

After a bite to eat for breakfast they went out to search for Elendril. Reece insisted that Ggydren left the Staff behind.

"It will be perfectly safe here and it's too big to hide discretely."

First they went to the back of one of the buildings that had a shape-shifter show. It was still too early for the shows but after a short wait two women arrived.

"Excuse me," said Reece, before they could enter, "we're looking for a lady, a person like yourselves. She would only have arrived a few days ago. Do you know of anyone like that?"

"There was a woman by the name of Elendril..."

"That's her," interrupted Ggydren, "a good friend of mine. Is she here now? Do you know where she is?"

"No sir, she only wanted shelter for a couple of nights. She told us she had once been in the shows and wouldn't do it again. We looked after her until the day before yesterday when she went off to offer herself in the hiring fair."

"Hiring fair?" asked Ggydren.

"They happen three or four times a year. They bring together people looking for work with others, farmers mainly, who are looking for labour. There was one this week," explained Reece.

They quickly made their way to the square where the hiring fair was held but although they asked around, no one could give them any information about a woman called Elendril who had put herself up for hire.

"Don't be downcast," said Reece, "we've still another avenue to explore. Hired labour is taxable and should be registered at the town hall. If the farmer or whoever it was hired her is an honest fellow, we should find a record of it there."

The official in the town hall was difficult at first but became more amenable when Reece passed him a groat. They had no luck again, however, for no one called Elendril had been registered that week. Not knowing where else to turn, they wandered back to the square to ask again and when that proved fruitless they decided to go for a bite and a drink in a nearby inn. There their luck turned for at the table next to them a couple of locals were chatting.

"Old Bill Higgins thinks he might have hired a shape-shifter the other day. Said she had that look about her. He's a crafty one that Bill, knows that she'll want to keep it quiet and he'll be able to get away with paying her far less than the going rate. Won't have registered her either, so he won't be paying tax on her too. Lucky sod, wish I'd found her first."

"I don't think old Bill ever pays the going rate on anything. Have you seen the state of his place?"

Ggydren had just taken a mouthful of beer when he heard them, kept it there while he listened and choked on it when he finally gulped it down. After a burst of loud coughing that got the attention of everyone, Reece indicated to him to keep quiet.

"Don't say anything my friend," he whispered. '"Everyone in Buggiton knows of this Higgins fellow. A bad lot by all accounts. He lives a mile or so out of town but tends to spends most of his days in here drinking. It seems we need to pay him a little visit."

They finished their drinks and left. Ggydren was anxious to go to Higgins' place immediately but Reece said no.

"It'll be a good walk and Matilda needs some attention first. In any case I want to think about this. If we just turn up at the Higgins place and ask about Elendril he'll realise he has someone valuable on his hands. If only a fraction of what they say about him is true, he'll try to turn it to his advantage. I very much doubt if he'll let us come away with Elendril without having paid a hefty sum for her."

"We have the Staff. We can force him to hand her over," said Ggydren.

"Yes and broadcast your Staff of Power all over Buggiton. No, I don't think that's a viable option. I was thinking that maybe we could get to his place once it's dark, that way we could see what's what without being seen ourselves. Maybe we could even bring Elendril away with us if we see her alone."

Much later that day they set out. Ggydren had been persuaded to leave the Staff behind again. Reece carried a small pouch.

"What's that?"

"Dog food."

By the time they reached the farm the light had gone completely and with only crescent moons it was difficult to make out anything at all. As they approached the gate a terrific sound of barking erupted. The dogs rushed up to the gates and stuck their noses though the railings, snarling ferociously. The back door opened and a shape, silhouetted by a light behind, appeared.

"Shut up you stupid hounds; bloody rabbits set you off every time."

The door was banged shut but the barking continued. Reece felt inside his pouch and threw handfuls of the contents over the railings. Pretty soon the barking stopped.

"Special dog food," explained Reece.

"Poison?" asked Ggydren.

"My own concoction, just a little something to make them sleepy. They won't be bothering us again for a bit."

Ggydren climbed over the gate and then opened it up for Reece. One or two flickering lights could be seen in the windows of the farmhouse but Ggydren noticed another feint one some way apart and to the side.

"Probably a barn," said Reece. "That may be our best chance. He's unlikely to share the house with farm hands."

The door was barred from the outside. Ggydren lifted the bar and pulled the door open a fraction.

"Who's there?" asked a voice from within the gloom.

"A friend," answered Reece. "Is there anyone here called Elendril?"

Something stirred in the upper level.

"I'm Elendril, who wants me?"

Ggydren was overjoyed.

"It's me, Ggydren; I've come to get you."

Very quickly the pair were reunited and embracing lovingly.

"I wasn't sure you'd come or if they'd even let you out of Aughphalia. How did you find me?"

Reece interrupted before Ggydren could answer.

"There'll be plenty of time for explanations later. Right now we need to get away before those dogs wake up."

While this had been happening other people had been emerging from the shadows.

"Take me too," said one of them, "it's like a prison here. The overseer treats us like slaves in the day and they lock us up like dogs in the night."

Other voices muttered in agreement. So it was that half a dozen people made their getaway from the Higgins farm that night. Reece led the way for some time but when they had reached a cross roads just outside the town he turned and gathered them round.

"I'm sorry but we came for Elendril and I have no room for more. You must go your own ways now and trust to luck and good judgement. Remember that you are indentured labour and Higgins has the law on his side. My advice is to split up and go in ones or two's. A crowd would be more easily noticed."

So they parted with the others and soon after Reece, Ggydren and Elendril arrived back at the shop. After introducing himself properly to Elendril, Reece made some excuse and left them alone. Ggydren and Elendril were overjoyed to be together again and hardly knew what to say first, so for some time they just sat, hand in hand together, in silence instead. Eventually they relaxed and told each other what had happened since they were last together, although Ggydren was careful to avoid any mention of Elisiu, wanting to find the right time to tell her about that. Later still Reece reappeared with food and a bottle of wine to celebrate their reunion.

After midnight, while they were alone in their room, Ggydren told Elendril about Elisiu and all that had happened there. Finally, he explained how babies were fathered there and their fate. Elendril became very quiet and then tearful.

"It is worse than I ever could have imagined. Bad enough to find these things happening to my body as a girl and to be rejected and thrown out by the people I thought were my parents and then to wander the streets as an outcast. But to find out that my father, I mean, can I even call him a father, that this thing somehow engendered me and then ordered me away. It is too much, too much to comprehend. I know I am different, separate from others, but to find I am some sort of freak, a monster even..."

Elendril paused, deep in thought. Ggydren held her to him but said nothing, knowing no words that could ease her pain. Finally she spoke.

"Will you stay?"

"Pardon?"

"Stay, will you stay with this monster?"

"You are not a monster and no different now from when I first met you. Of course I'll stay. I've left Aughphalia because of you and I'd gladly do it again, without hesitation. The future is unknown. We'll have to find work and somewhere to live but we can make a go of it in Morgrnvia. It's not so bad here. You can be freer than in Aughphalia, not so many rules and regulations, not so boring. Only not in Buggiton, I don't like Buggiton and its shape-shifter shows. We'll go somewhere else, the capital maybe or out in the countryside, somewhere where they don't exploit sha... they called it transmutation in Elisiu, I think transmuter is kinder than shape-shifter."

Ggydren spoke gently and lovingly and she felt his affection and was reassured but later, while he was sleeping soundly next to her, her thoughts turned to Elisiu again and she felt utterly wretched.

In the morning Ggydren packed his bag and they descended the stairs intending to take their leave.

"Nonsense," said Reece. "I wouldn't think of it. You are welcome to stay as long as you like. Well, for a while at least. I like having guests. Besides, I've been out already this morning to fetch bread and Higgins is in to town complaining to all and sundry about last night's events. He's even offering a reward. People are looking for you, Elendril, and the others who escaped. Better not to show your face for a few days until things have died down. There is another thing Ggydren. You have the Staff and I have explained the prophecies. Something big is happening and you are part of it. I doubt if you could just walk away and settle down in some quiet quarter, even if you wanted to. Decisions have to be made."

"What sort of decisions?' asked Ggydren.

"Well, what to do with the Staff, for one thing and what do about your friend Clive. You left him to find Elendril. Well, you have found her now and he is walking into danger."

Ggydren felt a twinge of guilt.

"I'm not criticising you, just saying that things have changed. You are a Staff-holder now."

"I don't want the Staff," said Ggydren, "you can have it."

"Me? I think not. I'm an old man, much too old to be carrying a Staff of Power around. For better or worse, it is in your hands Ggydren."

"But what am I supposed to do with it? And how can I go after Clive now? He could be anywhere. I'm not cut out for this sort of thing. I thought it would be good fun to go on a quest but I'm seriously having second thoughts. It's been a disaster."

"Let me make a suggestion. Why don't I invite a few of my friends from the secret society I told you about to come round? A few more minds might come up with a solution."

Ggydren looked at Elendril. She nodded.

"Alright then, we'll rely on your hospitality for a few more days and hear what your friends have to say. Do you think you could arrange it for tonight? The sooner the better as far as we're concerned."

"I'll see what can be done. The shop won't suffer for being closed this morning. Perhaps you'd like to meet Matilda, Elendril. I expect Ggydren has told you about her."

Reece was away for most of the morning and Elendril spent ages with Matilda. It seemed she became wider awake in Elendril's presence and the two had much to talk about. Ggydren was left on his own and found himself fretting about the situation. All he had wanted to do was to find Elendril and he could have done that without taking the Staff; it had played no part in his escape from the Council Office or from the nasty, tall, thin man in the cave, or in Elendril's rescue, come to think of it. He wished he'd never taken it because the chances were that it was going to get him involved in something complicated and dangerous. He even found

163

himself quietly cursing Clive because of all the nonsense that had happened since his arrival.

'By rights I should have had nothing to do with him; it was my day off.'

Later, Ggydren regretted his thoughts, he'd let Clive walk into danger alone and there was now no telling if he was alive or dead. At length Reece returned. A meeting had been arranged for that evening but at a friend's house. In the meantime Reece opened up the shop, Elendril went upstairs to Matilda again and Ggydren volunteered to buy food, first donning his woolly hat with the false horns. Later, when they had eaten and were waiting to leave for the meeting Ggydren noticed how quiet Elendril had become. It seemed clear that the knowledge of her parentage was weighing heavily and Ggydren did not know what to do or say to ease her mind. It didn't help, of course, that they no longer had a home and were effectively fugitives in a foreign land.

At last it was time to leave for the meeting but as they prepared themselves, Reece received a message that several of the escapees from the Higgins farm had been apprehended nearby and it was not safe for Elendril to be outside. So Ggydren and Reece set off alone leaving Elendril behind. The meeting house was nearby; Reece nodded discretely towards the symbol on the wall. Inside four others were already gathered and a little later two more joined them. If Ggydren was hoping for a lively meeting with a positive plan of action by the end of it, he was sorely disappointed. He was by far the youngest person there and no one, including Reece seemed to have the faintest idea what to do for the best. The meeting broke up in disagreement after little more than an hour.

Reece was also downcast and suggested a beer in a local tavern before they returned home. One beer turned into several and Ggydren quite forgot that his woolly hat with its candle wax horns disguised him as a Morgrnvian. He had only removed it for a few seconds before Reece urgently told him to put it back on. Even so several people had already looked his way with surprised expressions. A little later Reece opened the door to his shop. Ggydren called out to Elendril, thinking she was upstairs with Matilda but received no reply. Finding Matilda alone, he looked for Elendril in their room and found her sitting on the bed, looking forlorn.

"Something is wrong," said Ggydren, "you look so unhappy."

"I have decided," she answered, "I must go there, I must go to Elisiu to find out. If all you have told me is correct then I believe that one of those women must be my mother. I will confront her and ask how she could give me up, how they could smother their sons and give away their daughters. I must go. I do not ask you to come with me. I know you barely escaped from there with your life. I will go alone. I am sorry, Ggydren but I must. I will leave in the morning."

Chapter 13.

Clive looked up in amazement and horror at the Hinckle boys who loomed over him. He knew that his life was in danger but also wondered why they were called Hinckle boys when they were very obviously grown men and burly with it. He also felt slightly embarrassed to be caught in this situation, completely naked.

"Get out," ordered the Hinckle holding the rod. "Thought you could get away from us did you?"

"Well, yes I did and I will get out if you'd turn away for a moment. I find myself in the rather uncomfortable position of having nothing on."

"Dead men don't need clothes."

"I'm not de...oh I see what you mean. Couldn't we just talk this through? I think you already have what you came for."

"I told you, get out."

This time Clive felt an urge to comply and remembered what Angharind had said about the power of the command of the Staff-holder. He climbed out of the stream and stood there, covering his nakedness with his hands and shivering.

"How does this work?"

"What, the rod?"

"Yes, obviously the rod, what else am I holding? How does it work?"

"It goes bang and shoots up a shaft of light when you hit the ground with it."

"I already know that. I just did it, remember? But how do you control it? How do you use it?"

"I don't know."

"What?"

"I really don't know. I've been meaning to try to find out but I've never found the time to get round to it. Apart from banging it on the ground and having the shaft of light shoot up into the air like that, I'm completely ignorant about it. Look, do you mind if I put some clothes on?"

"Yes."

"Yes, you mind or yes, you don't mind?"

"Shut up. Where's your friend?"

"I don't know."

"What?"

"I don't know."

"How come?"

"He left to go back home. I don't know where he is now."

"A likely story. Are you going to tell me how this thing works?"

"Honestly, I would if I could. I really don't know."

"Then I'll just have to find out myself and it's curtains for you. This isn't the only weapon we've got. Henry, time for the sword."

The other Hinckle drew a large sword from its scabbard and moved threateningly towards Clive.

"Surely you don't need to kill me. It's not as if I'm any sort of threat, especially now that you've got the rod."

Clive realised that he was shaking.

"Shut up and behave like a man. I hate whingers. Get on with it Henry."

167

Henry moved closer to Clive who was gripped by blind panic. He should have run but it didn't occur to him to do so. He closed his eyes to await his fate.

Clive heard a twanging sound, followed by a kind of whoosh. He opened his eyes again and saw Henry in front of him, completely still and with the point of an arrow sticking out of one side of his neck and the shaft of it going into the other. Henry stayed in that position for a second or so and then started to teeter. Finally, he fell backwards onto the ground, dead. Henry's companion had already started to run when a second arrow, then another and yet another, hit him in the back. He staggered on for a few yards and then fell to the ground, still clutching the rod and groaning. Clive looked around. From the cover of a bush emerged a man holding a bow and drawing a sword. He looked quite a bit younger than Clive and was rather garishly dressed in green breeches, tunic and feathered peaked cap, so that Robin Hood instantly came to Clive's mind. The man walked up to the groaning Hinckle and plunged the sword into his back. Then he wriggled it round a bit, as if to make sure. Clive was both relieved and horrified. He was not used to seeing people killed, even if they had been intent on his own death, and it was not a pleasant sight. The newcomer pulled out his sword and the three arrows and walked towards Clive, who didn't know whether to smile or make a run for it. The man may have just saved his life but he might just as well be intending to take it too and then make off with the rod and whatever other goodies the Hinckles might have about them. The man smiled at Clive.

"I'm Bengough, pleased to meet you."

"I'm Clive," said Clive, feeling relieved as he figured that people who wanted to kill you weren't generally pleased to meet you.

"That's two villains you'll not have to worry about."

"Yes but one of them was only wounded. Did you have to finish him off like that? I've never seen a person killed before. It's not very pleasant."

"Just putting him out of his misery and in any case, we didn't want him reporting back and having a squad of soldiers come our way, did we?"

Clive noticed that Bengough didn't have horns.

"I see you aren't Morgrnvian. Me neither."

Bengough didn't answer. Instead he walked up to the Hinckle called Henry and retrieved his other arrow. This was rather more difficult than with the previous three; he had to pull from the pointed end and the whole arrow eventually came out bloody and gory. Clive had to look away.

"I think we ought to get you dressed in this fellow's clothes, he's near enough your size. It would be better not to be wearing Aughphalian garb; I expect the enemy already has people out looking for Aughphalians."

Bengough washed his sword and arrows in the stream. Clive put on his underpants and the two of them relieved the dead Henry of his tunic and breeches.

"Hurry up. We don't want to be here when they come to investigate."

Clive hurried up. The breeches were rather loose about his waist but felt as though they would at least stay up after he had put on Henry's belt. Finally, he put his own boots back on and wondered if his new outfit made him look rather dashing or just plain stupid. While wondering it occurred to Clive that Bengough was holding the rod.

"Do you mind if I have that back? It's rather special."

"So I saw. Metal rods don't usually send bolts of lightening up into the sky. It must have been visible for miles around. We really should get away. Here, have your rod. Peculiar though, I thought only Staffs of Power could do that," said Bengough, with a knowing smile.

"Where shall we go? Shouldn't we bury them first? It's not nice to just leave them."

"They'll be found soon enough and their own kind can bury them or leave them for animals to dispose of. I have a little hiding place a few miles away. We should be safe enough there. Follow me."

Bengough set off at such a pace it was difficult for Clive to keep up, let alone speak, so after a trek across open ground of at least an hour he was none the wiser about the man who had saved his life. Just when Clive was almost at the point of exhaustion they came upon a small copse, within which Bengough had erected a simple shelter of branches and leaves to keep the rain off.

"Home, sweet home. Well, not really but we should at least be safe enough here for tonight. I'll just go and get us something for supper. You could make a fire while I'm gone."

Bengough was away for half an hour while Clive gathered wood from the copse for a fire. He still hadn't managed to get it going before Bengough got back, carrying two rabbits, already skinned and cleaned, some green leaves and a small sack of mushrooms.

"We'll eat well tonight. Here, let me help you with that fire. Not practised in outdoor survival skills eh? Never mind we'll have it going in no time."

And he did. Within a few minutes the fire was taking hold nicely.

"You didn't answer my question about your lack of horns."

"I'm sorry. I didn't know it was a question. What did you want to know?"

"Who are you, where you come from, what you do, why you saved my life, did you just happen upon me by accident; any information along those lines. You see, I'm not sure about any of this; where we are, how I got here, the rod, Aughphalia, Morgrnvia, Besanto, everything to do with this place. It's around two hours since we first met and in that time you have saved my life, done away with the two men who wanted to kill me, led me here and gathered a meal and still the only thing I know about you is your name and I don't even know if it's your first or last one."

Clive realised that he was going on a bit. He tended to do that in tense situations.

"Try to calm yourself Clive. All will be explained in good time. I don't have horns because I'm not from here."

"So you're Aughphalian?"

"Not from there either."

"Where else is there?"

"Rather a lot of places, actually. I take it that you are Aughphalian, not having horns."

"No," said Clive, hesitating to say where he was from through fear that Bengough would think he was mad.

"No? Well, this is getting interesting. Where are you from then and what are you doing here?"

"I'd like to ask you the same questions. You go first."

"No, I think you should. I saved your life after all."

Clive pondered for some time, wondering whether it was wise to tell the truth.

"Alright, I'm from a place called Ealing, in a country called England, on a planet called Earth. I was in a plane, that's a thing that flies but isn't a bird or a drago..."

"I do know what a plane is. Are you trying to be difficult?"

"You do?"

"Of course I do. They were the principal means of intra planetary travel for many years. And although I've never heard of Ealing, I know all about the Earth and England. After all, we're both speaking English."

"We are?" asked Clive in a state of relieved shock, if such a state is possible.

"Of course, English, the official galactic language, originated on the planet Earth and gradually spread to all inhabited planets before intelligent life on Earth itself was destroyed through wars and general ecological mismanagement. Standard school boy history. Of course that was hundreds of thousands of years ago."

It was quite a bit to take in, quite a lot, in fact. Clive considered the idea that intelligent life had long since died out on Earth for some time before concluding that Bengough was the one who was mad.

"Look here, I'm not trying to be difficult but that's...that's impossible, quite impossible."

Clive was tempted to say 'ridiculous' instead of 'impossible' but was wary of offending a man who had already killed two people, at the very least, that day.

"The point is that I'm English, from Earth and I'm not fifty years old and I was there just a couple of weeks ago, along with millions of other people who were also very much alive, so the Earth couldn't have been destroyed thousands of years ago, could it and who are you anyway?"

"Actually, I think we are both telling the truth. If you are from Earth before it was destroyed then there are an awful lot of things that have happened since that you don't know about and it will take so long to explain that I think I should get on with the cooking first and we'll discuss it all after dinner. Would that be okay, Clive?"

Clive didn't like the rather patronising way Bengough said 'Would that be okay, Clive' but decided just to nod in agreement. He watched as Bengough produced a tripod and chain, cooking pot, plates and cutlery from a sack and then set about preparing a rabbit stew with all the ingredients he had hunted and gathered. As Bengough worked, he hummed a tune that sounded to Clive almost exactly like 'The Happy Wanderer', a song he had last heard over thirty years ago as a Boy Scout and he wondered for a second time, if someone somewhere wasn't filming this for a TV show where you were set up to be humiliated in front of millions of people. He looked around for hidden cameras.

The cooking took an hour or so. There wasn't much space inside the shelter and Clive didn't fancy the idea of sleeping cuddled up next to Bengough, so he used the time to unpack his rucksack and erect the tent just outside. By the time he

173

had finished the daylight had gone completely and Clive sat down on his blanket, near to the fire for warmth. If the cooking took an hour, the eating was done in a few minutes and the food was good and filling. Afterwards Clive waited in anticipation of what Bengough would say. His feelings towards the man had been rather negative up till then, despite him having saved his life and he still knew absolutely nothing about him but, sitting there, Clive at least felt confident that Bengough would be good to have around if danger arose. Bengough seemed in no hurry to start his explanation. After finishing his food he took out a pipe, filled it, lit it, sat back and smoked.

"Smoking kills," said Clive.

"I know," said Bengough, "but who wants to live forever."

A few minutes later, Clive waiting and pipe finished, Bengough spoke.

"There's such a lot to tell you it's difficult to know where to start. Tell you what, you start. Ask me a question."

Clive thought. He decided to start with easy questions to put them both at ease.

"Your name is Bengough?"

"Bengough, yes, I already told you."

"Is that your first or last name?"

"Last."

"What's your first?"

"I'd rather not say."

"Why not?"

"Because I find it embarrassing. I don't know what my parents could have been thinking."

Clive thought it better not to press the point.

"Where do you come from?"

"Hesppalis."

"Hesppalis?"

"Yes Hesppalis, a planet in the Andromeda galaxy."

"How did you get here?"

"Space buggy."

"Space buggy?"

"One man, outrider craft, despatched from the mother ship."

"Mother ship?"

"Inter-planetary spaceship."

"Inter-pl...."

"Oh, please stop repeating everything I say. Since Earth was ruined things have moved on. We have had the ability for space travel for thousands of years. You even had it to a certain extent on Earth for a bit. Now we can travel in space and in time. That is why you can be from a planet that no longer exists; well, not as a place that can support life anyway. We travel in mother ships using warp drives and wormholes. They can take us from one part of the galaxy to another or even to adjacent galaxies, which is how I can come from Andromeda. We're still working on how to get further afield. I'm a sergeant in the Inter-Galactic Special Police Force. I was ordered here to investigate reports of potentially fatal intrusions. Basically I've come to find out what you are doing here with that thing."

Bengough pointed to the rod.

"This thing?"

"Yes. Where did you get it and what are your intentions?"

"Intentions?"

"Yes, intentions. That thing is dangerous. In the wrong hands it can wreak havoc. Do you know what it is? How did you get it? What do you know about it?"

"It's a metal rod, as you see, but it can also turn into a Staff of Power and it can send shafts of light or lightening into the sky. My friend Ggydren said that several of them were made in Aughphalia long ago from the branch of an oak tree that became suffused with stuff from a meteorite. That's really all I know about it. Ggydren says there is another one hanging up in the town hall in Aughphalia and we saw what we thought to be one hanging up in the Chamber in Elisiu which is a place inside something called the Cerridwine, which is something like a giant jellyfish, only really gigantic, with living beings, well women actually, but not exactly normal, inside it. That was here in Morgrnvia, close by in fact. Also, there may be one in Besanto but I'm not sure. I got this one when the plane I was travelling in on Earth crashed into the sea. Everyone else was killed but somehow I survived and ended up with this. It came off the plane. Eventually I washed up on the shore in Aughphalia, met Ggydren and we came through a tunnel to get here. There, I think that about sums it up."

"Sounds reasonable."

Clive was taken aback. He was feeling increasingly exasperated, angry even. This Bengough seemed to accept everything he said, even though it was all totally ludicrous.

"Reasonable? It's not reasonable at all. It's totally off the wall. None of it is possible and your talk of time travel and wormholes, it's all just stuff and nonsense, science fiction nonsense at that. Tell you what, if you came here in a so-called space buggy, then where is it, eh? Tell me, no better,

176

show me where it is and also, if you come from some sort of advanced civilization, why are you dressed up like Robin Hood and hiding out here in the wild? It's all bonkers."

"It's just over there," said Bengough, pointing to a boulder, "only it's disguised, of course."

"Disguised eh, but of course, it would have to be disguised, wouldn't it and I suppose there is some perfectly good reason why you can't show me what it's like when it's not in disguise."

"No."

"No, no what?"

"No good reason."

Bengough took a small rectangular object out of his tunic pocket, pointed it at the boulder and pressed a button on it. Slowly at first but with gathering speed, the boulder began to change shape until it resembled a small, sleek aircraft.

"Good gracious!" exclaimed Clive.

"And I'm dressed like this person called Robin Hood, whoever he was, because we aren't allowed to reveal ourselves to the local populations, so we have to wear appropriate apparel and use the relevant technology. Do you think I enjoy looking like this?"

"Sorry," said Clive, feeling slight remorse for having doubted Bengough and totally dumbfounded by what he had been told and just seen.

"You say that when your plane crashed and that was on Earth, you were washed up in Aughphalia with this rod?"

"Exactly."

"Then it is fairly obvious that you must have entered a wormhole at some point during the process because Earth and Aughphalia are in different parts of the galaxy."

"Really?"

"The puzzling thing though, is how you came to arrive here with the rod because it was placed on the Earth for the very purpose of keeping it apart from the other ones. In fact the whole thing is rather worrying because the chances of your plane crashing directly into a wormhole are infinitesimally small. I'm afraid that it looks as though you were brought here by some malign purpose and my guess is that it is more interested in that thing than in your wellbeing. You were probably just being used as a carrier. Tell me about the tunnel you went through to get here and why you came here anyway."

"It's difficult to explain. The tunnel connects Aughphalia with Morgrnvia and people pay money to go back and forth through it. I don't mean that that is difficult, just that Morgrnvia shouldn't be there at the end of the tunnel, it should just be the other side of Aughphalia. Do you think the tunnel is a wormhole?"

"And a very special one at that. Two-way wormholes are very rare. Was there a part in the centre where you became disorientated?"

"The wobbly bit?"

"Well, this is beginning to fit together. What made you go into the tunnel?"

"Ggydren posted a letter through the door, asking if I could go on a quest to get home to England and the reply said yes, but first I had to go to Besanto and rescue a princess that the Baron had captured."

"Who sent the reply?"

"I've no idea."

"Didn't it occur to you to find out before accepting the challenge?"

Clive felt under pressure. He struggled to answer.

"No, I mean no, not really. You see I was confused. I'd already been through a lot. I just wanted to get home."

"In all probability it was the Baron or one of his minions. It looks as though you have been brought from the Earth to take the rod to Besanto where it will join its companion. You have no idea what it is really?"

"The rod, it's a Staff of Power but just in a different shape."

"Actually, far from being a Staff of Power, it is a particularly nasty instrument of mass destruction, a super enhanced, miniaturised, laser weapon, and if it was to be joined together with the other three, they would combine to become a Long Distance Planetary Obliterator. LDPO's are prohibited throughout the known universe, as are their component parts. Possession of them is punishable by death. Only one set of component parts has ever been made and once made they can never be unmade, so when they were discovered and their maker punished, they were transported to four far-flung parts of the galaxy and disguised. Myths were invented and circulated among communities to explain their existence, hence your story about the branch and the meteorite. There is another one here in Morgrnvia, about a man who learned to travel to a spirit world where he gained great powers and endowed the Staffs with them. Actually that myth is not too far off the truth. Do you fancy a hot drink? I'm not allowed anything stronger when I'm on duty but I could make us some tea."

Clive nodded in agreement and Bengough started rummaging through his rucksack again. Clive was glad of the break. There was a lot to take in. After finding himself in the fourth volume of Lord of the Rings, he now appeared to be in an episode of Star Trek; warp factor four and all that. He knew that travel in space and time was something to do with quantum physics, Einstein and Stephen Hawking, and that time went slower the faster you went, so theoretically if you went fast enough you could arrive in the future but that was basically as far as his knowledge went and even so, he didn't really understand any of it.

'Mind you,' thought Clive, 'that boulder did turn into a thing that does look like a space buggy might look, so perhaps it is all true. It's quite exciting really.'

Then Clive remembered that possession of the thing he possessed and which he had thought to be a Staff of Power, was punishable by death and he decided that, exciting though it was, this wasn't really the place for him.

"Bengough?"

"Yes, Clive."

"Do you know how I can get back to the Earth? Not the Earth as it is now but Earth at the time I left it."

"I would say it's just about impossible. It would mean finding the right wormhole and that could only be done by trial and error. We've documented all the ones we've found so far but none of them would return you to Earth. You'd just have to travel through space searching for wormholes and trying them out but that would be quite dangerous because any one of them could transport you to a place where the air is toxic or the inhabitants are non-human and hostile. In any case it's also impossible because you haven't got a spaceship and you can't use mine because then I'd be stuck here."

"Couldn't you fly up to your mother ship, tell them about me and have them send someone down to pick me up?"

"Not allowed, I'm afraid, strictly no unauthorised personnel allowed onboard. The Captain wouldn't allow it."

Clive felt dejected. There didn't seem to be any possibility of him ever getting home and he was stuck here in a place that was hundreds of years behind, or was it ahead of his own time, and where some malevolent force was out to get him. Also, there was so much that didn't make sense, such as how do you disguise a super enhanced laser weapon as a wooden staff or a metal rod. Clive asked Bengough about it.

"Something to do with molecular reconstruction but beyond that I haven't a clue. Physics was all double Dutch to me at school."

"And why is this one a rod sometimes, instead of a staff?"

"I think they have the ability to adapt to the technological circumstances in which they find themselves. I suppose when things on Earth got beyond the wooden staff stage it changed itself. It's probably confused now to find itself back in a less developed place, so it doesn't know whether it should be a rod or a staff."

"Why don't you take it back to your mother ship with you? Surely that would stop it joining up with the others and becoming a ..."?

"A Long Distance Planetary Obliterator. No, I couldn't possibly do that. Take an enhanced laser device onto a mother ship loaded with sophisticated electronics, state of the art armaments and not to mention the crew of thousands, well it would just be asking for trouble. I'm sorry; it will just have to stay here."

Clive was feeling desperate. Surely there must be something he could do to persuade Bengough not to leave him there, all alone in a place that only just seemed to have passed the Middle Ages and where the people had horns. He had an idea.

"So you are a police officer?"

"Yes, Specials, I told you."

"And you can arrest people?"

"Of course, if they've broken the law."

"Then what happens?"

"I look for other people who've br..."

"No, not to you, to the people you've already arrested?"

"They get put on the mother ship to be taken for trial."

"So you've get prisoners up there right now?"

"About a hundred."

"And what are their conditions like?"

"To tell you the truth, almost better than ours. It's a source of some discontent."

"So I take it the prisoners are not authorised personnel?"

"No, how could they be?

"Then couldn't you just arrest me?"

"I already told you the punishment for possession of one of those things is death. You wouldn't want that, would you?"

"But couldn't you just arrest me for something else, something fairly minor?"

"But you haven't broken any laws."

"Couldn't we just pretend?"

"Oh yes and when they found out it would be me in the clink."

"So what are some fairly minor crimes for which you could arrest me?"

"The most common one would be insulting the Supreme President of the Inter-Planetary Council."

Clive thought about it for a few seconds.

"What, that fat, ugly, half-witted, bird-brained, effeminate ignoramus who only got where he is through blackmail and corruption and whose only interest is in lining his own pockets?"

Bengough stared at Clive in amazement, then, after a few seconds he began to laugh.

"Oh, that was good, very good but it's not going to work. Besides, he is a she and what about the rod?"

"Couldn't we just leave it here?"

"You can't just leave a super enhanced laser device lying about. It would be the height of irresponsibility."

"Well, we could bury it."

"And what if someone dug it up?"

"But they'd think it was just a rod. Most likely they'd just bury it again."

"No, I'm sorry. It won't do. Those things have a force field that can be detected from miles away. Whoever brought you here might well be able to find it too."

'Well that's it then,' thought Clive dejectedly, 'I'm stuck here on this planet for the rest of my life. The quest was just a trick to get me to take the rod to Besanto. The obvious thing would be to get rid of the rod but I'm not allowed to do that because it would be 'irresponsible'. Well, it wasn't very responsible to kill a plane load of people to bring me here, was it? And while I have the rod the Baron or whoever the enemy is will know where I am because it gives off some kind of signal, so it looks like I'm doomed. It's just not fair. I treat myself to a nice little walking holiday in Madeira and I end up on the other side of the universe with zero options. So what happens next? Do I just stay here and wait for them, whoever they are, to find me and if I leave, where will I go to and how will I live? It's not even as if I can blend in with the local population, not having horns.'

"Bengough?"

"Yes, Clive."

"What do you think I should do? When you're gone I mean."

"I'd get myself as far away from Besanto as possible, if I were you."

"When do you think you will be leaving?"

"I have to report back in the morning."

"Oh dear, couldn't you stay a little longer?"

"Orders, I'm afraid."

Clive sat in silence for several minutes, contemplating his predicament.

"Bengough?"

"Yes Clive."

"Ggydren said that William or whoever it was, was able to use the rod to kill two people. He was able to direct the flash so it didn't just go straight up in the air. Do you know how he was able to do that?"

"Yes, Clive."

"You do? Do you think you could show me? It might come in handy if the enemy finds me."

"Of course, Clive; good idea. I was just thinking that I really ought to make sure it is what I've been talking about anyway. Here, you put some more wood on the fire and I'll get us a bit more light."

Bengough went over to the space buggy and pressed a different button on his remote control. The cockpit began to open up and Bengough reached inside to fetch a torch. Clive was curious and walked over to take a look. The interior resembled what Clive believed a Formula One racing car would look like. There was certainly no room for two. Back by the fire Bengough told Clive to strike the rod on the ground. He did so and a beam of light shot up in the air.

"Now examine the rod. Tell me what you notice."

Bengough shone the torch and Clive looked at the rod. It was only then that he noticed the same Ж symbol that he had seen when it had been a staff.

"That is the key," said Bengough. "But it only shows itself once you have let off an initial beam or some sparks. If you press it down while striking the rod on the ground again, the beam is delayed until you stop pressing. It gives you the opportunity to direct the beam at whatever you want. Here, have a go but make sure not to point it at me or the buggy. That tree there would do."

Clive felt both trepidation and excitement. He pressed down on the symbol and felt it give slightly under his touch. Then he struck the ground with the rod and pointed the rod at the tree. When he released his finger from the symbol a beam of light hit the tree, causing it to smoulder.

185

"My word!" gasped Clive.

"That is what whoever you told me about must have learned how to do and actually it's what brought me here. The mother ship is equipped with instruments that can detect those flashes. They warn us that the thing has been used in some way. That in itself is not particularly worrying but I was sent here because a number of flashes have been detected recently. Firstly, there were some in and around Besanto. Then there was one in Aughphalia, and now some from the same device, this device, in fact, here in Morgrnvia. And this device was last known to be half a galaxy away on Earth. And if what you have also told me about the other Staffs turns out to be correct, that makes it all even more worrying. These things are meant to be kept far apart, yet you've brought this one here from Earth, so that means there are two here for sure and if what you saw in Elisiu is one and the one hanging up in Aughphalia is too and that is only a wormhole away, then we have all the makings of a LDPO in very close proximity and you can bet your breeches that all this hasn't happened by accident. When I report this back to the Captain and he reports to the Admiral and he reports it to his bosses, I wouldn't mind predicting that there will be a specially convened meeting of the Supreme Council and you know where that might lead."

"Well, no actually but go on, tell me."

"Sorry, I was forgetting. I did say before that we're not allowed to reveal ourselves to the local population but it's more than that. We've learned from bitter experience that intervening in other planets' affairs can have very unexpected consequences, sometimes disastrously so and the Inter-

Galactic Code of Law reflects this. However, the 96th Amendment states that if there is a realistic danger of the component parts of a long distance planet obliterator being joined together, the Council can, indeed it has the obligation to act decisively."

"Yes?" asked Clive.

"Yes," answered Bengough, "the Council can order the destruction of the planet on which the LDPO is in danger of being created."

"That's terrible," said Clive. "You aren't allowed to intervene here but you are allowed to blow the place up. That doesn't sound right to me."

"Less chance of unintended consequences, you see. It's all been carefully thought through."

"So you can blow this planet up to stop someone on it blowing up another planet?"

"That's right."

"Then what's the difference between you and them? You're both blowing up planets and killing loads of people."

"It's a matter of self defence, Clive. When we blow a planet up, and it's only ever been necessary once or twice by the way, we are protecting life on many other planets. We have to get right up close to the planet and drop a device on it and then we have to hot foot it out of there to escape the blast wave. A person with a Long distance planet obliterator, however, could target a planet light years away and go on targeting any other planet they care to. Fortunately that's never happened so far but there's always a first time. In any case what really worries the powers that be is not the actual use of the LDPO but the threat to use it. We're talking blackmail here but on a grand scale. We'd have to pay up, what other choice would we have?"

"So, if you're worried that someone or something is trying to bring the component parts together here on Morgrnvia, do you have anyone in mind?"

"Oh, there are lots of possibilities. You see the Inter-Galactic Federation is not universally popular. It has only been around a couple of hundred thousand years and its formation meant that local planets and alliances had to give up their independence. There have been a number of short lived rebellions, not too much of a problem if they're simply planet based, but there are also a number of inter planetary terrorist organisations and any one of them would give their right hand to get hold of a long distance planetary obliterator."

"Does that mean that the Baron in Besanto is something to do with one of those terrorist groups?"

"We don't know. The Baron has been around for thirty odd years and has always been something of a nuisance to the king here but that's nothing special. We have no information linking him to any particular terrorist group or affiliate. I wanted to go in and take a look for myself but the official policy is still to wait and see. It might just all blow over."

Neither Clive nor Bengough spoke for a bit. Clive was looking at the rod and wondering how it could be so dangerous. Yes, it had singed the tree but that didn't make it a super enhanced, weapon of mass destruction. He asked Bengough about it.

"I'm not really supposed to show you but I don't see how it can do any harm so long as you promise not to tell anyone else."

Clive promised.

"Press the symbol three times in quick succession, wait a few seconds and then do it again."

Clive did as he was instructed. The rod began to react. He could feel it vibrating and getting warm. After a few more seconds it started to glow and to grow bigger in his hand. Very soon the thing was glowing so bright that Clive couldn't really see it any more. It was so disconcerting he dropped it. On the ground the thing continued to glow brightly, then, all of sudden, the glowing ceased. Clive looked down in astonishment. What had been a simple metal rod had turned into something that instantly reminded him of the laser weapons used in Star Wars. It was now about five feet long, tapering towards one end and with bands of coloured light, orange, green and yellow, that pulsated and moved along its length.

"Good gracious!"

"Pick it up," said Bengough. "The thick end is the handle."

Clive picked it up. Bengough pointed to four buttons just above the handle.

"These are the controls. If you press the first one it sends out a beam of laser light, like the one before but much more powerful and with a far greater range. The next one converts the beam into a fan shape that hits a much wider area. The final button has to be pressed six times to stop it being accidentally used. Basically it sends the thing into super enhanced laser mode."

"What does that mean?" asked Clive.

"It allows the operator to send out an incredibly powerful beam," answered Bengough. "It would destroy anything in its path for a distance of many miles, so it could be used against a city, for example, or a battalion. It would basically have the same effect as a thermo-nuclear weapon."

Bengough suggested that Clive should have a go, as long as he only used the first button.

"Point it down so it doesn't light up the sky and just fire a quick burst. Here, let me find a suitable target."

Bengough shone his torch about and found a large rock between the trees.

"There, that should do. Just a quick burst."

Clive pointed the rod towards the boulder. Slightly hesitant, he reached down towards the first button with one hand and pressed it. An intense beam of light shot forward and almost instantly the boulder shattered into thousands of pieces.

"Good God!" exclaimed Clive.

"That's enough for now, I think," said Bengough. "Oh, I forgot," he continued, "the fourth button is the off switch. It only takes one push."

Clive pressed the fourth button and the device instantly turned back into a rod. Clive was still amazed at everything that had just happened. He realised that if the boulder had been a man he would not just be dead but totally obliterated. Somehow Clive found that realisation reassuring, empowering even. At least he could put up a good fight if the enemy came.

Soon after that Bengough said it was about time to turn in. Clive crawled into the tent and wrapped himself in the blanket for warmth and comfort. He put the rod by his side. Lying there he thought about the day's events and all that Bengough had said. It was dreadful to think that the Earth was some kind of dead planet but it had all taken place so long ago in the past, or was it into the future, that he felt no particular sense of grief. Indeed, it was reassuring to think that Earth people had succeeded in leaving the confines of their planet and spreading the English language throughout the galaxy.

"Bengough, are you asleep?" called Clive from his tent.

"Nearly," answered Bengough from the shelter.

"You know you said that English is spoken throughout the galaxy?"

"Yes."

"Does that mean that there are people throughout the galaxy who are descended from humans, from Earth people?"

"No."

"No?"

"No, I told you that the Earth is uninhabited by sentient beings. Everyone died. Scientists had been warning for ages that there was too much pollution in the atmosphere and that eventually life would become unsustainable but people and governments took no notice. It was too difficult to change, too easy to carry on the way they were and some people said it was all just a conspiracy anyway. In the end it only took a little shove to send it over the edge."

"Little shove?"

"The history books tell of an unfortunate coincidence. Two nuclear powers going to war and using their weapons against each other, and several volcanoes erupting and spewing vast amounts of toxic smoke and gases into the atmosphere, and all within a few days of each other. The resultant dust and radiation was just too much. Millions of people basically suffocated. Plenty of people survived but not enough of them

191

were sufficiently skilled or knowledgeable to maintain the infrastructures. The whole system broke down. Finally the power stations and nuclear facilities that should have been turned off quickly deteriorated and sent huge quantities of extra pollution into the air. Everything died. There was one small outpost, a moon colony, but that depended on supplies from the Earth and everyone there died too. I'm sorry, Clive but as far as I know you are the last person from Earth alive in the galaxy, indeed in the universe."

"Oh dear," said Clive, not knowing what else to say.

"There's one good piece of news though," said Bengough.

"There is?" said Clive.

"At least the destruction of life on Earth served as an example for people on other planets. A good many have taken heed and avoided that fate."

'Not much compensation for so many dead people on Earth,' thought Clive, although he didn't say it out loud.

Clive lay awake thinking.

"Bengough?"

"Yes Clive. I really do need to get some sleep you know."

"Just one more question. You see there's one thing I still don't understand."

"Yes?"

"Then why does everyone speak English?"

"Radio waves. Three or four hundred years before the end of the Earth, electro-magnetic means of communication was invented and pretty soon there were hundreds of types of different types of devices all pumping out radio waves across the universe. Mostly the language used was English. This happened first on Earth, so when receivers were invented on other planets they were bombarded with information in English and, when they made contact with each other, it became the obvious common means of communication. Gradually English became the universal language. Obviously there are many forms of it now and many new words that have come about but it is customary to use Classical English, as I have been doing, when meeting strangers from other worlds."

"But I don't think they've got as far as radios yet, here in Morgrnvia or in Aughphalia," said Clive.

"Education," said Bengough.

"Education?" asked Clive.

"The Council decided that as everywhere was going to speak English eventually, they might as well start doing it as early as possible. Nowadays all planets where life exists are monitored and where primitive humanoid forms reach the language stage, robotic teachers are implanted to encourage the speaking of English."

"But you said that you aren't allowed to intervene in other planets."

"I know, it's caused a lot of controversy."

"I don't suppose you also teach those primitive humanoid forms, as you call them, to use weapons to achieve dominance. An ape is made to pick up a bone, for example and use it to kill a rival ape."

"Oh, that hoary old chestnut. Definitely not."

Clive wondered whether he should have found all this information comforting, after what he had been told about the fate of the Earth. He didn't but later, still trying to get to grips with the knowledge that he was the last person from

193

Earth, it did occur to him that if the English language had not spread like that his present situation would be infinitely more difficult and, just before he fell asleep, he wondered if Bengough might be a robot.

Bengough woke Clive early next morning; very early, it was still dark.

"I have to get off now, Clive. I'm not supposed to let the locals see the buggy, so I have to go before it gets light. Remember, head away from Besanto and try to avoid using the rod. I've left you my emergency rations, enough for a couple of weeks and my bow and arrows. The arrows are heat seeking, so you don't need any expertise. I really am sorry I can't take you with me but I will explain your situation to the Captain to see if something can be done. Can't promise anything though."

"Would you really blow this planet up?" asked Clive.

"Well, not me personally and besides only if it looks as though the four components are close to being joined together and that isn't something to worry about at the moment, especially if the one in Aughphalia stays where it is and you keep well away from Besanto."

"So, will you be able to find me again if your Captain agrees to do something?"

"As long as you have the rod, yes. We're able to track it from the force field and from any flashes and, given the situation, we'll be keeping very close tracks on it. Goodbye, Clive, I hope we meet again. I've enjoyed our brief time together. Keep well clear when I lift off."

With that Bengough opened up the space buggy, climbed in and manoeuvred himself into position. A few minutes later the engine, surprisingly quietly, started up and the craft rose vertically into the air. With no lights showing, Clive lost sight of it before it sped off to join the mother ship, somewhere in near space.

Chapter 14.

Clive crawled back into the tent and wrapped himself in the blanket; it was still dark and there was nothing much else he could do. He felt alone and vulnerable. Until Bengough had arrived he'd still had a lingering hope that none of this was really happening but Bengough's boulder had turned into a spaceship and he had seen it fly away and there was more than one moon, so he really was stuck on some faraway planet with no prospect of returning home. Clive thought to himself that all his hopes had been thwarted, and then found himself thinking about the word 'thwarted'. It was a strange word. He said it over and over again and each time it sounded stranger still. He wondered if there were any more words in the dictionary that started with the same three letters and realised that he would never know because he would never again have a dictionary to look in and check. Eventually he fell back to sleep.

When Clive awoke again it was light, almost too light, the sun was quite high in the sky. Still, he saw no reason to hurry. He unpegged the tent and placed it just outside the copse where it could dry in the sun and he wondered how Bengough thought he could manage to carry two weeks' supply of rations, along with everything else. He soon found out. Next to the bow and arrows was a very small container with fourteen little sachets inside. The labelling said to consume one a day, directly from the sachet or mixed in water, and that exceeding the recommended dose was not advisable. Clive tried one and found it had a pleasant banana flavour. Breakfast, lunch and dinner were over in a flash. Clive pondered his next move. Clearly he had to walk in a direction away from Besanto but where? He consulted the map. Buggiton was still the nearest place of any size. Reece was there and Ggydren a little way beyond and the journey there would allow him to find out if Bob was still alive. Trianja, another possibility, was further away to the north and to its west, along the coast, were three or four more towns, at still greater distance and with hilly terrain in between. Clive chose Buggiton; at least it was familiar. He was a little concerned that he was taking the rod nearer to the Staff in Aughphalia but decided that that wouldn't be a problem, as Aughphalia was actually who knows how far away and on a different planet. He prepared to set off and went to get the tent. The copse was on a slight rise and from it Clive had a good view of the land. He planned to avoid the road and head out in a slightly northerly direction in order to avoid the enemy and to be well clear of the spot where the Hinckle brothers had been slain. As he was finishing packing away the tent Clive noticed something glinting in the distance. Instantly he crouched down low to watch. Something was moving, maybe a mile away. He lay still for a good few minutes until he was in no doubt; a squad of soldiers was headed directly his way.

Clive hurriedly crawled back into the trees. He was slightly shaking in trepidation and wondered whether this was a time when it would be absolutely necessary to use the rod. He considered it for a second or so and then dismissed the idea. He wasn't a fighter. He would probably get it all wrong. The only thing to do was to run from the other side of the trees, where they would cover his exit. It meant going away from Buggiton but that couldn't be helped. All that mattered was to escape the danger. Grabbing what he could, his knapsack, the bow and quiver and his rod, Clive ran though the trees and down the slope. The countryside ahead was open and with little or no cover available but some way ahead was another hill. If he could reach it and be over the top before the soldiers got out of the copse then he might still have a chance.

Clive ran. He ran and ran and ran. He ran till he thought his chest would explode and his legs would seize up. He wasn't used to running. The last time he could remember running was at school and even then he was never chosen for any competitions. The final uphill bit was excruciating but at last Clive reached the top (it wasn't high enough to be called a summit) and looking behind him, saw no sign of soldiers. He flopped down to rest for as long as he dared and then, after a couple of minutes, struggled forward again. Over the rise the prospect was more encouraging. The land ahead was wooded with plenty of cover. He might still be able to get away. This time he walked, as quickly as possible but at a pace that was sustainable. He walked with the rod in his hand, the knapsack on his back and the bow and quiver slung over one shoulder. It was a heavy load but not quite as heavy as before; in his rush to get away he had dropped the tent and had neglected to pick up his sword and scabbard. As he walked, he thought. The squad had come from the direction where he had been attacked the day before. Probably they would have come across the corpses of the two Hinckles and undoubtedly, since they were coming in his direction, they were after him. He was being hunted and perhaps among the hunters might be the remaining brothers, intent on revenge. That they would find Bengough's shelter was beyond doubt and in it the things Clive had left behind. It might delay them a few minutes but no more; they would soon be off again, knowing their quarry was near.

All that day Clive walked onwards, hardly stopping for rests, often looking behind to check but always seeing nothing. Towards the end of the afternoon Clive realised that all he had had to eat that day was the sachet of banana flavoured goo and was surprised that he felt no hunger or need of food. He kept to a straight path or as straight as he could go, except for once when he came to a broad and gently flowing stream where he quickly took of his boots and waded in a few feet, then made his way downstream a couple of hundred yards before getting out on the other side and rebooting himself. All this in the hope that if they were skilled enough to be following a trail or even his scent, then they might be frustrated, at least for some time. As darkness fell Clive wondered if he should use the rod to light his way but decided against it. They might see it and besides, he was exhausted. He found a spot where he was hidden from sight, wrapped the blanket around him and fell asleep almost immediately. For how long he slept, Clive had no idea but it was still night when he awoke but with enough light from the moons to press ahead slowly. He was very stiff from the day before but this eased as he walked on. After an hour or so, while it was still dark, he reached into his rucksack for another sachet and wished for some real food.

Later, when it was light, Clive consulted the map again. If the stream he had waded in was big enough to be the river running adjacent to the Great Forest, then he was headed into wilderness, with no sign of habitation, on the map at least, until the coast of the Sea of Angeas. He reckoned that he might have just enough of Bengough's rations to reach it. He also figured that the next river marked on the map could act as his guide. If he followed its course he would eventually arrive at a town or settlement. Clive pressed on for all the hours of daylight but felt increasingly weary from the unaccustomed exertion, with legs aching and blisters on his feet. He checked behind less frequently than before, not having seen the enemy since that terrifying glimpse the previous morning. Still, he dared not rest in case they were following.

Sometime on the third day, Clive looked out from the brow of a tall hill and saw a river below and some way off. It followed a tortuous path, twisting its way through the valley, disappearing from sight behind one hill and re-emerging further on. Clive guessed it must be quite fast flowing. It was a reassuring sight. Even if it was not the river on the map it would surely take him to the sea. The descent to it was quite steep and hard going but after half an hour or so he had reached its banks. As he did so he heard a shout from behind and looked up to see figures on the brow off the hill he had just descended. One was clearly pointing his way. The enemy was on him.

Clive rushed forward in blind terror. His thoughts were scrambled. Images of home, the cat, Mrs Elphick came to mind. Then he thought about the rod, how this really might be the time when he would have to use it, to take on the enemy and defeat and slaughter them. He had run maybe a few hundred yards when he spied an obstruction in the river ahead, partly blocking its flow, some sort of beaver dam perhaps. Nearing it he saw that one of the bits of flotsam was a sizeable log, maybe six or seven feet long and broad too. Instantly he saw it as a chance. He plunged into the river and pulled at the log. It came away easily from the rest and Clive pointed it into the river's flow. Then somehow he scrambled onto it and with a foot pressing against the river bed below, launched it and himself. The river picked up the log at once and Clive felt it to be moving forward. Indeed, by the speed with which the river bank was passing by, Clive knew he was being carried at some speed. Surprisingly, it was not too difficult to maintain his balance; his weight seemed to give the log some stability but there was no way to steer, so all Clive could do was to hang on and hope for the best.

The log, moving swiftly, seemed to hug the centre of the current, sending occasional splashes of water onto Clive. Pretty soon he was soaking wet and cold too but he also knew that he was moving faster than the enemy could run and that the longer he could keep afloat the greater the distance he would put between himself and them. At some point Clive tried to get into a sitting position but that only caused the front of the log to tip upwards and Clive had to lie down again immediately before he capsized. So it continued for at least an hour until the channel widened, the flow lessened and the log suddenly grounded itself with a bump, sending Clive tumbling into the water, although by then he was already so wet that it made no difference. Clive pulled the log towards the bank to lodge it more firmly in the mud and then hauled himself out of the river. He stood up and stretched, rubbing his hands to try to warm them up. He looked around but there was no sign of the enemy or anyone else. He debated what to do. At that point the valley had widened out and Clive thought that perhaps the river had finished its mountainous run and was entering its final, lazier meander to the sea. The soldiers were perhaps a few miles away; maybe more than a few but he doubted whether he could get much further on foot today. He was freezing and his sodden load was twice as heavy as before, so much so that Clive wondered if he would be able to get it on again, should he take it off. The enemy, on the other hand, would be dry, conditioned to marching and following the river and would pretty soon catch up. So to Clive the choices were to walk away from the river into the wilderness where, with nothing to guide him, he might get completely lost and wander around forever or to get back on the log.

Back on the log Clive realised that the river was not entering its meandering phase, quite the opposite in fact, for the river and with it the log, began to gather speed. The valley through which the river flowed was narrowing and within a few minutes it was no more than a thin, tortuous gully. All Clive could do was to hang on for dear life as he was swept along at frightening speed. To get off or fall into the water could be fatal; he would not be able to swim against such a current and his load would drag him down. It got worse, for suddenly, the river took a steep downward course and entered a series of rapids. Clive had seen programmes about white water rafting and had never had the slightest inclination to have a go himself but now it seemed he had no choice. The water around him boiled, the log was tossed about and narrowly missed several big boulders and Clive knew that his chances of survival were decreasing by the second. He should have felt scared but there was not even time for that. All he could do was to cling on and hope. Finally, just when he was beginning to think that he and the log might come out at the other end unscathed, the log hit a boulder and went one way round it, while Clive crashed into the water, going the other way. Clive thought he was drowning. The water churned him round and round and each time he managed a few gasps of air the torrent pulled him down again. As he approached death again, Clive wondered if Mrs Elphick was still feeding the cat, then realised that she couldn't possibly be, as she, and everyone else on Earth, had been dead for hundreds of thousands of years.

It was over much more quickly than it had begun. One moment Clive was being rushed along, the next he seemed to be in free fall and then he felt himself splashing down hard and descending deep. It took all of his strength to fight his way back to the surface and breathe but Clive was immediately aware that he was no longer in a raging torrent. When he opened his eyes he saw a broad expanse of much calmer water in front of him. Clive was in a lake or at least a broad pool that was enclosed on three sides by almost sheer walls of rock, down one of which came the waterfall that he had just descended. On the fourth side there was nothing except an edge over which the river flowed. By some stroke of fortune, on one side, before the rock wall rose up, there was a small ledge sticking up a foot or so out of the water. With one final effort Clive swam towards it and grabbed it. Not having the strength to pull himself up, Clive remained still for a few minutes. Then he took off the bow and quiver and threw it onto the ledge. Getting the backpack off was more of a struggle but without its sodden weight Clive was finally able to haul himself out of the water and onto that tiny bit of dry land.

Clive stood up and looked around. It wasn't an encouraging prospect. At least there was no sign of the enemy. The pool glittered beautifully in the afternoon sun but Clive shivered almost uncontrollably in his soaking wet clothes. There and then he stripped off, hoping to get warmer that way. Then, in need of some sustenance or maybe just comfort, he drained the contents of another banana flavoured sachet into his mouth and swallowed. At length the shivering subsided and the sun warmed Clive. He began to feel a little better. He had no idea how he was going to get out of this predicament but at least he was still alive. He studied the rock walls. They looked far too difficult to attempt to climb for someone whose only successful ascent thus far in life had been up a ladder. No prospect of escape that way. He looked towards the pool's edge. Undoubtedly it was another waterfall but was it just a small survivable drop? He would have to find out. At the very edge of the pool, where it spilled over to the unknown depth below, the rock wall curved to form a small lip that jutted up and pushed the water towards the centre of the gap. If he could swim to that without the current sweeping him away then he might be able to see over and beyond. It was worth a try.

Clive lowered himself into the water. It was cold, much colder it seemed than when he had been on the log or swept off it but perhaps it was just that his mind had been too preoccupied then to notice. He swam towards the lip, keeping away from the centre of the pool where the flow was strongest. Reaching it without difficulty, he grasped it and pulled himself up to peer over. The view was far from encouraging. The new waterfall was much higher than the previous one and its descent was not sheer, for after about twenty feet it crashed onto an outcrop of rock before falling away to a pool far below. Clive realised that nobody could survive such a fall and felt a sudden twinge, actually it was much more than a twinge, of despair. He turned to swim back but then had another idea and turned again to pull himself up much further in order to look back up at the hillside. To his relief he could see that, although steep, it was not vertical and that it might just be possible, indeed it was the only possibility, to climb right onto the lip and then clamber onto the slope.

Clive swam back to the ledge and noticed that the daylight was beginning to fade. He realised that his means of escape was far too dangerous to be attempted in the dark and that he was there for the night. There was nothing else to do, so he unpacked all his gear and, together with his clothes, laid it out in the hope that it might be dry by morning. It was only after he had done all that that he thought about the rod and looked around for it. The thing was nowhere to be seen. Frantically he tried to think when he had last been aware of it and remembered the difficulty he had had clinging onto the log with the rod in his hand. That was all. Somewhere between that last memory and his present situation he had lost it. Clive told himself to keep calm. Was it such a bad thing? He had offered it to Bengough and suggested that they could bury it. Losing it had been an accident, not an act of irresponsibility and without it he might well be safer. If the Baron in Besanto or indeed the squad of enemy soldiers was tracking him through the signals it gave off, then they would surely turn their attention away from him and towards finding it. Yet the rod also afforded him protection. He had been scared to use it so far but he could use it if needs be, provided, of course, that he still had it. Clive remembered that Bengough could also keep tracks on him by way of the flashes and Bengough had also promised to have a word with his captain about him. But where might it be? Most probably it was lying at the bottom of the river somewhere or lodged in some crevice in the rapids. Then again, maybe it was in the pool. Most probably he had lost the rod in the frantic moments after he had entered the rapids and been knocked off the log. If he had been swept over the waterfall, perhaps the rod had too. Clive made up his mind. He would dive down into the depths of the pool to search for the rod. If it wasn't there he would go on without it.

Clive considered himself to be a competent swimmer and had once come third in a race in a school swimming gala but diving down was another matter, given that it involved holding his breath. There was no point in waiting, the sooner he got in and searched, the sooner he could get out and get dry. He lowered himself into the water once more and quickly he swam to the centre of the pool. Then, taking a deep breath, he headed for the bottom. It was too murky too see anything but he reached it quickly enough and then felt his way along for the few seconds that he could manage before surfacing again for air. This process he repeated several times, gradually getting nearer to the turbulence where the waterfall crashed into the pool. There he suddenly felt a long, round, thin shape and instantly knew that he had found it. He grabbed the rod and swam back to the ledge.

Clive felt very pleased with himself but faced the challenge of spending a long cold night on a small ledge in the middle of nowhere. Still dripping wet and shivering uncontrollably, Clive decided to do running on the spot in the expectation that this would dry him and warm him up. He knew that anyone seeing this would think him completely mad but then no one was likely to see him. Clive ran on the spot until he ran out of puff, which was a good ten minutes. By then he was dry and warm, sweating even. He quickly got cold again and, knowing that running on the spot on and off for the next twelve hours was not a realistic possibility, he wrapped himself in his damp blanket and tried to arrange his other things in a way that would shelter him from the breeze. Then he lay down and tried to go to sleep.

That night on the cold, hard slab of rock was one of the most miserable Clive had ever endured. He shivered though the first few hours and when what little body warmth he gave off had dried at least that part of the blanket touching him, the roar of the waterfall kept him awake. He was up and stretching at first light, running on the spot again to ease his stiffness and to warm himself up. A little later he dressed in his still damp clothes and packed up as best he could, eager to be off. It was only when he was nearly ready to start that

Clive, with a very sinking feeling, realised that he had to swim to the lip to make his way out. Reluctantly he undressed again and then decided to divide his belongings into three bundles. That way he might be able to hold a bundle out of the water while propelling himself with one arm. It proved easier than he anticipated. He reached the lip with the fist bundle and carefully pushed it onto the adjacent slope. Eventually, after he had deposited all three bundles, he went back one last time for his bow and arrows and the rod and, placing them next to the bundles, carefully climbed onto the lip and out onto the slope to join them.

Clive might have emerged from the mountain tarn but his immediate situation was precarious. The slope was too steep to stand upright and just looking down was enough to make him feel giddy. Moreover the wind out there was fierce and biting and the still wet and naked Clive was soon freezing again, with no possibility of getting dressed there or even repacking his belongings. Somehow he managed to extract his belt from one of the bundles and use it to tie them together and then to manoeuvre the bow and its quiver over his head and one shoulder. Then, clutching the bundle in one hand and his rod in the other, he began to edge his way, not directly upwards but slightly sideways as well to counteract the gradient. He moved slowly, almost painfully so, aware that any slight mistake could send him plummeting and fearful that any glance downwards would cause his head to spin with vertigo.

Eventually, as Clive neared the summit, the steepness of the slope declined and the going became slightly easier. Clive became aware of a hollow ahead and made for it. There, slightly out of the wind, and able to move freely, Clive threw down his load and took out his clothes. It was a relief to get dressed, even if the clothes were still wet, and not only because it afforded some protection from the wind and cold but also because Clive was unaccustomed to being outside and naked and felt uncomfortably conspicuous, even with no one else about. It struck him that he had already been observed twice in that state since the plane crash and that it would just be his bad luck to be seen so again, especially by a Hinckle or by others of the enemy. Clothed once more, if damply, and with no sign of company, unwanted or otherwise, Clive relaxed and had breakfast. Then he carefully repacked his belongings. Finally, Clive stood up to survey the landscape. From that height and in the clear air, he could see for miles. Ahead were low hills that seemed to peter out into a broad plain that continued far into the distance. Clive was not sure if the touch of blue beyond was the sea but he hoped so. He recalled that his map, which was still too wet to safely uncurl, showed settlements on the coast and that was where he must surely go, now that Buggiton was beyond reach. In all that expanse ahead Clive could see no sign of habitation, no roads or tracks, no villages, not even any isolated farms. That was a bit worrying but also a relief; at least none of the enemy was in sight.

Chapter 15.

Ggydren held Elendril gently in his arms.

"There is something else,' she said, 'I have decided that I will never change shape again. It is a curse. It has ruined my life. I will do it no more. That horrible man in the cave, when he said that shape-shifters were despised, it made me angry but deep down, I knew it was true. That was when I decided and that is why I put myself up for hire, and why I didn't use my powers to get away from Higgins. I want to just be like everyone else."

Just then they heard an urgent knocking on the door and Reece walked in without waiting to be beckoned.

"It's very bad news. One of the people from the meeting is downstairs. He came to warn us. A contingent of soldiers has arrived from Aughphalia. They are looking for a person they call a dangerous villain. They are looking for you, Ggydren. You are no longer safe here. We've been seen together by too many people and your little slip in the inn won't have helped at all. Tonight or tomorrow they will know about us and they will come here. You must go now, for your own safety and for mine. My friend downstairs has agreed to take you in for the night, but then you must get away from Buggiton. Gather your things now. They could be here at any time. And please make sure you take that thing with you," he said, glancing at the Staff.

Reece left and Ggydren turned to Elendril. She looked anxious but he smiled.

"That's settled then. I'm coming with you."

There was little time to thank Reece for his help and hospitality. He positively pushed them out of the back door and shut it immediately behind them. Their new companion said nothing except to follow him and keep quiet. The lane at the back of the little garden was unlit but he led them quickly through it and other back streets. At one point they had to cross over the main road that ran through Buggiton and he beckoned them to wait while he checked it. As he turned back to them he gestured to them to move in close to the wall and, at the same time they became aware of the sound of footsteps. Within seconds a group of soldiers was passing in front of them. At its rear, and carrying a flaming torch that lit up his face, was their leader. It was a long, lean face that Ggydren recognised immediately.

The squad passed by without looking their way and a few minutes later Ggydren and Elendril were inside the safety of their guide's home. He took them down to a cellar and explained that its other door opened onto steps at the back of the house which led to the garden. It might be a way of escape should the need arise. Then he left them in total darkness to fetch some things to provide a little comfort for the night ahead. He returned within minutes with a candle, blankets, food and wine, then left them. The cellar was simply that; there was no furniture and certainly no bed but there were sacks of wheat and barley that were comfortable enough. The food was basic, bread without butter and apples and pears, washed down with the wine. For their personal needs they opened the door to the stairs and used the garden.

Ggydren slept well; the beer and the wine saw to that. Elendril woke him at first light and they crept out, not waiting to give thanks to their host. All was quiet with just a few birds twittering, the start of the dawn chorus. The little garden backed onto others and they had to climb fences before they came to a street. This took them directly into the main square, a place they had hoped to avoid but still as yet deserted, so they walked across and saw a sign pinned to a notice board. In the dim light of dawn they could just about make out that it gave Ggydren's name and description, said he was a fugitive from justice in Aughphalia, might be carrying a carved staff and possibly be accompanied by a shape-shifter called Elendril. It offered a substantial reward for his capture. They hurried on.

During the few minutes it took to reach the outskirts of the little town Ggydren considered the Staff. It was quite cumbersome to carry and, without its wall hanging cover, very conspicuous, especially to anyone who might have seen the notice. He wondered whether he should simply ditch it in some place where it would be easily found. Maybe if the Staff was recovered that would satisfy the person who was after him but then maybe not. Also Ggydren found a strange reluctance to part with it. Perhaps he might be the one to make the forces of darkness quake in his presence, then smite them down and bring peace and prosperity to everyone. He certainly didn't think he could be the envoy of the dark spirits, full of malice and evil intent. The only malice he felt was towards the nasty man who had given him the sack and had him carted off. Then a more serious thought struck him, that they were going to Elisiu, where he would certainly not be welcomed, nor Elendril too. The Staff had proved its value there, when the ladies in the Chamber had succumbed to its power and they were clearly afraid of what it might do to the Cerridwine, having warned Clive against its use more than once. Well then, if it had been useful there before, it might be again. Ggydren resolved to hang onto the Staff come what may.

Some way out of Buggiton and on the road to Mickelling, they came upon a farmhouse and asked if they could buy food. The farmer's wife was friendly and provided freshly baked bread, cold meats and cheese and a flagon of mead. A little further on they stopped to breakfast a little way off the road for safety. While they were eating Elendril asked Ggydren about the powers of the Staff and he gently prodded the ground with it to show her the sparks it gave off. Then he showed her the symbol and told her what Reece had said. In doing so his finger pressed the symbol and he felt it give slightly under the pressure. Ggydren pressed the symbol again, at the same time tapping the rod against the ground. Nothing happened, no sparks flew off, but when he released the symbol the sparks appeared. He did it again, this time hitting the Staff harder against the ground, then lifting it and pointing it towards a small tree before releasing the symbol. The resulting flash set the tree alight.

"Well, I'm blowed," said Ggydren, suitably astonished, "so that's how you actually use it. That's what William must have done when he burnt up those two people. This could come in very handy if we run into any more Hinckles. I only wish Clive knew about this too."

Another thought crossed Ggydren's mind, that if the nasty, thin faced, tall man was still looking for them he could use the Staff to teach him a lesson or two. Ggydren smiled at the prospect.

They walked on and by evening came to the farm where Ggydren and Clive had spent their first night on the road. Ggydren knocked and asked permission to sleep in the barn again. The farmer was generous, refusing the money that Ggydren offered to pay. Later, when he brought them food, he talked about his fears for the farm after what had happened to Mickelling. If the enemy came this way, his farmhouse was the only building for miles around and he was sick with worry about what they might do. Ggydren could appreciate his concerns; the killing and destruction in Mickelling had been indiscriminate and the farmer had a wife and daughters.

During the second day, mindful that the enemy might be close, they tried to set a course away from the road but adjacent to it. As they walked the weather turned. A cold wind blew and clouds obscured the sun, although thankfully, any rain held off. Ggydren remembered that he and Clive had camped the second night but that was in fairer weather and with a tent and cooking equipment and a flint to start a fire. When dusk fell, he and Elendril looked for some sort of shelter for the night but found nothing that offered any comfort. In the end they had to make do with a small hollow, within a copse, where they were at least afforded some protection from the wind. Still, when night came they shivered in the cold and Ggydren decided to use the Staff to try to make fire. He gathered logs and fallen branches and piled them up and then, holding in the symbol, he tapped the staff gently on the ground and pointed it. The sparks made little impression on the damp wood, so he did it again but with greater force. The resultant flash triggered flames that took hold and within minutes a fire was burning strongly, so they had some warmth that night, if nothing else to cheer them up.

Towards the end of the fourth day Ggydren and Elendril came within sight of Mickelling. They approached cautiously, keeping away from the road and via the back garden of the ruined inn, as Ggydren had done before. This time he found no one. The village was deserted; even the old lady was gone. Ggydren wondered if the soldiers from Besanto had returned for more captives or if the survivors had decided to leave to seek refuge with the King. There was no way of knowing. In the fading light the village looked like some long abandoned place where time had taken its toll, yet he knew that only shortly before, the place had been thriving, the buildings intact, the people at ease. With the daylight fading Ggydren realised that they would have to stay there the night and quickly checked the few remaining, untouched cottages, until he found one that was set well back from the road and with a pantry that contained a little food. There he soon had a blaze going in the fireplace, while Elendril prepared a broth of vegetables and potatoes. It was their first hot meal in days but neither took much comfort from it; they both felt uneasy, that they were trespassing and taking advantage of someone else's misfortune or even tragedy. Not only that, Mickelling was less than a day away from the Great Forest and within that lay Elisiu. Elendril especially was preoccupied with what she might find there, while Ggydren wondered whether he should try to persuade her to abandon her intention to confront the women. In the end he didn't but he spent a restless night worrying nonetheless.

They left Mickelling early the next morning, again keeping away from the road, whilst keeping it in sight. Ggydren half expected to see enemy soldiers at some but there were none. Nor were any other people about and when Ggydren thought about it, he realised that they had seen no other travellers or traders since leaving Buggiton, a sure indication of troubled times. Before midday the Great Forest was in sight, far off at first but gradually looming larger. Elendril insisted that they stop to eat what little food they had before entering and they found a small thicket where they would be hidden from view and which might have been the very one that Clive and Ggydren had rested in before. Ggydren wondered if the pause meant that Elendril was having second thoughts but far from it, she tried to persuade Ggydren to let her go in alone.

"There is no point in you going in alone," he told her, "I know what to expect and that will be of use and I have the Staff and I can use its power of command. They'll try to frighten us away but I can order them to take us to Elisiu and I reckon they'll obey. I told you about Angharind, the one who spoke up for me and Clive. Maybe she will again, for us this time, if she is still alive and maybe, we might find your mother."

"I want to see all of them," said Elendril. "I want them all to know how they ruined my life and the lives of goodness knows how many others. I want to see if they can feel shame, if they have any shred of decency. As for my mother, well I doubt if there will be any way of knowing which one of them she is, if any. In any case, I don't know what I'd feel if I did find her."

The food was quickly eaten and, in the chilly breeze, they were keen to get on, if apprehensive about what lay ahead. As they walked out of the copse a shock awaited them. There on the road, directly ahead, was the squad of soldiers from Aughphalia, led by the nasty man from the cave. They were spotted immediately, the man pointing towards them and shouting out orders and the soldiers immediately running in their direction and drawing their swords. For a few seconds Ggydren was gripped by panic but then he remembered the Staff and his previous thoughts of what he would like to do to the nasty man with it.

Ggydren beckoned to Elendril to stand behind him, then held up the Staff and ordered the soldiers to stop. They did, maybe because of the power of the command of the Staff-holder or maybe because Ggydren's defiance surprised them and they didn't know quite what to do. It was a few seconds before their leader caught up. He looked at Ggydren with contempt and spoke.

"Well, well, look what we've got here, Ggydren and his little shape-shifter, one a common criminal, the other an abomination of nature. I see you've sprouted horns Ggydren but you don't deceive me. Your time is up. I'm taking you and the Staff back to Aughphalia; that creature can stay here and rot. I am not one to be made a fool of and take it lying down, Ggydren and by some stroke of luck or trickery on your part you did make me look rather foolish in Aughphalia. Well, I have you now and my revenge will be all the sweeter when I return with you to face trial. By law, as you are already no doubt aware, a wronged party can dictate the punishment of the wrongdoer. I will have you hanged. Now, lay down the Staff, and any weapons you have, immediately; hesitate and we will be quite within our rights to kill you here and now."

The man had a self-satisfied sneer on his face as he spoke. Ggydren's reaction was not what he expected.

"Well, well, what have we here indeed," he said calmly, "a fool and a nasty one with it. Before I have the satisfaction of dealing with you, I want you to tell me your name. You see, from now on whenever I remember your ugly face, I'd like to be able to put a name to it."

"Deal with me? Deal with me? Are you stupid? Do you think that you and that thing are any match for me and some of the best and most highly trained men of the King's personal guard? I am Imbert, the Secretary to the Council and I order you to lay down that thing."

"If you make one move against me I will use this thing, as you call it, against you," said Ggydren.

"What, sparks and flashes in the air, what good will that do you?" responded Imbert.

"Not only sparks and flashes in the air but this," said Ggydren, banging the Staff into the ground, then pointing it just to the side of Imbert and the soldiers and releasing the button. The beam of light that shot out went within a few inches of Imbert and singed his clothes and his eyebrows. He screamed in surprise and terror and then, together with the soldiers, began to back away.

"That's it," said Ggydren, "back away, right away and don't come back. I reckon it's me who's within his rights if there's

218

any killing to be done but luckily for you, I'm a merciful sort. So get on your way Imbert, go back to Aughphalia and tell 'em you've failed again. Don't try to follow us. I will use it against you the next time I see you."

Imbert stood motionless for a few seconds, a look of exasperation on his face and then backing away, beckoned to his soldiers to retreat. Ggydren and Elendril watched them until they had disappeared into the distance.

"My word, I enjoyed that," said Ggydren, embracing Elendril. "I reckon that's the last we'll see of them. Such an horrible man that Imbert. I had a great urge to kill him after what he said about you. Perhaps I should have but I've never killed anyone yet and I hope I never have to. Killing's not for the likes of simple souls like me. Well, my Elendril, the time has come. If you really are determined to go through with this plan of yours, we might as well get on with it. The Great Forest awaits, let's see what it has in store."

Chapter 16.

On the third day since his escape from the tarn, Clive was feeling despondent. The terrain, though flat, was difficult, boggy in places and with tall grasses for most of the rest. The weather was deteriorating, not raining but getting chillier by the day, with overcast skies and an almost continuous stiff breeze. On top of that the only living things he had seen since the pool had been birds high up in the sky. The two nights he had spent in the open had been awful. With no wood to make a fire and no shelter from the weather, all he could do was to simply huddle up inside his blanket and try to sleep as best he could. He wondered how long he could keep going like this, whether his food would run out before he reached wherever he was headed and whether wherever he was headed would be the sort of place he would want to be.

Later on that day things took a turn for the better however. Clive came across a small oasis of trees within the barren landscape and, within the trees, a stream. Perhaps most important of all, the land around the trees was pockmarked with rabbit holes. Clive immediately pictured himself beside a fire, beside the stream and with a rabbit barbequing on a spit. He realised that this would involve killing a rabbit and that he was not used to killing anything, except aphids and the occasional slug, and that he would also be required to skin and gut the poor creature and that that would also be venturing into unknown and very messy territory. On the other hand, he was mightily fed up with banana flavoured goo and he had the means in the form of the rod or arrows to do the deed. He decided to go no further that day. He would build a fire instead, set up a camp to make himself as comfortable as possible and become a rabbit hunter. Clive found the prospect quite exciting, rather like the weekend camping trip he had once enjoyed as a twelve year old boy scout.

The first task was easily achieved; there was plenty of dead wood lying around, sparks from the rod did the rest. The second proved more difficult; his camp eventually consisted of nothing more than piled up dead leaves which at least offered the prospect of being softer to lie on than the ground. The third looked more and more like an impossibility. Clive sat on a log, at the edge of the wood, bow in hand, with arrow in place, as still and as quietly as he could, for as long as possible but no rabbits appeared. He had no doubt they were there, the rabbit poo proved that, but they were obviously taking no chances with him about. Finally, well into the afternoon, Clive gave up and put some water on to heat up so that he could have a decent, if soap less, wash. While his back was turned rabbits emerged from their holes, dozens of them, and began their evening graze. Fortunately they were still grazing when Clive turned again in their direction. Avoiding swift movements he carefully picked up his bow, placed the arrow in position, pulled back the string, aimed and fired. The arrow shot straight ahead but then veered off as it sensed a target. One poor rabbit seemed to jump in the air, twitch and drop dead. Clive felt instant remorse at what he had done. He walked over to the rabbit and wondered whether the proper thing to do would be to bury it. He thought about it for a while but decided that would only increase the severity of his crime; he had killed the rabbit for food, to simply bury it would mean that the poor creature had died for nothing. No, the only thing was to press ahead and prepare dinner.

Clive very gingerly picked up the rabbit. It was warm and limp in his hand. He had no real idea of how to prepare the creature for eating, so he cut off its head, trying not to look and feeling slightly queasy as the knife crunched through bones. Not wanting to look at a severed head, he threw it on the fire. Next, Clive took the remaining part of the rabbit down to the stream, pulled out the arrow and cut into its stomach and forced out the innards. Then he skinned it using his fingers to separate the skin from the flesh. Finally he washed it clean, together with the arrow, in the running water.

'There, that wasn't so bad,' said Clive to himself before throwing up.

Later, having consumed a whole roasted rabbit and feeling mightily content, Clive shot another and cooked it so that he would have some cold meat to keep him going the following day. Next morning and after his best night's sleep for days, Clive debated among himself whether to stay there and hunt more rabbits or move on. Reluctantly he decided on the latter, there being little point in hanging around all day with nothing to do, until the rabbits came out.

The weather that day was just as bad as before and Clive, once more, felt himself fall into a slough of despondency. He pondered over the word 'slough', saying it to himself over and over again and decided that it was nearly as strange as the word 'thwart' that he had pondered over earlier. Clive told

222

himself to stop pondering over stupid words and think about what he was going to do whenever he got to where he was going. The following day, after a long cold and mostly sleepless night and with the second rabbit having been eaten down to the bones, it was back to the banana flavoured goo. Clive wondered how much worse things could get.

At length Clive began to notice signs of habitation; fields that had been planted, the odd cottage here and there, a proper track to walk on. Then, looking down from a low rise, he saw a town and beyond it the sea. Clive hurried on, spirits raised and eager to make contact with people again. The first person he saw was a man coming in his direction. Clive introduced himself, saying he was a traveller and would the man tell him the name of the place and could he please recommend somewhere to stay. The man stared at Clive, especially at his head and said nothing. Then he walked on. Clive was disappointed but thought that perhaps the man was simple and that things would improve.

The next people Clive saw, as he entered a broad street, flanked on either side by wooden buildings, were a group of children playing. They saw Clive and stopped playing. Then they started to point at his head and started laughing. One of them adopted a monkey like pose, with hands tucked into his armpits and started to make monkey like sounds and movements. Then they all started doing it. Clive walked on and the children followed, all the while doing monkey impressions. It was rather disconcerting and certainly not the reception Clive had been hoping for. Finally Clive came to a market square with food stalls and people milling about. They looked up when they heard the monkey sounds and the children's laughter and they stared at him too. Clive couldn't understand the situation at all. He wondered if something had fallen onto his head that he was unaware of and which was making them stare but then, all of a sudden, he realised what it was. They were staring at his absence of horns. Presumably the children thought that this reduced him to the status of an ape.

Clive became angry. The children continued to mock him and none of the adults had the courtesy to try to stop them. They just stared in silence. Clive stopped and made up his mind to speak.

"My name is Clive"' said Clive, addressing the people. "As you can see I am a stranger here and different from you in that I don't have horns but then nobody does, where I come from. I assure you that I am a man and not a monkey. I was hoping for a decent welcome after many days on the road and, quite frankly, I am very disappointed. Now, do you think that one of you could direct me to an inn where I might find a night's lodging? I am tired and in need of rest and a good meal."

The people continued to stare, although the monkey impressions subsided. One of the townsfolk walked up to Clive and handed him a banana. Then everyone started laughing and making monkey impressions. Clive tried to ignore them and started to walk on. They stood in his way. Clive turned to go back but found that way quickly blocked too. Clive was surrounded. The impressions and the laughing had stopped but there was nothing welcoming about their faces. Presently, one of them stepped forward.

"Whoever you are, you aren't welcome here. Proper people have horns."

"But you must have seen people without horns before," said Clive. "Haven't you seen Aughphalians?"

"Can't say we have."

"But you must have, it's not that far away."

"I said we haven't and we haven't. What ship did you come in on?"

"Ship? Come in on? No, I walked here. I'm a traveller. I came from Aughphalia and through Buggiton to get here. "

"You don't expect us to believe that, do you? Your sort comes from over the ocean and you aren't allowed here. That way," said the man pointing, "is the way to the harbour and we'll give you a few minutes to get there and back on your boat before we take the law into our own hands. Now get going."

Clive was thoroughly perplexed. All his hopes had been pinned on this place. Now he was being confronted by an increasingly hostile crowd. Saying nothing else, he began to move in the direction that he had been shown. The crowd parted to let him through and watched as he walked away. Fortunately they did not follow. Within a few minutes Clive could smell the sea air and soon found himself at a little harbour. There were a number of small fishing boats and a couple of larger ships. Other than a number of large seagulls it appeared deserted. On one side of the harbour wall, a rocky slope led upwards and out to a headland. Clive looked around to check that he was alone, then walked on and scrambled up the slope. Half way up he found a place where he was completely hidden from view and sat down. He needed time to collect his thoughts and make decisions and he consumed the last sachet of goo.

Clive thought. He thought and thought but he couldn't think of anything that could help his present situation. The people here were hostile and who knows what they would do if he went back and they did take the law into their own hands. Yes, he had the rod but he could hardly take on the whole town with it. If he went back the way he came he would be walking into danger and if he struck out for Trianja, well that was just too far to go with little or no money, no food and no shelter and it was getting chillier and how chilly did winters in Morgrnvia get anyway? They had thought he'd arrived by boat, presumably from some warmer place where they grew bananas and where the people were hornless and apparently, looked like monkeys. Should he try that but what if 'over there' proved hostile too and how could he get on a ship with no money to pay for passage? It was all too difficult. There didn't seem any way to turn.

Clive heard voices and peered over a rock to see. Children were playing on the harbour wall and seemed to be coming his way. Quickly he gathered his things and set off again, up the slope and over the headland. On the other side, Clive saw a broad bay with a few cottages strung out along a coastal track. Clive headed down to the track. He was minded to cross over so that he could avoid the cottages but nobody seemed to be about, so he took a chance. At the third cottage something caught his eye; carved into the wooden wall, right up by the eaves was something familiar. Clive looked at it. He stopped and looked again to make sure. It was the same symbol that was on his rod. It couldn't just be coincidence. It must have been placed there deliberately. Clive considered the situation for just a few seconds, his spirits and hopes suddenly rekindled. He knocked on the door and waited. The elderly lady who opened it, looked surprised and alarmed at seeing Clive. She went to shut the door but Clive put his foot in the doorway to stop her.

"Please don't shut it yet," he said urgently, "I don't mean to worry you. I mean you no harm. I saw the symbol on your wall. I have the same one, here on my rod."

Clive prodded the ground quite gently with the rod and a few sparks flew off. Then he pointed out the symbol to the lady. She ran her finger over it.

"Well, there's a thing," she said and told him to wait.

A few seconds later a man appeared. He looked agitated.

"What's all this about then, an offlander with a rod with the sacred symbol? Here let me see."

Clive showed him the symbol.

"If by offlander, you mean that I came from across the sea in a boat, well I'm not one and I didn't. It's difficult to explain but I'm in need of help. Would you help me?"

"Don't know about that. I've never seen the symbol on a piece of metal before. You're supposed to get them on Staffs of Power."

"It is a Staff of Power," said Clive, "only it's in a different form. Here, see."

Clive gently prodded the ground again with the rod and little sparks flew up.

"My word, goodness me," said the man, "this is a surprise and not half. Maybe it really is a Staff of Power. You'd better come in; quickly now, before anyone sees you. They don't like

227

offlanders round here and even if you're not, then you certainly look like one."

Inside the man introduced himself as Rolund and his wife as Mergania and asked Clive to explain himself. Clive thought it best not to mention Earth, or the plane crash, or Bengough and his space buggy, or anything to do with Elisiu. He gave Rolund the impression that he was on a mission to rescue the Princess in Besanto but that he had been forced to take a diversion. Fortunately Rolund had heard of Aughphalia and apologised for the behaviour of the townspeople. They were, he said, an isolated community, mainly fishermen and traders, and always wary of strangers. Their only experience of people without horns was indeed of a primitive people across the sea, where they traded for tropical woods and fruits.

Rolund also explained that the society of which he was a member, believed that a Staff-holder would one day come to destroy evil and bring about a time of peace and prosperity. The most evil thing around at the moment was the Baron in Besanto, who seemed intent in embarking on all out war against the King and, as Clive was a Staff-holder, on his way to Besanto, even if he was a bit off course at the moment, then it might all be beginning to fit together. On the other hand, not all Staff-holders had good intentions, so it was necessary to be cautious. Clive explained that it was almost a certainty that the Baron also had a Staff and, as he was known to be evil, then Rolund need have no doubts about him, Clive that is.

Clive asked where he might go next. Rolund suggested Trianja as the King ought to be informed of the Baron's possession of a Staff, and the King would be able to afford

228

Clive the protection and assistance he needed. Moreover he knew that a ship was leaving for Trianja the following morning and the captain, a good friend, might be persuaded to take Clive along, as long as the crew, a superstitious bunch, could somehow be deceived into thinking that Clive had horns. Clive remembered the hat that Reece had given him in Buggiton. He rummaged in his backpack until he found it.

"I have this," he said. "It was given to me by a kind man in Buggiton called Reece who gave us some camping gear. He said it might come in handy."

"It wasn't a bookseller called Reece, was it?" asked Rolund.

Clive nodded.

"Well this really is interesting. Reece is also a member of our little society, the leader in fact. If he trusted you then you must be genuine. Here let me have that hat. We need to stuff the tufts with something to make them look solid."

"Maybe candle wax," suggested Clive.

Rolund insisted, much to Clive's relief, that he stayed for the night. His hosts provided a room, warm bedding and a hearty fish stew, not to mention agreeable conversation. At some point Rolund went out to find the captain and make the arrangements for Clive's voyage. He returned saying that it was all agreed and that the captain would even accompany Clive to the royal palace, to speak on his behalf in request for an audience with the King. After all Clive had been through, it seemed almost too good to be true. Clive slept soundly that night.

The ship was to sail at first light and it was still dark when Rolund woke Clive. Together they made their way to the harbour, where the ship was being readied. It was a three-masted vessel, something akin to a galleon of olden days, thought Clive. The crew of twelve were hauling supplies on board. One of them looked closely at Clive, a quizzical expression on his face. Captain Branna welcomed Clive and said he could share his cabin during the voyage, and that it would be better if he kept out of sight as much as possible. He explained that he had told the crew that Clive was an important envoy of the King and was not to be disturbed. If they found out that Clive's horns were not real there could be trouble. Unfortunately that happened even before they had set sail. The sailor with the quizzical expression had been one of the men in the town square the previous day and he recognised Clive by his face and his apparel. He had informed the rest of the crew of his suspicions and every one of them downed tools and refused to set sail until Clive had been brought before them and deprived of his hat, so that they could know the truth.

All this happened while Clive was below deck but he heard every word, even above the squawking of seagulls. Captain Branna tried to argue with them but to no avail. They would not set sail until they were satisfied. To have an offlander on board would be a bad omen and risk catastrophe. Reluctantly the captain went below and apologised to Clive; he would have to leave or the ship could not sail. Clive gathered his things and followed the captain. On the deck the sight that confronted him was worse than he could have imagined. The crew were gathered on the prow and a large and obviously hostile crowd had assembled on the quayside, alerted by the standoff and the argument onboard.

'Well, that's it then,' thought Clive, 'if I stay the crew will kill me and if I leave the crowd will. Not exactly a comfortable choice.'

Clive stood still. Seagulls were flying overhead. They gave him an idea. He put down his things, including the rod, took up his bow and placed an arrow in position.

"Listen here," he shouted at the crew, "I am not an offlander. I come from Aughphalia and I have important business with the King, who will be mightily annoyed if you delay me. So I am staying on this ship and you are going to sail it and me with it to Trianja. Just so as you know, let me tell you that I am an excellent shot and I will shoot anyone who lifts a finger against me. If you want proof of my skill then look above your heads."

With that Clive pointed the bow towards the sky and the seagulls and in the same moment and seemingly without taking aim, he fired the arrow. Seconds later a seagull crashed onto the deck. Clive took another arrow and put it in place. Then he pointed the bow at the crew, almost all of whom had expressions of surprise or fear or both.

"Now get this ship under way at once. That's an order."

Albeit reluctantly, the sailors began to go about their allotted tasks and within minutes they had cast off and the ship was in motion. Clive remained standing, bow in hand, as the harbour faded from view. He felt quite pleased with himself, proud in fact, that he had acted so decisively and successfully but then it occurred to him that he couldn't spend the whole voyage pointing his bow at the crew. He considered the predicament and then started to shout again.

231

"Oh and by the way, you crew, I have another weapon too, so don't get any ideas."

With that he put down the bow, picked up the rod, banged it hard on the deck, pointed it out to sea and fired it. The crew stared in amazement and didn't get any ideas for the rest of the voyage, which was just as well because Clive spent most of it with his head over the side being seasick and quite unable to defend himself, should the need have arisen. The voyage lasted three days.

The harbour Clive sailed into was much bigger than the one he had left, with dozens of ships moored. Trianja too was a much more substantial place than Buggiton. The streets were narrow and bustling, the houses wooden, with overhanging upper stories and some with windows open onto the street and wares on sale within. The place had a positively medieval air about it. Captain Branna was true to his word and led Clive to the Royal Palace, which was set apart from the other housing and surrounded by strong walls. At the gatehouse the Captain spoke to a guard, who spoke to another guard, who summoned the Steward, who spoke to Captain Branna. At length, the Steward departed and the Captain and Clive remained waiting outside. It was a good twenty minutes before he returned and a door opened to allow the pair into the courtyard. They were shown to a waiting room within the Palace and there they waited again. After what seemed like ages, Captain Branna was summoned and led away. Clive remained waiting. As he waited, it occurred to him that the Captain would tell the King that he had been on a mission to Besanto to rescue the Princes, and he wondered if the King would be annoyed to find that he had no intention of resuming his mission and that, on the contrary, he wanted to stay as far away from Besanto as possible.

Eventually Clive was summoned too. A valet led him through a series of rooms and corridors until he reached another room that was filled with people waiting to see the King. Fortunately for Clive, who was anticipating another long wait, the valet knocked on one of the pair of large doors at the end of the room, opened it, and motioned to Clive to go through. The room inside, befitting a palace, was palatial. It was vast, with windows that reached from floor to ceiling and walls adorned with tapestries and portraits of what, Clive presumed, were previous monarchs. As Clive stepped in he was immediately flanked on either side by heavily armed guards. At the far end of the room was a dais with a throne and on the throne sat a rather short, fat man whose feet didn't reach the floor. He didn't look much like a king should look but it was obvious to Clive that he was the King because he was wearing a crown and seated on a throne, while everyone else on the dais, including Captain Branna, was standing. They all looked at Clive and waited, while he, encouraged by the heavily armed guards, stepped up to the dais and stopped. He was feeling distinctly nervous, never having addressed a monarch before or even having seen one, except on the telly.

Clive waited and so did everyone else. Eventually one of the people spoke.

"It is customary to remove ones headwear and bow when entering the King's presence."

"Oh dear"' said Clive, hastily removing his woolly hat with its candle wax horns and bowing down as far as he could go.

"I'm very sorry. I should have known. I'm not used to meeting kings or important people. In fact I don't think I've ever met anyone really important bef...."

Clive realised he was babbling and shut up.

"You can get up now," he heard a voice say; "bows usually have a downward movement followed by an upward one. You don't have to prostrate yourself."

It was the King speaking.

"It is also customary to put down one's weapons before entering the throne room," continued the King, "but then we are told that you are from Aughphalia and not familiar with our conventions, so it will be overlooked this time. Now I understand, from what the Captain has said that you were on a mission to rescue my daughter, a very laudable thing in itself, I might add, but that you have temporarily abandoned your mission to bring me important news of a new weapon that the Baron has acquired."

"Yes," said Clive, wondering if the King knew about Staffs of Power.

"Yes, Your Majesty," corrected the King.

"Sorry, Your Majesty," said Clive.

"Well?" said the King.

"Oh yes, sorry Your Majesty but I think the Baron has a Staff of Power."

"And what makes you think that?"

Clive thought it best to keep quiet about Bengough's revelation that flashes from a Staff in Besanto had been detected on the mother ship.

"I have been told that the Baron has a new weapon that can kill unseen and from afar, using fire."

234

"And who told you that?"

"A man called Reece in Buggiton, Your Majesty."

"Is that all? It's not a lot to go on."

"Excuse me, Your Majesty, but that's what a Staff of Power can do, kill at great distance using fire, or the power of light anyway. It would be a very powerful weapon in the wrong hands."

"Yes, yes but these Staffs of Power are the stuff of legend, not of reality. I know that some people believe in all that nonsense but really."

"But they do exist, I know, they really do."

"How do you know?"

"I've got one."

Clive didn't know why he said it. It just came out.

"You've got one? Where is it?"

Clive held up the rod.

"That thing?"

"Yes, Your Majesty."

Clive saw the smiles on everyone's faces except the captain's.

"It doesn't look like an ordinary staff, let alone a Staff of Power," said the King.

"I assure you it is, Your Majesty. It might not look like it now but it can do incredible things."

At this point the captain intervened to support Clive, explaining what had happened on deck.

"Let's have a demonstration then," said the King.

"What, in here?"

"In here is as good as anywhere. Aim it at that tapestry," directed the King.

Clive couldn't believe that he'd been directed to destroy what was obviously a valuable tapestry but did as he was told. He pressed the symbol, banged the rod on the carpet and fired at the tapestry which burst into flames. For a few seconds there was pandemonium as guards and servants rushed to put out the fire before it spread to adjoining tapestries.

"Sorry, Your Majesty," said Clive, feeling rather guilty and wondering just how much the tapestry had been worth.

"What else can it do?" asked the King.

"I'm not allowed to tell."

"You're not allowed to tell what?"

"What else it can do."

"No, you're not allowed to tell, Your Majesty."

"That's what I said," said Clive, not getting the point.

"Never mind," said the King, "why aren't you allowed to tell?"

"I promised the man who told me."

"Who was that?"

"I can't tell you that either," said Clive, thinking it best to keep Bengough a secret.

"Then, can you tell me how to use the thing?"

"I'm afraid not. It was a sort of general promise that covered all possibilities."

"I could make you tell me," said the King.

"Could you?" asked Clive.

"Yes, I could have you tortured."

Clive didn't quite know how to respond to the King or how he would respond to torture. But he did feel himself getting rather agitated.

"That's not very fair"' he blurted out, "I come all this way to warn you about a dreadful weapon, not to mention the rescuing your daughter bit and you threaten to have me tortured."

Everyone, including the King looked at Clive with horrified expressions. Clive realised he had overstepped the mark. The King's expression changed from surprise to annoyance but then, after a very long few seconds, he smiled.

"Bravo, well said Clive," he said. "I do need putting in my place from time to time and none of these sycophants would dare to say anything like that, especially given my reputation for tantrums and cruelty. But please do try to remember the 'Your Majesties', I'm a bit of a stickler for protocol."

"Yes, Your Majesty," said Clive, relieved.

"Well now, you won't, or rather can't tell me what else that thing can do, or how to make it do it, so as far as I can see, you'll just have to come with us and bring it along. Actually it's very useful you turning up like this, the army is ready and we march against Besanto tomorrow. You'll need an official position. Let me see, the captain here says you are an amazing shot with that bow of yours, so I'll put you in the King's Own Archers, in fact I'll make you the Commander of the King's Own Archers. The present one is a doddery old fool who couldn't hit a target even if he was standing next to it, whereas you'll be able to lead by example. There, that's all settled then. You are my guest tonight Clive. You will have a royal bedroom and dine with me this evening."

With that the King clicked his fingers and the guards to either side of Clive turned and escorted him out.

Clive was still slightly in shock when the guards delivered him to his room. Apparently he was not only going to the one place that Bengough had told him not to go to but he was also going to war. He considered making a run for it but guessed that getting out of the palace would be much more difficult than getting in and besides, what was the point, where would he go? On top of everything he was supposed to command a company, or was it a division or even a brigade, of archers. Clive sat on the bed and felt like crying, every turn in his journey seemed to be for the worse.

'However,' thought Clive, suddenly feeling more positive, 'tonight I'm going to dine with a king. That can't be bad.'

Clive anticipated the various courses that might be on offer and realised that, after three days of seasickness and hardly eating anything, he was starving. A knock at the door announced the arrival of his personal servant, an aged gentleman called Aubalard. The servant was carrying the uniform of the Commander of the King's Own Archers and urged Clive to try it on for size in the bathroom. Clive hadn't realised he had a bathroom, or even taken any notice of his room, but then he looked around and saw that it was spacious, lavishly furnished and much nicer than his own bedroom back home.

'Perhaps it's not always for the worse,' thought Clive, 'even if it is only for one night.'

The servant retired from his room and Clive, finding a bath in the bathroom and hot water from the hot tap, treated himself to the luxury of a long, lazy soak before trying on the uniform. It fitted him well. Clive rather admired himself in the mirror and thought that while it was a tad ostentatious, it was only what one would expect for a Commander. Back in the main room Aubalard had reappeared with another uniform. Apparently the King had changed his mind about Clive's position. Instead of the Archers, he was now to be a soldier in the King's Own Personal Bodyguard. Aubalard explained that the King had decided that, in the event of imminent danger to himself, he wanted Clive and his weapons as close as possible, instead of somewhere at the rear with a load of archers. Clive tried on his new uniform. It fit well but it obviously didn't convey the status of a Commander. Clive didn't know quite what to think about his new position. It was quite an honour to be so near to the King but it was also an obvious demotion and it seemed to place him in even greater danger than before.

Aubalard returned later with yet more clothes. Clive was concerned that he had been moved rank again but it turned out that these were for immediate wear. Clive's own clothes were to be laundered and made ready for him in the event that he returned from the war alive. Clive tried them on. They fit well and were quite comfy. Aubalard asked Clive if he would like anything to eat before dinner but Clive, anticipating a feast, declined. Aubalard said he expected that Clive would want something later, which Clive thought rather strange given that he intended to have eaten his fill by then.

Dinner was at 8.00pm and a squire escorted Clive to the dining room, advising him not to sit too near the King if at all possible. The dining room was of stately size and had three long tables, all already partially occupied and one slightly smaller empty one, raised up on a dais, with what was obviously the King's throne on the middle. Several of those

239

seated gesticulated with their eyes that Clive should seat himself amongst them. It seemed that he was not sufficiently important to sit at the high table. Clive was rather surprised that none of the tables were set with cutlery, nor condiments of any sort, just plates and napkins. Presently the King arrived and everybody stood. The King surveyed the room and called for his Chancellor. The Chancellor was asked why he was not sitting at his rightful place on the high table and ordered to move. This process continued until there was only one place left, right next to the King, who then called for Clive. Clive felt honoured and took his place with pride.

Clive waited in anticipation for the first course. In fact there was no first course, if by that one understands that there would be others to follow. There was only one course; bananas. Bunches of them were brought out on silver platters and the King told everyone not to wait on ceremony but to tuck in and have as many as they liked. Clive's heart sank; bananas again after so many days of banana flavoured goo. Aubalard later explained that the King frequently went on faddish diets and expected everybody else to join in. Half way through his second and final banana, Clive noticed a horrible smell. It continued throughout the meal, often accompanied by loud noises. Clive realised why nobody wanted to sit on the high table and certainly not next to the King, who said little during the meal but consumed much. At one point he remarked that Clive was a strange name for an Aughphalian but that Aughphalians were quite strange anyway, which probably explained it. Shortly afterwards the King announced that as they were going to war on the morrow, everybody should have an early night. With that he left and everybody else did too. Back in his room and preparing for bed there was a knock on the door. Aubalard entered bearing a covered tray.

"I anticipated you might like a little something before bed but please don't tell the King," he said and uncovered a dish of venison stew, with boiled potatoes and peas. There was also a carafe of red wine. Clive ate all the food and then drank all the wine. Next morning he went to war with a hangover.

Chapter 17.

Clive went to war with a hangover and on a horse. His only previous experience of riding, animals that is, had been as a child, on a donkey, on the beach in some seaside resort. He hadn't liked it much then and it was even worse this time, on a bigger beast, and with a hangover. The constant movement made him feel sick and the horse's girth seemed to force his legs out at some unnatural angle which made them hurt like hell after only a few minutes. By the end of the day he was aching all over and his buttocks were raw due to the constant rubbing against the saddle. Clive's horsemanship did not even border on competence. The horse stopped to graze whenever it pleased and broke into a trot whenever it felt like a little more exertion. Fortunately for Clive the horse seemed to enjoy the company of other horses, so it never led him too far astray. The track they followed led them south away from the coast and actually away from Besanto at first but after a few days they came to a fork in the track and turned left towards their destination.

Only the bodyguard rode, about a dozen of them. Everyone else walked, except the King, who was carried in an elaborately covered, horse drawn wagon. Clive had presumed there would be cavalry units but it turned out that the only cavalry unit had been the one that had already been wiped out trying to rescue the Princess. It didn't look like much of an infantry to Clive. Half of it didn't seem to be wearing uniforms or to be properly armed and the rest didn't march along neatly in step but just formed an amorphous mass that trudged along. The King didn't lead from the front but positioned his wagon safely in the centre. At the rear were various other supply wagons and the camp followers. Clive noticed, during the day, that a succession of camp followers made their way into the King's wagon.

The closest rider to Clive was Wilfred. Clive remarked that there didn't seem to be any generals and was told that the King, intending to direct all military matters personally, didn't see the need for them. Wilfred added that nobody had much confidence in the King, who had never been to battle before, but not to tell anyone that he had said so. It wasn't long before they stopped for lunch. Everyone else got sandwiches but a table was set up for the King on which were placed various dishes of roasted meats and pies. Apparently the King had decided that it wouldn't do to go to war on a diet. Everyone else finished their lunch in a couple of minutes and then had to wait ages while the King dined. Sometime around mid-afternoon, which wasn't very long after they had set off again, the King declared that they had gone far enough that day. Clive was quite pleased because he was really sore by then. An elaborate marquee was erected for the King, into which were carried carpets, furniture and a bed. Everyone else was to make do as best they could. All in all, the day didn't inspire much confidence, if any, that they were headed for anything except disaster, if they ever got to where they were going, that is.

Subsequent days followed the same pattern. Clive noticed that the army seemed to be getting smaller. Wilfred agreed and added that only an idiot would willingly follow the King into war but not to tell anyone that he had said so. He also let slip that he would like to get away himself, except that his absence as a bodyguard would be noticed by the King, who really did have a bad temper and a cruel streak. Clive asked him about the Baron in Besanto. The Baron had apparently been a thorn in the King's side for a long time, having been unwilling to pay taxes that, he maintained, would only be frittered away. However, in recent times, that was within the last year or so, the Baron had become much more than a nuisance and seemed determined to force an all out war, which, given their present situation, he was obviously on the point of achieving. No one was sure what had brought about this change in the Baron but it might have something to do with a new advisor who was rumoured to have won the Baron's favour.

By that time they reached the fork in the road Clive and his horse had grown somewhat accustomed to each other. Clive had learnt to make it move most of the times he wanted it to and in the direction he wanted it to go and was able to tolerate and even enjoy the occasional unplanned canter. Moreover his body no longer ached horribly every minute he was on it and he had perfected a sitting position with his knees high up and his feet pointed forward in which he no longer felt that he was about to be split in half by the wide girth of his mount. It was at this point that the King decided that they were near enough to danger for him to want Clive, his rod and his bow and arrows much nearer to hand, so Clive was relieved of the horse and installed at the side of the King's wagon driver.

Up on the wagon Clive was much more aware of the goings on inside it. Clive considered himself to be broad minded but the King's behaviour set a new standard in debauchery that even Clive found to be quite disgusting. On the other hand being on the wagon meant that he shared the same food as the King when it came to mealtimes, so he was no longer forced to suffer the increasingly stale sandwiches, and there was even enough left over for him to be able to secrete some away to give to Wilfred, with whom he had become quite friendly. In this new situation Clive was required to sleep at the entrance, or rather just outside the entrance, to the King's marquee with instructions to kill any unauthorised person who tried to get in. In the middle of the third night out from the fork in the road, Clive's slumber was disturbed by sounds which he took to indicate that someone was approaching in a very stealthy way. Clive was immediately overcome by panic that this would prove to be the sort of unauthorised person whom he was authorised, not to say instructed, to kill, that is if he wasn't killed himself. Clive was tempted to cry out to wake up everyone else and put off the would-be assassin. He was just about to do so, when he heard a whisper.

"Psst, Clive."

Clive was somewhat taken aback to hear his own name. He suspected a trap but then decided that a would-be assassin would probably not know his name or warn him of his presence by using it.

"Psst, Clive," whispered the voice again before adding, "it's me."

"Me?" asked Clive.

"Me," replied the whisper, "yes me, Bengough."

"Bengough?" whispered Clive, incredulously.

Bengough crawled up to Clive and lay down beside him.

"Hello Clive," whispered Bengough.

Clive was overjoyed.

"Have you come to save me?" he whispered hopefully.

"Not exactly to save you. More to warn you."

"Warn me?" whispered Clive.

"Really, Clive," whispered Bengough, "it is very irritating to have you repeat as a question, everything I say. Now listen carefully, I have been doing some investigating on my own and it appears that there is a super enhanced laser device in Besanto that was supposed to be somewhere in the Orion Nebula. Now these things can't move by themselves, so you know what that means?"

"Someone brought it here?" whispered Clive.

"Exactly," whispered Bengough, "and I've a hunch who that someone might be."

"You have?" whispered Clive.

"Sticky Fingers Maclean," whispered Bengough.

Clive was about to repeat the name as a question but forced himself not to.

"Sticky Fingers Maclean is one of the most wanted men in the galaxy. There's an enormous bounty on his head," whispered Bengough. "He and his little gang of space pirates have made a fortune by intercepting private, and even Federation spaceships, and holding them for ransom. Now Sticky was also known to be hiding out in the Orion Nebula but sources tell us he has moved on. If he has managed to get hold of one of the four devices and has brought it here, then it is worryingly near to the other three."

"So you think he intends to get hold of the others too and make a ...whatchamacallit?"

"Yes, that's exactly what I think. He's planning on making a long distance planet obliterator."

"So the Baron is really Sticky Fingers Maclean," whispered Clive.

"No," whispered Bengough, "the Baron is the Baron. I think he is under the influence of Sticky."

Clive thought.

"That fits," he whispered "Someone told me that the Baron has a new advisor. Maybe it's this Sticky. What are you going to do?"

"It's more a question of what are you going to do. I told you we aren't allowed to intervene."

"Except to blow us all to smithereens," whispered Clive.

"Let's hope it doesn't come to that. There's more Clive. Since we last met, all four of the devices have been on the move. The one in Besanto has been going westwards and the one in Aughphalia has crossed into Morgrnvia and joined up with the one in Elisiu and they're going westwards too. The four devices are nearer than ever to each other."

"Where do you think this Sticky is now?" whispered Clive, half fearing that the two of them were on a collision course on the same track.

"Somewhere between Buggiton and Mickelling, I would say. There have been large scale troop movements out of Besanto and this probably means that the Baron is marching against Buggiton or Trianja or both."

"But we're marching against Besanto. Trianja is undefended." whispered Clive.

247

"In that case it's probably best to keep marching," whispered Bengough, 'but there is another possibility."

Clive sensed that what Bengough was about to whisper would not be to his liking.

"If you were to capture Sticky and alert me, then the Captain would send me down with a unit to arrest him. It would be the best possible outcome and what's more, I'd get a big share of the reward."

"And if Sticky Wicky or whoever he is already has three devices when I catch up with him, wouldn't your captain want to blow this planet up, along with him and everyone else, including me, rather than take any chances by sending a unit down?"

"I have to admit that that's a possibility but he's a fair man and he'd get a share of the reward too if we were to take him back alive."

"So, on the one hand you're advising me to carry on to Besanto, where the danger to me has decreased and on the other you're advising me to desert and walk in the opposite direction into all sorts of danger."

"Yes, that's about it Clive, I'm afraid but it's your choice entirely. You don't have to consider me or the reward that I could really do with having."

"So the reward is that important is it? Have you got any plans for what you intend to do with it?"

"Pig farming; I'd start a pig farm."

"Pig farming? You'd prefer to be a pig farmer than an inter-galactic policeman?"

"Every time. Lovely animals pigs, not the hybridised bacon factories on feet that are so common nowadays but the originals, outdoor bred and all that."

"Like Gloucester Old Spots?"

"You know about pigs, Clive? A kindred spirit? Yes, like Gloucester Old Spots, the finest breed of pig in the galaxy or at least they were."

"We've got them on Earth; in fact I think they might have come from there."

"They do or rather they did, before life on Earth was destroyed."

An idea was forming in Clive's mind.

"So all you'd have to do to make your dream come true would be to find a way to get back to Earth as it was and you could get hold of some breeding sows and a male and take them to wherever you wanted and you know what?"

"Go on."

"There is a pig farm right near to where I live that has Old Spots. I could show you; if you took me with you, that is."

Bengough was quiet, pondering the possibilities.

"I've already told you, Clive," he whispered after a bit, "it would be very difficult to get back to Earth; it might not be possible."

"You already told me it would be impossible, so merely being very difficult is a big step in the right direction and in any case, you mentioned alerting you, how would I do that?"

"Let's say seven flashes of laser into the sky, one after the other. We would detect that and I could inform the captain that it was a signal from you."

249

"And the captain would agree to take me on board so that we could set about finding the Earth?"

"Maybe, I can...."

At that moment Bengough was interrupted by the bugler sounding the early morning reveille call and had to make a hasty getaway. Clive was left wondering what he should do next. He hadn't decided by the time the army set off again.

Before the end of the day, Clive was clear about two things. Firstly, that he would not be going off alone to confront the Baron and Sticky Maclean because that would be a confrontation in which he was sure to come off worse. Secondly, if he continued to Besanto with the King and he didn't get killed there, they would eventually have to leave anyway and face the Baron at some point. Being clear about things did not make it any easier to reach a decision but, that night, lying in position outside the entrance to the King's marquee and hoping against hope that Bengough would make a return visit, Clive suddenly remembered the poor group of prisoners he and Ggydren had seen outside the Great Forest and the pall of smoke that lay above what they took to be Mickelling. If the Baron was headed for Buggiton and Trianja and they were undefended, then he feared the worst would surely happen. Clive decided that it was his duty to persuade the King to turn away from Besanto and defend his threatened towns instead. This decision gave Clive another problem for he could hardly tell the King that he was privy to information given him by a member of the Inter-Galactic Police Force.

Next morning the King required Clive to have breakfast with him. Once again he tried to get Clive to reveal the secrets of the rod and once again Clive politely refused. The situation did, however, give Clive the opportunity to ask the King if he had considered the possibility that the Baron had lured him towards Besanto, so that he could attack Trianja. The King dismissed the idea. Clive suggested that riders could be despatched to make sure the Baron was still in Besanto. The King dismissed the idea. Clive informed the King that he had a hunch that the Baron was marching on Buggiton. The King said that hunches alone would not divert him from his path and added that the Baron was more than welcome to Buggiton anyway. In the end Clive had to settle for the status quo; they were heading for Besanto and the Baron and Sticky Fingers would have to wait.

Over the course of the next week the army continued to trudge forwards and continued to get smaller. The King continued to avail himself to the dubious pleasures of the camp followers and Clive continued to hope that Bengough would reappear and whisk him away in a space buggy built for two. By the end of the week they were well into the foothills and caught their first glimpse of the Besanton plateau, high up in the distance. A few days later the going became so arduous that the King had to abandon his wagon and had himself carried on a litter instead. When he fell off he had the litter bearers flogged and reluctantly took to his feet but, not used to such exertion, he had to stop frequently for rests and snacks to keep up his strength. During all this time there was no sign of the enemy but the King gradually moved further and towards the back of the army, just in case they showed up.

During what must have been the fourth week of their march, the remains of the army finally arrived at the gates of Besanto, to find them firmly shut against them. The army waited for orders from the King and, for some strange reason that Clive did not understand, the King told Clive to direct the attack. Clive explained that he had never attacked anything in his life and didn't really know what to do. Anyway, hadn't the King said that he intended to direct the attack personally? The King interpreted this as impertinence and threatened to have Clive flogged too. Clive made his way to the front of the army and looked ahead. The two enormous wooden gates were set into a gatehouse, with twin towers and battlements. The gatehouse was flanked on either side by a jagged wall of rocks which continued into the distance as far as the eye could see. Every hundred yards or so, a turret rose up above the rocks. The place seemed pretty much impregnable. Clive made his way back to the King, explained the situation and suggested a siege. The King said Clive was a coward and called for the floggers but Clive agreed to go and have another look to see if he could come up with something.

Clive walked alone towards the gates and noticed that he hadn't seen any signs of movement on the ramparts or anywhere else for that matter. While he was also pretty certain that Bengough would be correct in saying that the Baron had left, he was also sure that the Baron wouldn't have taken absolutely everyone with him, so there were sure to be dangers within. Clive considered using the rod against the doors. This was sure to be effective and very impressive but Clive wondered if it would be showing his best hand too soon. He continued to walk forward. A few yards from the gatehouse he stopped and looked upwards for any signs that the machicolation was being prepared to jettison burning oil or rocks on him. There were none. Clive walked right up to the door and knocked.

"Who's there?"

Clive remembered about the power of the command of the Staff-holder and gripped his rod firmly.

"My name is Clive and I am the emissary of the King, who is here with a large army. I order you to open these gates or we will break them down and show no mercy to those within," said Clive, trying to sound as authoritative as possible and feeling rather pleased with the result.

A small window within the door opened and a face appeared.

"There's no one here. Go away."

"Not exactly no one," said Clive, "you're here and where there's one there's sure to be more. Where's the Baron?"

"Gone to war against the King."

"That's strange," said Clive, "the King is here and so is his army. Look, see."

"Well the Baron isn't here and I've got strict instructions not to let anyone in while he's away."

"We've come about the King's daughter whom the Baron kidnapped. Surely he hasn't taken her to war."

"Of course not but I've got strict instructions about her too."

"Look, you may have your instructions but I don't suppose the Baron anticipated that the King would arrive with an army. It seems to me that your choice is to let us in or have us force our way in and if we have to force our way in, the King is not going to be too happy about it. I wouldn't fancy your

253

chances if he finds out you're the one who wouldn't open the door. I'll tell you what, why not let me in to have a talk with the King's daughter? We may be able to work things out without the need for bloodshed. What do you say?"

"I'm not sure. The Baron would have my guts for garters if he finds out."

"Well, I promise that I won't tell him."

"It could be a trick, I open the door and your army rushes in."

"Let me have a word with the King. I'll explain the situation and maybe he'll agree to withdraw a little."

"No, I'm sorry. It won't do. No army has ever been able to capture this stronghold. It's more than my life is worth to open the doors."

Clive decided that it might be time to show his best hand.

"The Baron's new advisor, does he have a weapon that can kill from afar using flashes of light?"

"Well, yes actually. It's very impressive. Some of your lot already copped it."

"I've got one too and I'm going to use it to burn down the gates if you don't let me in."

"I don't believe you. Where is it then?"

"Here," said Clive holding up the rod.

"What, that thing? Come off it."

Clive struck the rod against the ground and a flash of light flew up into the sky, accompanied by an awesome cry of surprise from the army behind.

"Convinced now?"

The expression on the face in the window was one of surprise.

"Alright then, but you still have to get your army moved back. I'm not taking any chances, and just you, nobody else."

Clive explained the situation to the King. The King dithered. While Clive's suggestion was perfectly reasonable it would mean that Clive would emerge with all the glory and he with none and that was not part of his plans. Also, knowing that the Baron had left and taken his army with him, the prospect of attacking a virtually deserted fortress and capturing it was very tempting. Clive finally convinced the King by suggesting that an attack might endanger his daughter's life. Maybe the Baron had given orders for her to be slain in such an event. The King saw the possibility and reluctantly ordered his troops to move back a couple of hundred yards.

Clive walked up to the doors again. One of them opened a few inches to let him in. As it did so the King ordered the army to attack. The door closed again before it even got half way.

"Well, that was pretty sneaky, I thought I could trust you," said the guard, who was actually the Steward and in charge of things while the Baron was away.

"I can assure you that I had no part in that. To tell you the truth I'm not surprised. All in all, he's a pretty despicable character," explained Clive, "but no harm done. Now where's his daughter?"

The doors opened into large open space that Clive, having enjoyed History lessons at school, knew to be a bailey. The keep rose up before him, a great stone structure, with all the typical features, portcullis, arrow slits, towers and battlements. Above the towers, to one side, a single circular turret rose highest of all, capped with a pointed roof.

"She's up there," said the steward, pointing.

The castle was manned by a skeleton staff. They eyed Clive warily but did not oppose him. The portcullis was raised and Clive cautiously entered the tunnel that led to the inner bailey, aware that such places were known as killing grounds. Safely through however, and inside the keep, he was shown to the spiral staircase. Clive climbed to the very top and out onto the battlement walkway and then through another doorway that led to another flight of stairs up to the turret. Finally and more than slightly out of breath, Clive reached a door. He paused a minute to rest and then knocked.

"Yes?" answered a voice.

"Are you the King's daughter?" said Clive, thinking it wouldn't do to rescue the wrong person.

"Yes."

"Good, I've come to rescue you."

"Go away; I don't want to be rescued."

"Pardon?" was all Clive could think to say, never for one moment having anticipated the daughter's response.

"You heard. Go away; I don't want to be rescued."

"But you must. Your father's here. He's come all this way."

"Then he can go all the way back again."

Clive suddenly remembered the quest. Actually he hadn't thought about it for ages.

"But I'm on a quest to rescue you and if I don't complete it I can't get home again."

"Look, I'm sorry about that but it's hardly my problem is it?"

Clive was flummoxed.

"But what about your father?"

"My father is a buffoon."

Clive could not have agreed more.

256

"But he loves you."

"The only thing my father loves is himself."

'She's spot on again,' thought Clive, warming to the King's daughter.

"Stand back," said Clive, "I'm going to blast open this door."

"Try using the handle, it's not locked."

Clive opened the door and looked in. The King's daughter was seated at a table, embroidery in hand. She was very beautiful, with long golden locks and only tiny horns.

"Hello," said Clive, "I'm Clive."

"Hello, Clive, I'm Gretchen," said the King's daughter, smiling. "Look, I'm sure you mean well but I'm not leaving; I like it here."

As she spoke she stood up and patted the rather large bump on her belly.

"And besides, I've got this to consider."

Clive's heart sank.

"I'm too late," he said, "I was supposed to rescue you before the Baron had his wicked way; you know what I mean, don't you, with you."

"Not the Baron," explained Gretchen, "his son and heir and it wasn't wicked, it was love. Prince Cenwynn and I are to be married on his return. Honestly, he's not at all like his dad. He's kind and considerate, he likes animals and children, and he hates violence."

Clive was stumped.

"Well, your father's not going to be too happy about this. How on earth am I going to tell him?"

"We'll have to think of something," said Gretchen smiling. "You seem a friendly enough sort. I wouldn't want him to have your head on a plate."

"He wouldn't, would he?" said Clive, already knowing the answer to his question.

"Sit down, Clive, and do have a glass of wine. We need to talk."

Clive sat down and sipped the wine. They talked and agreed a plan. Gretchen pulled on a cord to summon the Steward.

"Have another glass; he's a bit slow on the stairs."

Seven minutes later the Steward arrived.

"You'll be pleased to hear," said Gretchen, "that I've decided not to allow myself to be rescued."

"I'm very pleased indeed, ma'am, indeed it's a load off my mind."

"But my father, the King, won't be happy to leave empty handed, so I've decided to have the prisoners from Mickelling released."

"Is that wise, ma'am? The Baron was holding them as a bargaining chip, just in case."

"And so, I reckon, the Baron will think it a fair trade to give up the prisoners to save Besanto from being ransacked."

"Yes, ma'am, I see what you mean. I'll give the orders right away."

A few minutes later Clive prepared to take his leave of the Princess. He was rather taken aback when she kissed him lightly on the cheek and wished him well, saying that he was a bit of a sweetie. In response, and feeling rather chuffed, Clive pulled off his hat and bowed before her.

"Oh, Aughphalian?" she commented, noticing the absence of horns.

Clive decided it was easier not to explain.

Shortly afterwards, Clive emerged from the doors of Besanto with the group of men, women and children from Mickelling. A loud cheer went up from the army when they realised what was happening and Clive felt a surge of pride as he strode forward. The King was all smiles at first but the smiles soon turned to frowns.

"Where is my daughter?" he demanded.

"She thought it wiser to remain," answered Clive.

"Remain?" said the King, "There better be a very good explanation for this."

"She is with child."

"With child?" asked the King.

"She is afraid that to return in her condition would bring shame upon your royal highness and your royal house."

"So he had his way with her then?"

"It would seem so, Your Majesty."

"Did she put up a fight?"

"She is very delicate, Your Majesty."

"No fight eh, I might have expected it. In fact I bet she enjoyed it, the brazen hussy. I always had my misgivings about her. Well, at least she's doing the decent thing now. Can you imagine the embarrassment it would cause me if I had to take her home to give birth to a Besanton sprog? I shall disown her. She'll get nothing more from me."

Clive kept quiet but thought that the King was perhaps the most contemptuous person he had ever met.

The King ordered the army to turn around.

"Which way shall we go," asked Clive, "the same way we came?"

The King thought about the glory he would bask in, delivering the prisoners from Mickelling back to their homes.

"No, I shall make a progress through Mickelling and Buggiton to show my people their victorious leader," said the King.

"What if we run into the Baron?" asked Clive.

"I'm confident my people will have acquitted themselves well against him. His forces are sure to be sorely diminished, and I shall wipe those that remain from the face of this land."

"Don't forget he's got a Staff of Power," said Clive.

"So have you," replied the King, "and I have every confidence that you will better him if it comes to it."

"You expect us to fight it out using Staffs of Power?"

"And I expect you to win or, better still, perhaps you will all be blown to smithereens and I wouldn't have to concern myself with the Baron or Staffs of Power again. You'd be happy to sacrifice yourself for such a noble cause, I take it?"

"Of course, Your Majesty," lied Clive.

Chapter 18.

With no path to follow Ggydren and Elendril found the going hard. They had been inside the Great Forest for several hours, following a course that Ggydren hoped would take them to Elisiu, although he had no way of knowing for sure. He had thought they might be met by the ladies of the Cerridwine in some form or other soon after entering, but thus far they hadn't seen, nor heard a single living creature. Ggydren remembered that it had only been on the first night that he and Clive had been approached.

By the time the light began to fade they were tired out, hungry and thirsty. They looked for somewhere to stop and presently came to a slight clearing where the trees were not so tightly packed. Ggydren gathered wood and used the Staff to light a fire. At least they would have warmth. Ggydren thought that the Staff and the fire might attract the ladies but none came. That night they slept as best they could, backs propped up against the thick trunk of some tree that neither knew the name of. Next morning, hungry and stiff, they struggled on again. Wracked by hunger and thirst, they walked all morning until, to their dismay, they came to the edge of the forest again. They looked at each other in disbelief, and then walked out into the sunlight to discuss what they should do. It was in Ggydren's mind that enough was enough, they had tried and failed but Elendril was insistent, she would not give up until she had seen Elisiu. So they plunged into the Forest again, hoping that this time they would walk in a straight line and not round in circles as they had evidently done before.

Towards the middle of the afternoon Ggydren thought he could sense something, a feeling that they were being watched. He stopped and whispered to Elendril and they looked all around but saw nothing, at least nothing tangible. They walked on for at least another hour but the feeling persisted and with it came an increasing dread, a fear of the unknown. Suddenly Elendril stopped and held Ggydren back. She stepped forward and called out.

"I know you are there. Show yourselves."

They waited, nothing happened.

"Here," said Ggydren quietly, "let me give it a go with this," and holding the rod aloft, he repeated Elendril's words several times and each time more loudly, till he was shouting at the top of his voice.

Then they came, not in or twos or threes but all at once, save one and all in their womanly form. They stood before Ggydren and Elendril and their faces were full of anger and hatred. One of them, the same one who had spoken after the death of Bronghar, came forward. Her fury was focussed on Ggydren.

"You! You again. You, who broke our laws and brought such tragedy. You, who nevertheless was allowed to leave in peace. You, who promised never to return and yet here you are again and with a new accomplice. You, who knows the dire punishment for trespass and yet you trespass again. Are you mad, are you stupid? So you have a new Staff but if you think that thing will protect you, then you are mistaken,

262

nothing will save you from our wrath. We want no explanations, no excuses. You will both bear the brunt of the full weight of the law."

They started to move forward and as they did they began to change into hideous shapes, some into grotesquely deformed humans, some into serpents, others into snarling animals. Ggydren was overcome with terror. He raised the rod to bang it on the ground but Elendril grabbed his hand to stop him.

"Can't you see"' she screamed, "I am one of you, one of the children you discarded. I have returned. Take me to Elisiu. I will see Elisiu. I demand it."

The effect was instant; the creatures all stood still and began to change back into their human forms.

"Yes" said Elendril, regaining her composure, "I am one of you and I have come to try to find out and understand what kind of mothers would sacrifice their own children for their own selfish ends. You can tell now, I can see it in your faces. You recognise me as one of your own. Can you imagine how I have suffered, how we have all suffered, the daughters you cast out? Do you know the ways in which we are abused and mistreated, how we are despised? One of you may well be my mother; will you kill your own daughter after everything she has endured because of you? I have returned because I need to know how you could behave in such a way. I want to try to understand, So, I will have you take me there. I will see this place of yours, this Elisiu and the thing you call the Cerridwine."

They gathered round and their faces were no longer contorted in hatred but seemed to show surprise, bewilderment even. They whispered to each other for some time and it was clear to Ggydren that there was an argument, a difference of opinion about what should happen. Finally the same one stepped forward.

"We do see that you are one of our own but this has never happened before. What will you do if we show you Elisiu? Will you stay; we are one short since Bronghar died? Or have you come in search of revenge? Are you intent on our destruction? Tell us your intentions."

"I have no intentions," answered Elendril truthfully. "The possibility of staying has never occurred to me. I have to admit that I have come with anger but not with thoughts of revenge. I suppose I just want to see it, the place of my birth and the people of my birth, and I want to make you question yourselves for the suffering you have caused. That is all. Perhaps my hope is that I can make you change."

They whispered together again for some time. Eventually another stepped forward.

"My name is Rohanna. We have decided that we will give you safe passage and show you Elisiu but him, no," she said, pointing at Ggydren, "he cannot come. He is not one of us."

Ggydren looked at Elendril. He didn't quite know how to react. His initial thought was one of relief, that he didn't have to go in or place his trust in them again but then that was exactly it, he didn't trust them. They killed their own sons, got rid of their daughters, so what might they do to Elendril once they had her alone and in their grasp?

"I'm staying with her," he said. "If you take her you must take me too. We've been together for too many years. I won't let you take her off alone."

"My name is Elendril and I can vouch for him. Ggydren is a good man. He took me in when I was at my lowest point. He has protected me ever since and when they threw me out of his land, he gave up everything to follow and find me. He cannot go back. He means you no harm."

Again they debated. Again it seemed they were in disagreement.

"We do not doubt your sincerity but we cannot allow it. There is too much at stake. Already Elisiu is threatened from the north. The forest is being assaulted by soldiers from Besanto."

"Pardon me," said Ggydren, "but Besanto is my enemy too. My friend and I were pursued by brothers who were in the Baron's pay and the Baron has declared war on the King and already raised the village of Mickelling to the ground."

"That the Baron is your enemy is no comfort. What if these brothers have followed you now? It would make our situation even more fraught. I am sorry, you cannot come."

Ggydren suddenly remembered the power of the Staff.

"I am sorry too but I am coming with Elendril. I didn't want to resort to this but I do have the Staff and I've learned how to use it properly. I will use it if you force me to."

Ggydren held the Staff aloft.

"And you also know that the command of the Staff-holder is powerful, so I command you now; take us both to Elisiu."

The ladies stood for some seconds as if transfixed and then, without speaking, they turned aside and began to walk. Elendril and Ggydren followed.

As they walked Ggydren tried to count them.

'There were twenty four but Bronghar is dead. Angharind, kind Angharind, I don't think she's here, there are only twenty two.'

He called out to Rohanna.

"Where is Angharind? I don't see her. Did she recover?"

"Angharind is not dead but she mends very slowly. We do not think she is even out of danger yet. You gave her your word not to return and she nearly gave her life for you. See how you have repaid her."

Ggydren felt the slight keenly. Angharind had trusted them, him and Clive, and they had promised her that they would not return or even reveal the existence of Elisiu to anyone. He had returned, he had told Elendril and bought her with him and he had told Reece as well. Perhaps they were right to distrust him. He walked on in silence. At last they could see the Cerridwine ahead. He held Elendril's hand and he saw the amazement on her face, even though he had told her all about it, as the ladies walked right up to, and through it. Ggydren led Elendril forward and, hand in hand, they approached and went through the Cerridwine. Elendril gasped as she saw the wonder that was Elisiu and even Ggydren, who had seen it all before, was enthralled again. Yet he also sighed to think that a place of such beauty could harbour such horrible secrets.

Rohanna stopped and turned towards them

"Well, we are here. What would you have me do? What do you want to see?"

"I want to see it all," answered Elendril, "and then I want to question you, all of you. I want to know why you act as you do. If you feel remorse and..."

266

"But first," said Ggydren, interrupting, "please would you take us to Angharind. She spoke up for us before and defended me and Clive in the Forest. In fact I'm sure she saved our lives and it makes me sad to know that she hasn't recovered. I want to see her to show her my gratitude. Would that be possible?"

"If I were her I would not agree to see you. She trusted you and fought Bronghar because of you. Now that you are here, she will know that Bronghar's death and her suffering have been for nothing and she will be ashamed. The decision will be hers though. I will ask her for you."

"Well, that's telling me but thank you anyway," said Ggydren. "I can feel your contempt. In some ways I know that it is justified. It's true that I've broken my word but when I left here before it was me that felt contempt for you and the others. I was angry for Elendril, for what you've put her through. It seems we both have our reasons to be suspicious but I have not come with any thought in my head other than to help Elendril find the answers she needs. In the end, I will be as pleased to leave here, as you will be to see me go."

They stood and waited with the other women while Rohanna went to Angharind. At first no one spoke but then the others, curious about Elendril, began to ask questions about her life. Eventually one of them asked her if she had any birthmarks or other tell-tale features.

"One of us is certainly your mother and this may help us to know who she is. We always find it hard to give up our daughters and treasure the memory of such details."

Elendril showed them a mark on her arm just above the elbow, almost heart shaped and red in colour. They all studied it but none of them came forward to claim her and it struck Ggydren that Elendril's mother, if she was there at all, must be one of the three women not present, the dead Bronghar, Rohanna or Angharind.

Rohanna returned to tell them that Angharind had consented to see them but not on that day for she felt too ill and in need of rest. In the meantime she had asked that they be fed and given accommodation and for Elendril to be shown as much of Elisiu as she cared to see. So it was that Ggydren and Elendril were taken to Bronghar's empty home and food and drink provided. Later on Rohanna arrived to show Elendril around Elisiu but Ggydren, cautious as ever, insisted on going too.

"I know I've seen some of it already but I don't know how much and a second viewing won't do any harm."

Elendril seemed captivated by Elisiu. She smiled to see the gardens, all neatly tended and the abundance of produce ready to harvest, and she found the whitewashed buildings with their domed roofs delightful. Ggydren asked about the sacred grove that Angharind had mentioned the previous time but Rohanna said that some places were absolutely forbidden to them. Later, after darkness had fallen, Rohanna took them out again to see the wonder of the Cerridwine, in all its magnificent glory, as it glowed and shimmered and pulsated. Elendril was amazed and thrilled by its beauty. Inside again, Rohanna explained that she would take them to see Angharind in the morning and that the others had agreed to assemble afterwards for Elendril to question them.

"It will be a very special occasion for us, for seldom do we assemble together and leave the Forest unwatched. You may ask whatever you want and we will hold nothing back. We understand your reasons for coming here. You are a daughter of Elisiu."

Ggydren and Elendril slept in comfort that night. Ggydren kept the Staff by his side but otherwise felt no need to be on guard; somehow he found Rohanna to be entirely trustworthy. In the morning she took them to Angharind, saying that she was somewhat improved from the previous day and anxious to see them. Ggydren wondered if she would be friendly or hostile. Angharind was propped up in bed. Ggydren was shocked at the change. This Angharind looked haggard. She was thinner, much thinner, so much so that her face was sunken into its bones and she had hardly the strength to lift her head. Her flesh was still covered with scabs and bruises from her fight with Bronghar.

Rohanna arranged chairs by the bed and they sat beside her.

"It took a great deal of her remaining strength to transmute back into this form. She finds it difficult to speak but wishes to see the birthmark."

Elendril pulled up her sleeve and leaned forward so that her arm was just inches from Angharind's face. Summoning some inner strength Angharind raised her head, the better to see the mark and, with the gentlest of touches, placed her finger on it. She said nothing at all but her breathing became more pronounced and laboured and tears came to her eyes and by those tears they knew that Elendril had found her mother. Elendril cried too, leaning forward to gather Angharind in her arms and hold her close. She stayed like that for some minutes, gently rocking, before releasing her mother from her clasp, then rising to leave. Not a single word was spoken but outside Elendril wept more bitterly than she had ever done before and nothing that Ggydren could do or say held any comfort for her.

A little later, when the tears had stemmed, they were joined by Rohanna who had stayed inside with Angharind for some time.

"The others are all here now," she said. 'We are agreed that the Chamber is not suitable for you to ask your questions, so we have prepared a new place of assembly but there is something I must say first. Yesterday I said that we are one short and asked if was in your mind to remain here. Today I repeat the question. Will you stay, Elendril? Angharind wishes it and I think it will aid her recovery to have her daughter so near. I think the others will agree too and I wish it myself. But if you stay it must be because you accept Elisiu as it is and not with any intention to change it. We do have babies but there can never be more than two dozen here and you have to appreciate the meaning in that. Understand also that if you do stay, the Cerridwine will work its magic on you too; you will not age. Question the others first but, after that you must decide. As for you Ggydren," she said smiling, "that was well spoken yesterday. I am beginning to like you, even if you are a man. At the end of all this we will give you safe passage out of Elisiu again, be it with or without Elendril."

She led them to a place behind the Chamber that was circular in shape and with flower beds and ornamental shrubs. Seats had been arranged for everyone; all were occupied save three on which Ggydren, Elendril and Rohanna took their places.

Rohanna addressed Ggydren.

"Never before has a weapon been allowed in this place. That thing you hold is deadly to us. We do not ask you to give it up however, but only to place it on the ground beside you."

Ggydren did as he was asked and without reluctance; he was nearer to it than anyone else and had only to reach down for it if need be.

Rohanna explained that Elendril could question whoever she chose and would be answered truthfully. In return, they would also be allowed to question her to ensure her suitability, if she decided to remain. Elendril agreed and Ggydren was filled with a deep apprehension that despite everything she had said before, she would choose to stay, and he would lose her forever. Rohanna sat down and invited Elendril to ask her first question. Even before she had uttered a word there was a terrible commotion. Ggydren was aware of something behind him but his eyes were transfixed on the ladies around who had all jumped up, with horrified expressions. Then Ggydren saw a hand grab the Staff and whip it away. He turned and came face to face with Imbert and his squad of soldiers. Imbert held the Staff aloft, a look of triumph on his face which immediately changed to one of fear and amazement as the ladies began to transmute into terrifying forms. Whether it was intentional or maybe some reflex action, Imbert pulled the Staff down and struck it against the ground. A great flash of light flew upwards and tore into the very fabric of the Cerridwine. The effect was spectacular and disastrous. The gossamer fabric of the Cerridwine burst into flames that spread throughout it, rather like fork lightning spreads across the sky and, as the Cerridwine burned, so it melted in the heat and as it melted, great globules of molten fire fell to ground and one of them fell on Imbert and burned him agonisingly to death.

Several things happened at once. Ggydren, grabbed the Staff and then, reacting to the danger, pushed Elendril under the eaves of the Chamber, where they would be sheltered. The soldiers all ran off, although not all of them escaped the same horrible fate as Imbert, and the ladies in their various forms, scattered in every direction. It was all over in minutes. The Cerridwine was gone, completely destroyed, and with it Elisiu's future. Ggydren and Elendril were still in a state of shock when the ladies began to reappear, once more in womanly form. Ggydren, fearing their anger, picked up the Staff but they were too dazed to be angry. They just stumbled around, knowing their world was ending, knowing that without the Cerridwine and the being that had made it, they were just women, transmuters yes but just women and no longer immortal.

Elendril's first concern was for her mother. She grabbed Ggydren's hand and pulled him away towards Angharind's house. There another shock awaited them for Angharind looked older than just a few minutes before and she continued to age before their very eyes. Elendril held her hand and Angharind opened her eyes and smiled at her. Within less than an hour she died. Ggydren could only imagine Elendril's feelings of despair, to have found her mother so recently, only to lose her again so soon after. At least there was no longer a question of Elendril remaining, there was nothing to remain for; the Cerridwine was gone and Elisiu would die.

272

No longer under the spell of the Cerridwine, the ladies of Elisiu were also doomed. Almost immediately each began to show signs of ageing and, as the days passed, the ageing gathered pace. Soon they began to die and within a fortnight all were gone. Ggydren and Elendril stayed all that time, even though what was happening was horrible to experience. They gave what little care and comfort they could and buried the bodies. Rohanna was one of the last. She seemed to bear no bitterness towards Ggydren, even though he was wracked with guilt that he had brought all this on them. Elendril though considered herself to blame for she knew that she had been the one who had been determined to get to Elisiu and she had allowed Ggydren to accompany her. As the ladies withered and died, so too did Elisiu; inside that same fortnight it's gardens and lawns were decimated by cold and frost.

While they remained, Ggydren and Elendril thought long about what they should do next and where they should go. In the end they decided on Buggiton. Elendril wanted to spend her days giving help to the ladies of the shape-shifter shows and Buggiton was at least a place that was familiar to Ggydren. With Imbert dead, he doubted whether he would be troubled again from Aughphalia and Higgins would probably have already got over his loss of Elendril. It was also a comfort to Elendril to know that the shape-shifter shows would eventually come to an end; that was inevitable now that there would be no new shape-shifters born.

Elendril and Ggydren left Elisiu one cold morning. They had gathered provisions, blankets and utensils for the road, as much as they could carry and they also had the other Staff too, the one that had been hanging up in the Chamber. There was no point in leaving it there. Rohanna had spoken of the threat from Besanto and, sooner or later, it might have been found. Better for them, also, to have one each, in case of danger. The danger came on their third night out from the forest, not that they were aware of it. They were between Mickelling and Buggiton and had found a ruined barn that provided at least a little shelter from the storm they had seen approaching. The roar of the wind blocked out any other sounds, so they did not hear the marching of boots or the approach of footsteps. In the first light of day they awoke to find a Hinckle brother standing over them and sneering, their two Staffs in his clutches and behind him a unit of Besanton soldiers.

"Well, look who we have here," gloated the Hinckle, "one half of the pair we met before and a pretty little thing. The Baron will be very happy to get his hands on these two but first I've got some business to settle, two dead brothers' worth of business to be exact. I'm going to enjoy this."

Chapter 19

The journey down to the plain from Besanto was almost as slow as the journey up; the King insisted on frequent breaks and also on dining formally. As soon as the terrain allowed he took to his wagon or 'the royal coach' as he called it, and this permitted a better pace but it was still slow going. As they skirted the Great Forest Clive saw the damage inflicted by the Baron's forces, with whole swathes of trees cut down for lumber and he wondered if the ladies of Elisiu had been affected. Beyond the Forest lay the ruins of the deserted Mickelling. The prisoners that Clive had rescued searched in vain for any loved ones and, realising the hopelessness of the situation, decided to continue onwards with the King. Clive had expected the devastation, after all he had seen the pall of smoke before and guessed it to be Mickelling burning but even he was shocked to see such wanton destruction. The King said nothing.

Further on came messengers bearing even worse news; Buggiton and Trianja had surrendered without a fight and were now under the Baron's control. The King was furious and had all the messengers flogged and then flogged again, after one of them unfortunately let slip of the general feeling in Trianja that he had deserted it in its hour of need and left it undefended. That evening the King was in a melancholy mood, would speak to no one except to swear at the servant who served him at dinner and got very drunk. The following morning he was so hung-over he refused to move and lay in his bed in his marquee all day. Clive could tell the army or what was left of it, was not at all happy. The King, in fact, refused to move the following day as well. He informed Clive that he was considering what to do best and asked him for his opinion. As far as Clive could see the King had two options. The first was to try to attempt to liberate Buggiton and Trianja, although not necessarily in that order, and the second was to give up and go into exile somewhere. When it became generally known that the King was considering places where he could live out a comfortable exile, he received a delegation of soldiers who informed him that he would be deposed and decapitated if he did not take on the Baron. The King reluctantly agreed and the following day the army set out for Buggiton. The army would have preferred Trianja where most of them had loved ones but the King persuaded them that an attack on Buggiton first would be better. It would be less well defended and a victory would encourage people to join his cause. Actually the King chose Buggiton because it was nearer to Aughphalia in case he needed to beat a hasty retreat, and where he had useful contacts, including the Secretary to the Council, one Hieronymus Imbert.

The Battle of Buggiton was a one-sided affair that Clive watched from a safe distance, having been required to stay close to the King who did not intend to be anywhere near the fighting. The King had been correct in thinking that Buggiton would be sparsely defended, so there was really only one possible outcome, although his army, without generals or even experienced officers to direct things, made very hard work of it. The King celebrated the victory with a circuit of the shape-shifter shows and then finished off with a succession of camp followers in his marquee that he had required to be, rather ostentatiously, erected in the central square. Clive found Reece and learned that Ggydren, having escaped Aughphalia and on finding Elendril, had departed with her for Elisiu.

The victory celebrations continued for so long that, in the end, a company of soldiers ejected the King from his marquee, packed it up and forced him to ride in the direction of Trianja. The same soldiers, not approving the favouritism that the King had shown Clive, had him, Clive that is, demoted to the rank of private, not that Clive was aware of having had a rank to begin with. Thereafter Clive walked with the archery unit and well away from the King, a situation that suited him right down to the ground, as his contempt for the man had reached such heights that he had taken to daydreaming about what he would like to do to him.

The march to Trianja took a week and was entirely uneventful. They saw nothing of the enemy and not much of anyone else, since most that could had fled to safety elsewhere. As he walked Clive determined the course of action he needed to take. It was all quite straightforward really. Once he had come within sight of Sticky Fingers Maclean, whom he presumed would be at the right hand of the Baron, he would bang his rod seven times on the ground and the resultant flashes would summon Bengough to arrest him. It was as simple as that and, once done, Bengough would fly off with him, hopefully to Earth, but in search of Gloucester Old Spots anyway. As they neared the city, however, doubts began to grow in Clive's mind. Things were usually never as simple as he first hoped and they had certainly not been so since he had boarded the plane in Madeira, so something was almost bound to go wrong. Firstly, there was the question of how long it would take Bengough to arrive; it could hardly be instantaneous and what would happen in the meantime and what if he didn't arrive at all? Then there was the doctrine of non–intervention and whether that was compatible with the arrival at a place that had not yet experienced an industrial revolution, of the Inter–Galactic Police Force in a space ship or, at the very least, in a number of space buggies. Then there was the little matter of what the King intended of him and whether the army would overrule his intention to make Clive fight it out alone with the Baron's new advisor who was, in all probability, Sticky himself. The one redeeming thing about this situation was that there seemed to be no prospect of the four Staffs coming together, resulting in the destruction of the planet and of himself, by the mother ship, this understanding being based on the news from Reece that Ggydren had acquired a Staff of his own and was presently in, or somewhere near Elisiu and where the fourth was also located.

The army approached the gates of Trianja and stopped outside them. The soldiers brought the King up from the rear, placed him on a horse at the head of the army and demanded orders. The King, panic stricken, demanded that Clive be sent for and had him seated on a horse beside him. The King looked at Clive expectantly.

"I told you before," said Clive, not bothering with the usual etiquette, "there's no point in asking me what to do, I've never been in a war before. Actually I've never even been in a

278

fight, even at school. Perhaps you ought to issue an ultimatum."

"What kind of ultimatum?" asked the King.

"Oh for goodness sake," snapped Clive, "how many kinds are there?"

"Don't you take that tone of voice with me," snapped the King back. "Remember who I am."

"It's difficult to forget," muttered Clive, under his breath.

Just then, the gates of Trianja opened and a lone emissary rode out. The King looked at Clive.

"Well, go on then. Find out what he wants."

Considering it was only a lone emissary and with no noticeable display of weaponry, let alone a Staff, Clive thought it safe to obey. He rode forward and met the emissary half way.

"The Baron of Besanto declares," said the emissary, "that if you lay down your arms and submit to his authority, he will be merciful."

"How merciful?" asked Clive.

"The Baron of Besanto will only take revenge on those in authority and allow the general hoi polloi off."

'That's not going to go down too well with the King,' thought Clive, 'and I might be included in the former group.'

"And what if we don't lay down our arms?"

"The Baron of Besanto will slaughter all of you."

"All?" repeated Clive. "That's a pretty tall order."

"The Baron of Besanto has at his disposal an excellent new weapon that can easily accomplish the task."

"Oh yes," said Clive, "and can this weapon kill from a distance using flashes of light and did it come with the Baron's new advisor?"

"I'm not sure we are supposed to be having a general conversation," said the emissary, "but the answer to both questions is yes."

"Just one more question before I take your offer to the King. Does the Baron's new advisor ride at his right hand and what does he look like?"

"Sorry, that's two questions. Which one would you like me to answer?"

Clive thought.

"The second."

"The Baron of Besanto's new advisor wears a coat of fur. There, I think I've said enough."

The King was not amused.

"So you're telling me that if I surrender the Baron will have me killed and if I don't he'll also have me killed?"

"Only if you lose," said Clive, helpfully.

"Go back and tell him to get stuffed."

"The King says to tell the Baron to get stuffed," said Clive to the waiting emissary, who replied that the Baron was not going to like it. Just then Clive had an idea.

"Look, I've had an idea. Nobody wants a war. Why don't you tell the Baron that the King wants to parley and I'll say the same to the King? I would accompany the King and the new advisor could come out with the Baron and the four of us could try to sort something out. It must be better than resorting to violence straight off."

280

The emissary agreed to take the proposal to the Baron and rode back. Clive rode back too, in the opposite direction.

"What if it's a trick?" asked the King.

"It would just be the four of us and I'd have the rod," said Clive.

"Oh, I get your drift, good thinking," said the King, smiling. "We get the pair of them on their own and then you let them have it with that thing."

"Well, that's a possibility," agreed Clive, who was actually more interested in whether he would have time to strike the rod on the ground the necessary seven times before Sticky reacted with his own device.

The King agreed to the meeting and so did the Baron. Half an hour later the gates of Trianja opened again and two riders rode out. At the same time Clive and the King rode towards them. Clive noticed that the King was shaking and was quite impressed that he wasn't.

'Perhaps I was born for this sort of thing after all,' he thought and then corrected himself. 'Don't be silly, Clive, this isn't your sort of thing at all. Something's bound to go wrong. You need your head examined.'

As the approaching riders neared him, Clive could see that one of them had a small crown and the other was wearing a fur coat. Then he began to shake too and hoped it didn't show. The two pairs stopped a few yards apart. The Baron's companion sneered.

"Give up now before it's too late."

"I've got one of these and this is what it can do," replied Clive, hastily leaning down to bang the end of the rod on the ground seven times. The flashes shot up in the air.

"And I've got three of these," said the Baron's companion, bringing three Staffs of Life out of his fur coat and holding them up, "and I'd rather like to have yours as well."

Clive's feelings at that moment could be described as descending into panic. Several different thoughts went through his mind at the same time. That something terrible, maybe fatal, had happened to Ggydren and Elendril. That the whole planet he was on might be about to be obliterated at any moment and that he might have known it was stupid to expect Bengough to arrive so soon.

Clive desperately tried to remember the sequence of squeezes he needed to give the symbol on the rod to turn it into its more effective form. It was difficult to think clearly, given the situation but somehow he managed it and the rod turned in his hand into a glowing, super enhanced, miniaturised, laser device. Unfortunately the person opposite had done the same with one of his Staffs. They pointed them at each other, neither quite knowing what to do next. Meanwhile the King and the Baron were gasping in astonishment at what they had just witnessed.

Clive decided on a new approach.

"The game's up Sticky, Sticky Fingers Maclean that is. Your plan is foiled. I'm with the Inter-Galactic Police, you are wanted for space piracy and the mother ship is at this very moment sending down a unit to arrest you. I'm expecting company. I think it's you who'd better give up."

Sticky Fingers Maclean, for it was him indeed, was completely taken by surprise and moreover, it was quite clear to him the person opposite who knew his real name and of the existence of the Inter-Galactic Police and who was familiar with the true nature of Staffs of Power, was obviously telling the truth. He continued to point his device at Clive while he tried to think of what to do next. The King and the Baron were also somewhat surprised by the turn of events, indeed flabbergasted would be a more appropriate description. Neither of them had the faintest idea what was happening but both recognised a situation that was completely outside their own experience and control. The Baron thought it sensible to put some distance between him and his new advisor, whom he now realised was not quite, or was maybe even more than the person he had thought him to be. He turned his horse and rode slowly back into Trianja. The King was frightened stiff and galloped back to the army. Once safely out of the way he turned his horse to watch the standoff unfold.

Clive and Sticky continued to point their weapons at each other. Clive was desperately praying for Bengough to appear, even though he was not a religious person and not usually given to praying.

"You do know that even if they don't arrest you, the Force is authorised to destroy a planet on which the four laser devices are about to be brought together?" asked Clive. "So either way, it's curtains for you."

"Well, in that case it would be curtains for you too," answered Sticky. "I'll tell you what, you put down your weapon and then I'll put down mine."

"You must think I'm stupid," said Clive, "and besides, you'd still have two more. I'll tell you what, you throw down the other two first and then we'll decide what to do next."

Sticky thought about it and then threw down the other two Staffs.

"Right, what next?"

"I don't know, except that I do know that I can't trust you. Pirates aren't renowned for their trustworthiness."

"And I'm supposed to be able to trust you, am I? Who are you anyway and where did you come from."

"My name is Clive and I'm from the planet Earth. Why do they call you Sticky Fingers?"

"If you must know I have an issue with perspiration; I tend to do a lot of it in my line of work."

"What's all this about then, I mean this business with the Baron? Surely you're only here for the Staffs."

"That's true enough but I knew it would take time and it's a nice little diversion while I'm waiting. These primitive planets and their primitive people, it's so easy and such fun to create a little mayhem.... Oh, I see, you keep me talking while you wait for the reinforcements; well that's enough of that then."

They faced each other in silence, weapons pointed and ready, each keenly looking for any indication that the other was going to fire. After a while Clive's arm began to ache. He figured that Sticky's must be doing the same and it might boil down to who could keep their weapon pointed the longest. Ten minutes later, arm aching more than ever and still no sign of Bengough, Clive was beginning to feel desperate.

'This is stupid,' he thought to himself, 'we can't stay like this forever. It'll be dark soon and then what?'

He decided on a new psychological warfare approach.

"What's that on your face?"

"How do you mean?"

284

"On your face, there's something crawling on it?"

"Nah."

"Yes, really. I think it's a spider. Surely you can feel it. Doesn't it tickle?"

Clive was hoping that the suggestion of a tickle would cause that effect and that Sticky's guard would lapse, if only for a second. Sticky began to look distinctly uncomfortable. It seemed to be working. Then Sticky used the hand that wasn't holding the Staff to check his face.

"Good try, Clive," he said, looking distinctly comfortable again.

Just then the sound of hooves in the distance could be heard and they were gradually getting louder. They stopped somewhere to the side of Clive and Sticky. Neither dared to look in case the other took the opportunity to fire.

"Don't look now but it's me, Clive. Keep that thing pointed."

"Bengough?" asked Clive, almost overwhelmed by a sudden feeling of relief.

"Yes, Bengough," said Bengough, "sorry it took me so long."

"Who's Bengough?" asked Sticky, still looking straight ahead at Clive.

"Corporal Bengough of the Inter-Galactic Police, I've got you cornered."

"Make a move, Bengough and your friend's a gonner," said Sticky.

"Really Maclean, you're in no position to start making threats. Now be a good pirate and slowly put down your weapon."

"Or what?"

"Or I'll have to shoot you."

285

"No way. My finger is on the button. Shoot me and your friend gets it too."

"Who said he's my friend," said Bengough, "and why do you think I care if he gets shot? There's a nice fat reward for you, dead or alive."

That was not what Clive expected or wanted to hear.

"Hang on, Bengough," he said nervously and still pointing his weapon at Sticky, "don't forget I'm the one who knows where the Old Spots are."

"Are you going to put down that weapon Maclean?" asked Bengough.

"No," said Sticky.

"So be it," said Bengough.

Clive heard a twang, followed by a whoosh and saw the arrow enter Sticky's hand, the one with the finger on the button. Sticky's hand jerked and at the same time a flash of light issued forth from the weapon. The flash missed Clive by some way but continued onwards until it found a target in the form of the King, who was vaporised. A great cheer immediately went up from the King's army and Sticky, looking round, saw that Bengough was not alone and that at least a dozen bows were trained on him. He put his good hand up in a gesture of surrender and that was that.

Bengough and his men were all dressed in Robin Hood outfits but they didn't look particularly merry. Bengough picked up the Staffs and his men picked up Sticky. He was bound and gagged and carted off to somewhere out of sight, from where, presumably, he was moved up to the mother ship.

"You took a chance there," said Clive, "I might easily have been killed. Did you really mean what you said about me and not caring whether I got shot or not?"

"Of course not,' replied Bengough, smiling.

"It sounded convincing," said Clive.

"Just a bluff, honest."

"Are we off now then?"

"Off?" asked Bengough.

"To claim the reward, find the Earth and get your Gloucester Old Spots."

"I'm afraid not," said Bengough, "the reward will take months to come through, if I get it at all and then I'll have to apply for a discharge and that's by no means certain. It might be six months before you see me again, if ever. Besides, you've still got work to do here."

"What kind of work?" exclaimed Clive, feeling distinctly annoyed.

"Well, you seem to be at the head of an army that is about to attack this place. You can hardly leave now?"

"Why on earth not, it's nothing to do with me?"

"Really, Clive, where is your sense of honour? You just can't abandon them."

"Well, I don't see why not."

"Think of all those poor people inside, at the Baron's mercy."

Clive was going to say that he didn't see it as his responsibility to think about the poor people inside, when he remembered that two of the poor people inside were likely to be Ggydren and Elendril, that is if they were still alive.

"But what can I do?" he asked. "I kept telling the King I've got no idea about warfare."

"Well, you've got the rod and I'm going to be taking the other three away to be disposed of safely, so I think that gives you a big advantage, even without any experience. I'm sure you can come up with something."

Clive pondered his situation and what he could safely do without getting himself killed in the process. While he was pondering, Bengough announced that it was time for him to go.

"You really will come back for me, won't you?" asked Clive.

"I'll do my best, honestly," said Bengough.

"One last question," said Clive.

"There always is," said Bengough.

"You told me you were a sergeant," said Clive, even though it was not technically a question.

"I was," said Bengough.

"What happened for you to become a corporal?" asked Clive.

"I got demoted."

"I know that, but why?"

"Because I returned without the heat seeking arrows. Fairly primitive technology but of great antique value. Worth an arm and a leg but I thought they might come in handy for you."

"You did that for me?" asked Clive.

"Well, obviously."

"It's a good job they gave you some more for this mission," said Clive.

"Oh, these aren't heat seeking," said Bengough, "just ordinary ones; they wouldn't trust me again." As Bengough disappeared into the distance and Clive wondered at his archery skills, he noticed a figure walk towards him from the ranks of the army.

"Hello, Wilfred," said Clive.

"The soldiers want to know if that thing you're holding is the same as the one the Baron's advisor had."

"Yes," said Clive, "I think so anyway. Sorry about the King."

"Nobody else is," said Wilfred. "Anyway, in that case I'm pleased to tell you that the soldiers have made you Commander in Chief."

The new commander of the Morgrnvian Armed Forces wondered why everyone kept thinking he knew about fighting, and whether anyone else had ever gone from Private to Commander in Chief, without any of the ranks in between. As he was wondering, Wilfred coughed to get his attention and asked what the orders were. Not having a clue, Clive decided to play for time.

"Perhaps you could walk up to the gates for me and tell them I want to speak to the emissary again."

"Is that an order?"

"Yes but please be careful. Come away quick if they get nasty."

Wilfred walked up to the gates which opened a few minutes later to allow the emissary out.

"Hello again," said Clive, once Wilfred had returned with the emissary, "do you think the Baron is ready to surrender?"

"Certainly not," answered the emissary. "The gates of Trianja are strong and he's got plenty of food to withstand a siege and he has the population hostage. He thinks it's you who should surrender."

'Oh dear,' thought Clive, having hoped to avoid any violence.

"But he knows I've got this thing and he saw what it did to the King."

"Yes, but he's safe inside and you're out here."

Clive pointed the super enhanced laser device at the gates of Trianja and fired. The gates of Trianja exploded and when the dust had settled, nothing remained of them.

"There," said Clive, "now what were you saying about the gates of Trianja? Please go back and tell the Baron to come out with his hands up, or else."

Chapter 20.

The next few months were every bit as eventful for Clive as the last ones had been, except in a less traumatic way. On the very day of the Baron's surrender he was reunited with Ggydren and made the proper acquaintance of Elendril, whom he had previously known only as a lioness. Ggydren was in quite a bad way, having been roughed up by the remaining Hinckle brothers but took a great deal of solace in Clive's orders to have them incarcerated in prison. The dilemma of what to do with the Baron was easily solved, Clive had him relinquish his title and then sent him into an exile of boredom in Aughphalia. Clive found the Baron's son to be every bit as charming as Gretchen had described and realised that the marriage of the two would bring an end to the discord between Morgrnvia and Besanto. He sent for Gretchen, who being the dead King's only offspring, well legitimate anyway, was technically queen. Clive arranged for the coronation and wedding to take place on the same day and personally supervised the arrangements. He was particularly impressed with the sumptuousness of the coronation-come-wedding gown that he commissioned and which Gretchen was to wear, although this had to be altered after she arrived to accommodate the, by then, enormous bulge of her pregnancy. Indeed, there was a concern that the birth might take place before the wedding and render the status of the resultant child questionable but fortunately Gretchen gave birth to triplets the following day.

Queen Gretchen wanted to give Clive an official position in her government but, unused to so much attention and ceremony, he declined but accepted instead the offer of a very generous financial payment for services rendered. Thereafter he accompanied Ggydren, by then fully recovered, and Elendril to Buggiton, where they took rooms in one of the inns. One of the first things Clive did in Buggiton was to visit the bookshop with Ggydren, who pointed out the symbol on the wall outside. Reece showed Clive the Book of Transition and talked about the prophecy.

"It's completely fulfilled in all but a few minor details, my old chap,' he said, 'and it's quite clear that you are the person the prophecy predicted would overthrow the forces of darkness and usher in an age of peace and prosperity. There, what do you think of that?"

Clive, not wanting to upset the old man by saying that it was all a load of twaddle, merely muttered a thoughtful 'humm', and left it at that.

Clive was hoping that Bengough would show up at any time but after a couple of months he began to lose heart and realised that a more permanent domestic arrangement than the inn might be necessary. Luckily he found out that the Higgins farm was up for sale. Clive bought it and then had the farmhouse divided into two quite separate living spaces, where he, Ggydren and Elendril could all reside. Thereafter, Elendril devoted herself to the welfare of shape-shifters and Ggydren became a farmer.

In the many months that followed, Clive waited patiently but in vain for Bengough to reappear. He took to going out in the dead of night when no one was about and striking the rod on the ground so that it would send flashes of light into the sky to indicate his whereabouts but nothing came of it. With the nothing came an increasing foreboding that he would never see Bengough or Earth again or get back home to feed his unnamed pet. The foreboding led to unhappiness and the unhappiness turned to depression. Ggydren and Elendril noticed his general listlessness and kept telling him to buck up, which annoyed Clive who felt he had nothing to buck up for. He was, as he remembered from the title of a book he had once read, a stranger in a strange land and it didn't really suit him at all.

Eventually, after a couple of years, Clive did manage to buck up somewhat. As Reece got too old to manage the shop on his own, Clive went in almost every day to help and, given that customers were often few and far between, he had plenty of time for reading. He became particularly interested in the past of Morgrnvia, made copious notes and began to write his own history of the place. It frequently occurred to him that if he ever did get back to Earth, then this History of Morgrnvia might go down well as a piece of detailed science fiction, or was it fantasy?

Sometime into his third year in Buggiton Clive went out as usual in the dead of night to bang his rod on the ground. As he did so a familiar voice told him that there was no need to do that.

"I'm already here, Clive. Sorry it's been so long."

A little later, over a cup of hot chocolate in Clive's part of the farmhouse, Bengough explained that it had taken most of that time to get his share of the reward.

"They tried to say that I was just doing my job and shouldn't get anything extra and I had to take them to court. Well, you know how long-winded the legal system is, not to mention how expensive solicitors are, but I got there in the end. Then there was the time it took to buy myself out of the Force and the expense of buying a suitable vehicle."

"Yes, yes," said Clive, a little impatiently, "but can you get me back to Earth again and in my own time?"

"I think so. I've been trying out wormholes and I'm pretty sure I've found the one we need. Are you sure about the Gloucester Old Spots?"

Bengough told Clive to gather a few essentials, just a few mind, as there wasn't much room. As he was doing so, Clive was suddenly overcome with a sense of foreboding. Although he had dreamed of getting back to Earth, would that be such a good thing? Had he been really happy there, stuck in front of a computer screen all day, doing accounts, sending emails or at home, watching telly, feeding the cat, the occasional holiday, no real friends, hardly any family to speak of? His short time in Aughphalia and Morgrnvia had given him more excitement than in the whole of his previous existence. Ggydren, Elendril and Reece had become the best friends he had ever had and he doubted whether Queen Elizabeth would ever pop round for a glass of something, as Queen Gretchen sometimes did. Faced with these second thoughts he found himself in all of a dither about what to do. Just then Bengough called up that they really should be off soon, and had he thought about leaving a note for the others? Still undecided, Clive wrote the note anyway and left it on the mantelpiece where it would be found.

'Dear Ggydren and Elendril,

I don't know how to say this but I have the opportunity to get back to the place I originally came from. I hate to say goodbye but I feel I should go. Say my farewells to Reece and the Queen for me and please help yourself to any of my things you want.

PS You can have my half of the house too.

Best Regards,

Clive.'

A little later, by the back door, Clive told Bengough of his misgivings.

"But I've come all this way. I've been working up to it for ages. What about my Old Spots?"

Clive was pretty sure Bengough could find some Old Spots on his own but not wanting to let his friend down, he finally decided to go with him.

It was just starting to get light as they made their way out to one of the fields, in the middle of which was a massive boulder that hadn't been there before. Bengough pressed a button on a remote and the boulder turned into a spaceship, not a one man space buggy, but an enormous flying saucer.

"Goodness," exclaimed Clive, surprised by the size and the condition of it. "It's a bit dented. Are you sure it's up to the job?"

"It's certainly been around a bit, well a lot really. They're not cheap, you know, these things. This is the best I could afford, not even second hand, more like eighth but it goes like a bomb."

Clive hoped it wouldn't blow up like a bomb but kept that to himself. Bengough showed him where to climb onto the wing and opened a small window for him to clamber in. Inside it was remarkably cramped, given the size of the thing on the outside. There were two seats, one steering wheel and a whole lot of instruments. It was only when Bengough had started the engines that Clive suddenly had an important thought.

"Stop! We can't go yet. I've forgotten the rod."

"I thought that was deliberate," said Bengough. "We really shouldn't have one of those things on board. I remember telling you that last time."

"Well, I'm not going without it," insisted Clive. 'It's saved my life on numerous occasions and I'd feel lost without it."

Bengough relented and ten minutes later, with Clive, rod in hand, by his side, the spaceship rose into the air and shot off into near space and then, using warp drive, into distant space.

"How long is this going to take?" asked Clive when they had been going for an hour or so and also asking if there was another compartment where there might be sleeping, eating and   bathroom   facilities.

"No, this is all there is," said Bengough. "Warp drive is pretty quick. Journeys in this thing usually take just a couple of hours and we can always find somewhere to land if the need arises. I'm just having a little difficulty in finding the correct wormhole, that's all. I know it's around here somewhere."

Bengough handed Clive a sachet of emergency ration.

"Here eat this. It'll settle your stomach. It's a rather turbulent wormhole and this old thing doesn't have the stabilizers you get on more modern ships."

Somehow the sachet of banana flavoured goo was quite comforting. Clive had forgotten how sick of it he'd become before. He'd only just swallowed the last drop when Bengough announced that this was it and the spaceship plunged into an even more complete darkness than it had been in before. Then it began to shudder so violently that Clive was convinced it would shake itself apart. The shaking seemed to last an eternity but was actually over in less than a minute and it finished as abruptly as it had started. The spaceship emerged into bright sunlight and Clive, looking out of the window, could see the outline of what distinctly looked like the continent of Australia.

'My goodness,' he thought, 'I'm home.'

Before the final descent Clive had to admit that he had made up the bit about the place near him with the Gloucester Old Spots but assured Bengough that there were plenty of real places in England where he would be able to find them. Bengough took it quite well and said that he would have probably done the same, given the circumstances.

"I don't understand how you can take any pigs with you anyway," said Clive, "there isn't room to swing a cat in here, let alone a pair of breeding pigs."

"DNA, old chap," said Bengough. "I don't need the actual pigs, just some of their DNA. I can grow them from that."

Clive was quite impressed.

"We were on the verge of that sort of thing on Earth just before I left. There was talk of bringing back the dinosaurs. Where will you go after you drop me off?"

"With you, of course, I hope you have a spare room. We can search out the pigs together."

Very soon they were over the British Isles and Bengough asked Clive for his postcode to feed into the onboard universal navigation system to take them to his house. When they were a few thousand feet above it Bengough said that he better not land until it was night because it would give the locals too much of a fright and it was prohibited anyway. He put the spaceship into hover mode and suggested they have a nap while they waited. Bengough fell asleep almost immediately but Clive was too excited and spent hours thinking about his experiences since the plane crash and what it would be like to get back home again. Eventually he did drop off and it was almost light before either of them woke.

The size of Clive's back garden caused one slight hitch; it was smaller than the space ship. Bengough searched for a suitable spot and in the end got fed up and decided to make do with the local recreation ground, even though he realised that the sudden appearance of a boulder that was half the size of a football pitch, on the football pitch, was bound to cause a stir when discovered. It did and the local and national media had a field day. As they walked along the streets to his house, the thought struck Clive that his keys, wallet and much else besides, was in his carry-on luggage at the bottom of the Atlantic Ocean and he wondered if he would have to knock on Mrs Elphick's door in order to ask for the keys he had given her. As they rounded the last bend however and his house came into view, Clive could see that the front door was open. Inside they found Mrs Elphick, always an early riser, feeding the cat. She looked surprised to see them and not only because of the strange clothes they were wearing.

"You're back early," she said to Clive, "I was only expecting you on Friday."

Printed in Great Britain
by Amazon